DEATH BY DOODLEBUG

ALSO BY CAROL CAVERLY

DEATH BY DOODLEBUG

A THEA BARLOW WYOMING MYSTERY, BOOK 4

CAROL CAVERLY

ePublishingWorks!
love what you read.

Book and cover design by eBook Prep
www.ebookprep.com

November, 2021

ISBN: 978-1-64457-138-5

ePublishing Works!
644 Shrewsbury Commons Ave
Ste 249
Shrewsbury PA 17361
United States of America
www.epublishingworks.com
Phone: 866-846-5123

This book is dedicated to my husband, Donald Hart, for his extreme patience in difficult times. You made it possible for me. I love you.
AND
To Yvonne Montgomery, a beautiful writer, for all our weekly calls of encouragement, help, faith, and millions of laughs.

PROLOGUE

The black-dark night was soft and warm, just the way he liked it, the moon's tiny sickle lost among the clouds. He rubbed his gimpy knee, easing the pain. He hadn't been followed. Why would he have been? He'd told them he was going to town. And if they watched, well, that was exactly what he'd done. But now caution steeled him. Long after midnight, he saw no cars or eyes on the empty street, only dust and weeds blown by the wild Wyoming wind.

He turned his truck off Main and into the alley behind the old garage he'd spotted weeks ago. It sat in a weeded vacant lot along with a tractor's rusted skeleton. One end of the building's weathered boards leaned dangerously off-kilter, distorting the shape of the large opening and the ability of the only door still hanging to close as it should. *Fine by me*, he thought, sliding the truck through the open space and behind the remaining door. Always good to have a hiding place.

He took a small flashlight from the seat beside him and fished through the coverless jockey box for a piece of paper, finally tearing the back off a crumpled envelope. Snatching a pencil stub, he braced the paper awkwardly on the dashboard and scribbled a few words. He should have done this days ago like he'd promised. So, what the hell, he was doing it now. Better than never. Debt paid. There wasn't much time. He had to get out of here.

He opened the truck's door and swung his legs out, wincing when his weight hit the aching knee. Strong odors of mold, rust and dog piss made his eyes water. He threw his John Deere cap on the seat and grabbed a tattered straw cowboy hat from the empty gun rack on the cab's back window. Pushing the folded paper into his pocket, he rubber-necked the alley. He was too old for this crap, but the job could be done faster on foot. He didn't want his truck spotted. Dodging a sleeping dog, and two reeking garbage bins, he headed back to Main Street and crossed. Walking briskly, not too fast, he hugged the dark side of the streets. If some sleepless duffer looked out a window, he should see an ordinary guy out late, heading home to a mad-as-hell woman.

He saw the house he wanted and ducked behind a bush. The scent of lilac gave a moment's pleasure before he slipped up to the front stoop and slid the note between the edges of the screen door.

Done. Now, out of here. He'd be at Mickey's place on the Utah rez before daylight. He hurried, cutting between houses and yards back to Main, glad there weren't any dogs. Puffing from the effort, he forgot caution and stepped out on the street. Halfway across, truck lights caught him. Blinded, he stood as if paralyzed. The driver jumped out and grabbed his arm with a ferocious twist.

"You didn't do it, did you, you shit!" The man spat the words at him, his fist a smashing emphasis. "There's no toxic dump around here. You think I'm an idiot? Where is he?"

"He's dead, he's dead. Leave me alone." Dropping to his knees, his heart banged around his chest; flashing pains burned through his arms and neck. Then the kicking began.

The driver's last words spun dizzily through his agony. "Then you're dead, too, you old fool."

CHAPTER 1

I can't believe it. I am now that most pitied of women: she who is left at the altar. Me, Thea Barlow. And I hate every minute of it. I'm *not* a poor pitiful Pearl. I'm bewildered, sad, angry, a bit humiliated maybe, but mostly I'm worried to death about Max.

Max Holman, independent oilman and geologist, is not the kind of man who just doesn't show up. No. Even if he changed his mind about getting married—which I don't believe for a minute—he would have come right out and told me. Nicely, I'm sure, with an arm around my shoulder, and a voice filled with reason and concern about how I would take it, which wouldn't be well, of course. But that's not what happened.

What happened was me in my wedding dress, standing at the altar of the quaint Community Church in Garnet Pass, Wyoming, holding a wilting bouquet of baby roses and sweet peas. Best man, Rusty Metzger, had already slipped out the side door for preliminary searches. As the ex-sheriff of only a few days he still had the right connections to do serious checking.

My mother, the queen of social niceties, had a firm grip on my arm. She knew my feet, dancing nervously in their silver shoes, wanted nothing more than to bolt out the door, and jump in my car so I could carry out my own search for Max.

"Some of these people have come a long way to see you," she whispered in my ear. "We need to greet them. Play nice, dear."

Of course, Mother was right; so I followed her lead. Charlotte, ex-sheriff Rusty's wife, my best friend and matron of honor, helped with the chit-chat. I have little memory of who else I spoke to, or what was said. Obviously my mind was elsewhere.

I do remember pulling Charlotte aside, dear ditsy Charlotte, whose psychic powers run from seeing the energy colors, auras, that supposedly surround everyone, to visions, clairvoyance and all the other weird things out there.

"Where is he, Charlotte?" I asked her. "Can you see him?"

"Who? See who?"

"Max! Where is he?"

"Oh, Thea." She touched my cheek. "I'm sorry. I can't see him. It doesn't work that way. I can't make it happen. I'm so sorry."

I was sorry, too. Even more sorry to lose her when she and Rusty left for Utah the next day.

Even now, five days later, the scene at the church is embedded in my memory, popping up with alarming regularity to remind me of shattered dreams. Neither Rusty's professional searches through accident reports, hospital checks, bars, hang-outs, nor my more personal ones, were successful. I looked everywhere I could think of, and spoke to everyone who might have information about Max. Nothing.

I flipped the package I'd just finished wrapping, slapped on its mailing address, and placed it with its two mates on the kitchen table. The last of the wedding present returns. Such a pathetic job. At least it was something to do. Something to block the constant mind-pictures that deviled me: Max lying in a remote chasm somewhere, hurt, injured…or worse.

Small town Wyoming—and Garnet Pass was one of the smallest—was no different from small towns anywhere. The botched wedding created a field day for gossip and specula-tion which was just now, after close to a week, dwindling. The citizenry was pretty well split between those believing I'd been dumped by Max, and those who thought some-thing must have happened to keep him away. I tended to vacillate between the two, but not much. I simply could not believe Max would jilt me without a word. He was a very straightforward kind of person. Disappearing was not char-acteristic. But then, how well did any of us know another person? My self-confidence lived in the sewer these days.

I took the packages into the living room and put them on my desk next to the piles of books, folders and miscella-neous stuff I'd gathered over the years for research about the soiled doves, ladies of the night, and their houses of ill repute. They served as a dismal reminder that sooner or later—now that once again I was a single woman, or rather, still a single woman—I needed to get back to work. Write another article. Bring in some money.

I'd run a few story ideas by *Western True Adventures* magazine, my most dependable market, but they weren't any more excited by them than I was. The old-time whore-houses were my specialty and readers' favorite stories, but nothing had grabbed my interest other than an old-time madam on the east coast named Honeybell Forever, of all things, who tended to drift west periodically. I'd have to do a lot more research to see if I could find enough information about her to be worth an article. Sadly, the needed concentration and energy for such a project had disappeared with you know who.

And how about my little house? I looked at all the familiar nooks, crannies, and second-hand furniture. I loved my house. But what should I do now? The thought of staying here in Garnet Pass without Max was unbearable. I could write anywhere, go anywhere. But every nook and cranny of my body said leaving was impossible. I needed to stay here, search for Max, search for answers to my most burdensome questions: *Where are you, Max? And why, why ,why?*

Always restless, Max had finished his oil field business here several months ago. "To free up time for our honeymoon," he'd told me. I chewed on a fingernail. Could part of that restlessness be fear of being tied into a marriage? Worth a ponder or two, but no, I didn't believe it. We didn't date. We were constant companions. We enjoyed each other's company. I was a Wyoming newcomer, Max a Wyoming native. Even so, he didn't stay in one place long due to his oil business. Neither of us felt tied to Garnet Pass. We were simply together. Until now.

I half-sat on the desk, glanced at the telephone, looking for a message light, and checked my cell phone to make sure it was fully charged. I'd become something of a phona-fobe—if there is such a word. Whatever happened to Max had evidently happened to his phone as well. Gone. The possibilities of what such a disaster might be were numberless, each more ghastly than the next, and kept me awake at night.

Thankfully, a rumble from the street followed by the loud blast of Charlie Daniels going down to Georgia or somewhere, announced the arrival of Dale Anders in her rattletrap Dodge truck. Relieved from dark thoughts, I watched her out the bay window. Without slowing down, she turned onto the graveled two-track path to my stand-alone garage, jerking to a stop just inches from the lilac bush. One of these days, she'd hit it, and I'd have her neck.

But thank God for Dale. Last night she took the remaining batch of presents from local ranch residents with her to deliver this morning. Only a true friend would offer to take on the awkward task of returning wedding presents. She's the one bright spot in this whole wretched affair. If she hadn't catered the food for the wedding reception that didn't happen, we might never have met. I'd seen her before at the Glory Hole restaurant where she worked; a nodding acquaintance. We actually bonded over a spilled dish of potato salad at one of our consultations. The bowl bounced, spewing mayonnaised potatoes, onions, pickles through the air to land all over us and the floor. We ended with howls of laughter, sliding on slickened linoleum.

Dale's the kind of crazy woman I need to be around now. She makes me laugh. She's a fool for gold prospecting, loves exploring ghost towns, collects photos of outhouses, and is going to teach me how to pan for gold today when we finish with the presents. Beats sitting around moping and wondering.

I smiled as she jumped out of her truck wearing her usual scruffy Outdoor Woman uniform of ugly cargo pants with all the pockets stuffed full, and a worn flannel shirt over a tee bearing a caustic slogan.

Wild blond hair escaped from her floppy pony tail. I loved that she didn't care how her hair looked. I spent too much time worrying about mine. We hadn't know each other long, but so far we got along famously.

I timed it perfectly and opened the front door just as she pulled open the screen.

"You are now a free woman," she announced, stooping to pick up a piece of paper as she stepped through the door. "All packages delivered!"

"Thank you, thank you!" I gave her the old corny obeisance bow.

"And Max Holman owes me a hundred dollars for gas, wear and tear on my tires, and anything else I can think of. Not everyone was home. If not, I left the package by the door."

I couldn't help being curious. "Were there any comments?"

"Other than the, 'Oh, she shouldn't haves,' most wanted to know if anyone had heard from Max. That lady with the pet chicken asked how *you* were doing. About time. You're the person people should be thinking about. Not that jerk." I always knew what side Dale was on.

She plopped down on a chair. "Here." She handed me a folded piece of paper and re-scrunched her ponytail.

"What's this?" I unfolded the scrap.

"I don't know. It was stuck in the screen door."

I smoothed out the wrinkled paper. It was indeed a scrap, torn from an envelope. Penciled writing straggled haphazardly across the paper.

"Max!" I gasped. Dale jumped up and peered over my shoulder.

Hands shaking, I pointed to the first words. *Max ok*, it read. My heart began to pound. Max okay. Yes! Max okay!

"I *tried best al*" Dale said, reading what appeared to come next.

"Al?" I tried to pull my mind from the first two words. "Who's Al?"

"Beats me."

The letters of the next word staggered crazily, as if written by a drunken hand. I pointed to it. We squinted at the letters: *dugul,* then maybe a space and *bug.* "What on earth?"

"Well, if the guy can't spell, I know what a *doodle*bug is," Dale said, with a puzzled frown. "Is that a *hurry* that comes after, or *burry?*"

"I can't tell. And, what's that at the end? It looks like *deef.*"

"Or maybe *deep,*" Dale put in. Whether an *f* or a *p,* its long tail slithered down to disappear off the paper.

I busied myself spreading the note on the desktop, not wanting Dale to see how the sight of Max's name had brought me close to tears. "Might be someone's idea of a joke," I muttered.

"Maybe, but let's see what we have." She bent over the paper and read out loud, putting in periods where there weren't any. "*Max ok. I tried best.* Then comes *al.* Do you think it's a name?"

"Could be," I said. "As in, *I tried my best,* comma, *Al.* But, who knows? There's no punctuation, no capitals. But if whoever wrote it is talking to a person named Al, why put the note on my door?"

Dale shrugged. "Then comes *doodlebug hurry,* or *burry deef.*"

"Or deep. Buried deep. Yuk, I don't like that." I straightened, eyes closed for a moment. The words drew me back. "It does say Max is okay. The rest doesn't make sense. I tried best. That could mean that Max wasn't okay, but this person tried to make him so?" Anxiety dampened my brief shot of elation. Still, this was the first crumb.

It could be another form of the hate mail I got months ago when I served as chief suspect for the murder of one of the town's valued citizens. At that time, Rusty, the sheriff, told me to turn in any off-beat mail I got to his office. Only, this note didn't sound threatening, more like a teaser from someone wanting to take a poke at the town's most notorious newbie. Whatever, the simple sight of Max's name had set my heart off on a wild up-and-down race. I mean, this could be it! What I'd been breaking my neck trying to discover. Someone knew something about Max.

My first instinct was to call Rusty Metzger, but that wasn't fair. He wasn't our sheriff anymore. He was getting used to a new job with the law in Utah. He couldn't do much from there anyway. I wouldn't bother him yet, maybe when I knew more. He and his wife, Charlotte, had already gone out of their way to help us. They delayed their move to Utah by two days to stand up for us. I also knew that if Charlotte learned anything about Max, by whatever crazy means, she would tell me immediately.

A riff of excitement prickled my skin again, sending shivers up my arms. "Strange as it is, Dale," I shook the note in front of her face, "this actually mentions Max, says he's okay. I'm taking it to the new sheriff, whoever he is. Maybe it'll get them off their butts."

Dale looked surprised. "Are they looking for Max?"

"Hardly," I huffed. "It's not a crime to blow off your marriage. The department sent queries to other counties as a courtesy to Rusty, who was worried. But Max isn't considered a missing person." *Only by me.* I put the note in my jean's pocket. "We'll mail the packages, then give them a whiff of it and see what they think."

Dale shrugged. I knew what she was thinking. Firmly on the side of the dumpees, certain Max had walked out on me; she thought I should get on with my life. Max shouldn't be a concern of mine any more. She seldom said anything, but I knew her feelings, we just didn't talk about it much. In general, she didn't have a good opinion of men. Which was okay with me. It didn't change the way I felt.

Inside I was a mess. Outside I tried to keep my dignity.

With the three wrapped packages in hand, I rushed Dale out the door. "Come on, let's go."

CHAPTER 2

The nice thing about Garnet Pass is that everything is within walking distance. Even my little house was just two and a half blocks from downtown.

The sirens began when we left the Post Office. The town's faux squad car sped down the street, lights flopped on the roof flashing red and blue, whooper blasting out the open window. At the sound, doors burst open. People raced up the street, following the noise. Across from us, a man stepped out of the Glory Hole restaurant, leaned against the wall and watched the excitement.

"What's up?" Dale hollered at him.

"A body's been found out by the Park!"

"What? Max!" I whirled and joined the runners.

"Hey," Dale called. I paid no attention. Visions of crushed skulls, severed limbs, broken necks—all the things I didn't want to think about—reeled through my mind.

I ran between the crush of slow moving cars and trucks, pushed past people on foot, but when my feet touched the grass they stopped, unable to proceed. No, I didn't want to see...

Dale caught up with me; put a gentle hand on my arm. "You all right?"

I nodded. My arms quivered. I wrapped them around my body.

"Stay here, I'll go look." She pushed through the milling crowd, everyone vying to see who could get closest to the creek bank, the uniforms, the squad car. Somebody with a badge tried to shoo people away with little success. Dale slipped past him and disappeared behind a bush.

I felt people staring at me, thinking, "*There she is again. Always around when a dead body appears.*" I fought the paranoia, jerking my head around ready to stare anyone down, but no one was looking at me. Abashed, I took a couple of deep breaths, swung my arms a bit, trying to calm the tomtom drumming in my chest.

A hand brushed my shoulder along with soft words. "Don't worry. You're all right." Our friend from the Emporium, Johnny Onenote, now wearing a Sheriff's Posse vest and badge. I touched his crippled fingers as he passed, and relaxed a bit. A nice old man. He always managed to take me out of myself. One of these days I'd find the nerve to ask about his name.

Dale reappeared hustled by a deputy griping her elbow. She shook him away and ran to me, and spoke quietly. "It's not Max," and maneuvered us away from the nudgers behind.

I clutched her arm, nearly collapsing with relief. "Yes," I whispered. Then somewhat recovered, "Yes, I can see that now. Why after five days, after all that looking, would Max be here...dead. I don't know what got into me. Seeing his name on that note freaked me out. I'm sorry you had to go look. Not gruesome, I hope."

"No. I hardly got a glimpse. Just some skinny old guy

with scraggly grey hair. A bunch of bruises, a lot of blood. Let's get out of here. I need a beer."

"Yeah, maybe two. Each." I felt deflated, like one of those pricked balloons that squeals dizzily through the air and lands an empty, useless, wrinkled thing.

Out of the four and a half restaurants in town, two of which were really bars, The Glory Hole was where everyone gathered to hear news. Rather tacky, but I liked the place. Where else would you find a restaurant that offered flyswatters to battle the occasional hordes? But I'd also had my share of uncomfortable experiences there. Not so long ago, as a suspected murderer, I was the focus of everyone's interest. With the real murderer discovered, my notoriety diminished in the last months only to be revived by the farcical wedding that wasn't. I hesitated before pushing through the door, stomach jumping along with the clanking cowbell. All heads turned our way, silencing the buzz of excitement.

Dale raised a hand to the four men sitting at the corner table. "Hi, guys."

I didn't know any of them, but from the way they stared at me, or let their eyes slide away self-consciously, they knew who I was. To my surprise, I recognized the man in a suit who sat in the middle of the group. He owned a gift shop on the outskirts of Rock Springs. Max and I bought our wedding rings from him. I didn't remember his name.

A younger man with a considerable growth of black stubble aimed a question at Dale. "Did you hear what happened at the park?"

"Yeah, Cody, does anybody know who it was?"

"Not me." He looked at the older man sitting next to him who had a scraggly grey beard and wore a faded

Harley Davidson tee shirt. Dale touched his shoulder lightly.

"Hi, Walt." she said with a nice touch of deference.

He gave her a shy Wyoming nod. "I was down there, but they wouldn't let us get close, or answer any questions."

The jeweler spoke up. "I heard someone say it was a big shot from out of town."

A voice rose ethereally from a booth behind him, "He didn't look like a big shot to me." This caused a clamor. Like a herd of grasshoppers, people popped up from tables and booths to gather around the new speaker.

"Nor me either," Dale said. The man in the booth stood up. "Oh, hi, Stan, You recognized him?"

He lifted a shoulder. "Not really. Thought it might be a guy I saw driving a honey wagon awhile back."

I moved away from the conversation and chose a fly swatter from the umbrella stand by the door, and flapped it against my leg. No part of a conversation about bodies appealed to me. I envied Dale's easy way with these people, so I smiled and gave tiny nods of acquaintance to all who looked my way. Return smiles were a comforting reward. A reminder that my paranoia might be getting out of hand.

I jumped when the person sitting in the corner with his chair propped against the wall dropped the front legs to the floor with a bang. His sharp angular face was just this side of handsome and at odds with his broad shoulders and well-muscled chest and arms. Showing off? Not really, I guessed. He wore a soft loose shirt that didn't cling, but the rolled-up sleeves were stopped because of the thickness of the arms, not because he didn't want them higher. I had noticed him before because he seemed to be studiously not looking at me.

"Hey, Trig," he said to Dale, "How'd you—"

She jabbed a finger at him. "The name is Dale."

Whoa. She didn't like him.

He gave her an insolent smile, and me a wink. "How'd you get to see the guy?"

"What guy?" she demanded, jaw jutting out with a belligerent thrust.

"The body."

"None of your business." Her voice was as insolent as his smile. There obviously was no love lost between them. She turned back to the man in the booth and rudely gave him the answer to the other man's question. "There were a lot of people when we got there. I snuck around the law. What about you?"

"Me and George was the ones who found him. Called the sheriff." This caused a new burst of questions from everyone.

I gave Dale a move-on nudge, urging her in front of me, around another table and down the line of booths against the wall towards the back of the restaurant.

The words, "Looked like someone beat him up bad," followed us down the aisle.

We slid into the farthest back booth we could find. I checked for flies; none were apparent. When the girl came—Dale called her Christie—we ordered Modella and fried pickles. I put the swatter on the seat beside me. Gross, but better than flies.

"You must know everyone in town," I said.

"Well, I work here, remember, part time anyway, so I know most of the regulars. The guys in front are all prospectors in their spare time. I see them around now and then. Walt, the older man, hunts gold full time. He's the one who taught me how to pan for gold. Got me hooked. I was surprised to see Cody. I thought he was out on his claim. He's a real die-hard."

"I recognized the man in the suit. He has a gift and jewelry store close to Rock Springs. Is he a prospector, too?"

She shrugged. "I've never seen him before, but you never know. There are a lot of gold nuts in this part of the country."

"And what about the other one?" I teased. "An old boyfriend? I thought you were going to bite his head off."

She made an inelegant noise. "Jake the snake. Barf. We went to high school together in Casper. Long time ago. I always hated his guts."

"What did he call you? Trig? What's that about?"

"You had to ask." She grimaced and gave a half laugh. "Mom was a big Roy Rogers fan, so I got named after his wife, Dale Evans. All the kids in town knew the story and thought it hilarious. They called me Trigger after his horse." She shrugged. "I was never petite."

"I'm sorry I asked."

"Don't be. I'll tell you a secret." She grinned. "It's even worse. My name's really Roydale."

"No!" I could empathize. "I came close to being Theodosia. Dad insisted he wouldn't be able to spell it, so Mom gave in, and settled for Thea, but I think she always regretted it."

The beer was cold and smooth and the pickles were… well, fried pickles. Never my favorite, but they seemed suitable for the day. We gobbled them down And I, at least, felt revived.

I wiped my fingers on a napkin. "Speaking of names…"

Dale grimaced. "Oh, no, not him again."

"Yeah, Max. Seeing his name." *Max ok. Max ok.* "I'm

sorry, all I can think about is that blasted note." I took it out of my pocket and tossed it on the table. We both stared at it, then I tucked it back in my pocket. "I'm going to take it to the sheriff's office."

We guzzled the last of the Modella, threw some bills on the table, and took off.

CHAPTER 3

The sheriff's office was in the basement of the court house. I knew the way rather too well. In fact, for the short amount of time I'd spent in Wyoming, I'm on first name acquaintance with more sheriffs than most people in the state.

"I don't know who's in charge now that Rusty's gone, and I'd like to keep it that way, but now…" I let it dangle. We turned the corner towards the court house. From here we could see the crowds still milling around the park. I didn't want to think about that poor man. No more bodies for me.

We ran down the concrete steps and pushed through the door marked Sheriff's Department.

Rhonda, her hair teased in a tall pompadour, was at the desk, in charge, as always. "Oh, Thea," she said with a look of concern. "It's you. I was going to call." She nodded at Dale, and then looked back to me. "You doing okay?"

"Great!" The word came out rather more emphatically than I intended. I knew everyone in this office believed I was a jilted woman.

"Umm, well…" She looked away, hesitated a moment, then blurted out, "We got a call yesterday from Sheridan. They spotted Max's truck heading east."

My stomach lurched. My voice croaked like a beleaguered frog. "Was…were they sure it was Max driving? I mean, anyone could have stolen his truck."

"They actually stopped him, Thea. No warrant or anything, you know, just a courtesy for Rusty. Checked his driver's license and registration. Told Max to give Rusty a call." She spoke self-consciously, as if she didn't want to be the bearer of bad news. "So, yeah, it was really him. I'm sorry."

Give Rusty a call? What about me? If it really was Max, why hasn't he called? I didn't know what to say.

"I know how worried you were, Thea." Rhonda groped for words. "At least…at least now you know he's alive, and…and well enough to be driving." She raised her hands in a helpless gesture, as if she didn't know where to go from there. As in, poor thing, we knew all along you're one of those pathetic women, deceived, and left at the altar with ridicule smeared on your face.

Was it true? Had I been duped all this time? I couldn't think straight. The Max I knew simply would not act like that. We'd been on many adventures together. He had never treated me like a fragile woman who had to be protected from anything adverse. If danger occurred, we helped each other.

I turned away from Rhonda's look of pity, and tried to shake away Dale's hand on my shoulder.

"Well then." Rhonda cleared her throat and changed the subject. "Did you come in for something?"

"Well…I. Yeah." Still croaking, I held up the note clutched in my hand. "This was stuck in my door this morning. The sheriff might want to see it."

Angry, I scrunched the already crumpled paper into a ball and dropped it on her desk. Rhonda picked it up gingerly. "We're running our tails off now, as I'm sure you know, but I'll see that he gets it." She tossed it in a basket on her desk as the phone rang. Lifting the receiver, she held up a finger, signaling us to wait.

"Yes?" She reached for her note pad. "Possible homicide! Wow." A pause. "Deefy?" she asked with a note of incredulity, "What kind of name is that?"

Deefy! My mouth dropped open.

Dale grabbed my arm. "But that's—"

I shushed her, and while Rhonda still scribbled, I snatched the note out of her basket, and shoved it back in my pocket. Giving her a smile, I mouthed, "I'll be back."

Pushing Dale, I muttered, "I'm out of here. Come on."

"Okay, okay," Rhonda spoke into the phone. "I got it. I'll see what I can find."

With an over-the-shoulder wave, I ran out the door and up the steps.

Dale stumbled up behind me. "Thea, did you hear that? The dead man's name is Deefy."

"So?" I walked at a fast clip, my mind reeling with too much information.

"Do you think there's a connection to the deef on that note? It was at the end. It could be a signature."

I struggled to control the thoughts bouncing through my mind, from Max to Deefy, to Max, to homicide, to Max, Max, Max. Max driving half way across the state without me beside him. *Why didn't you call me? Where are you going? Why?* And a dead man named Deefy.

Was it really Max driving that truck? Did the cop who stopped him actually know him, or did the person look enough like Max's ID to pass?

My head was about to explode.

"Thea!" Dale insisted. "The note. Deefy. What about it?"

I increased my pace. I didn't want to think about the old man right now. "They could have been talking about someone else. It might not be the man in the park."

She trotted to keep up with me. "Oh, come on, who else would they be talking about today?" Dale took my arm. "What's the matter? Slow down."

"Okay, okay." I spotted the bench in front of the Bear's Den bar and headed for it. "I have to think." I dropped down on the hard seat. Dale sat beside me. I stretched out my legs, and tried to quiet myself.

I finally got out, "The word homicide scares me."

"Well snort," Dale said. "It's just a word."

"And I'm just worried about getting involved in another murder. I know a man named Deefy. So does Max. If the man in the park is the Deefy we know, and has been murdered after leaving a note on my door, then I could be connected with another murder. It hasn't been six months since they tried to nail me for a murder in Hog Heaven."

"But you were completely cleared."

"By the skin of my teeth. If I hadn't found that last piece of evidence, who knows what would have happened.

"Oh, come on. Rusty and Charlotte—the sheriff, mind you—stood up for you at the wedding." She clapped her hand over her mouth, rolling her eyes at the supposedly unmentionable word. I huffed, but the tension released. We both laughed. I rose from the hard bench and stretched.

"That was so scary back then, Dale. I don't want it to happen again. And Max was the rock I could always lean on. He's not here now. Neither are Rusty or Charlotte, for that matter. I'm going to wait a bit before I give the note to the sheriff. We don't need him anyway. We can handle this ourselves. Whoops," I gave her a quick glance. "I mean, if you want to help? You don't have to get mixed up in this mess if you don't want to."

"Are you kidding? Of course, I'll help. I'm as curious as you are."

"Wonderful!" I so didn't want to be alone with this. I smiled my gratitude. "I do need help. And one of the things that really puzzles me is this deefy business." I took the note from my pocket and unwrinkled it enough to see the deef dripping off the bottom of the paper. "It could be a name. Even so, I suppose there's a chance he's not the Deefy we know. It's a fairly common nickname, at least among the old timers. I've been told that, back in the old days, deaf was frequently called deef. At any rate, the man we knew lived around the Lander area. It's been several years ago. He was one of those men always looking to make some money. In and out of trouble. He got mixed up with some thieves and went to jail. Max felt sorry for him and got him a good lawyer. But I can't imagine Max ever getting involved with him again."

I put the note back in my pocket. "But now I think it's the *hurry* we should be concerned about. What do you think, Dale? Why say that if Max is driving across the state? And the writer wrote it twice. Why am I supposed to hurry, and hurry to do what?"

Dale rose too. "Or if the *hurry* is *burry*, as in, possibly, buried…"

"Not acceptable. That's another word I don't like"

We started back to my house. "Doodlebug's the weirdest thing on the note, Dale. You said you know what it is. So tell me about it."

"It's an old time gold dredge. They still have gold dredges—I have a small one myself—they just don't call them doodlebugs any more. Early prospectors made them by hand with whatever they had. It's just a piece of equipment that sucks stuff up from the bottom of creek beds, dumps it on a screen so it can be sifted with water to see if there's any color. There are hundreds of them around here."

"Oh," I said, rather stupidly. "Why on earth…"

"Mm," Dale said, "that's exactly what I thought. Why put it in the note? Was Max interested in gold?"

"Not that I know of, but he's full of curiosity about all kinds of things. Particularly if it dealt with any kind of geology or mining."

"Maybe it doesn't matter, but I wonder if that's what the note wanted you to look for."

"A doodlebug? You said there are hundreds around here."

"Hundreds of dredges, some enormous and some small. But not many that have survived from the old days that would still be called doodlebugs. I've actually seen one of the old ones, or the remains of one. In fact, that's what got me interested enough to read up on them. It was quite a while ago. I went out looking for a new place to pan and found this creek. I followed the stream bed a bit and saw a fancy wrought iron fence surrounding what looked like a big pile of junk. That someone had memorialized such a thing caught my interest. I didn't know it was the remains of a doodlebug until I read the plaque. Most of the words were worn off, but it said Doodlebug, and something like *miner's best friend*. Can't quite remember. I thought it might be part of an old ghost town, or settlement that wasn't well known. I didn't have time to investigate that day and never got back. We could go check it out if you like."

CHAPTER 4

Back at the house, first things first. I carefully spread the note out on my printer screen and made a copy, front and back. I should have taken care of it properly when it was found. It might be evidence. We'd already ruined it for fingerprints.

"Look at this, Dale." The crumpled paper was a mess. A deep wrinkle had creased *al* making the l look like a possible t. She peered over my shoulder. "Al might not be a name after all. Along with all the other mistakes, he could have forgotten to cross the t, making it at. "I tried best *at dugglebug.*

"Makes more sense, anyway."

"I want to get a look at that doodlebug. Okay?"

"Sure, if I can find the damn thing again. But look, Thea, I don't want you to be disappointed. We're not going to find Max. You do know that, don't you? I don't want you to get hurt again."

"No, I don't know that." I felt tired, wrung out. "I don't trust that sighting completely. If he were simply driving off somewhere, he'd call. Even if he was in some kind of a pinch he would have called and said, "Hey, I've got a problem, will you come with me while I figure it out."

With a pained look, Dale put a hand on her forehead, groaned dramatically, and rolled her eyes. "Why, why can't you accept that he's just another jerk? How can you have so much faith in him? Guys do this all the time."

"But Max wouldn't do it. I know he wouldn't."

"That's what every woman says before she gets a black eye, a broken arm, or a bullet between the eyes. I know you love him, but don't trust him. A little doubt would do you good." She looked truly distressed.

"Oh, Thea," she said. "I'm sorry, I shouldn't be talking like this."

"It's okay. I know you think I'm a silly romantic, and maybe I am. I do know that bad things can happen, that people you love can do horrible things to each other."

"He's hurt you enough as it is."

"But in this I think I'm right. Even when he and I were new together, Max stood by me, and we've been through some crazy, frightening times. He never doubted me. Even when I was unsure of him, he gave me breath. Now it's my turn. I'll stand by him until I find I can't." I sounded like an operetta; I should burst into song.

As usual, Dale picked up on my thoughts quickly. "Stand by me, la de lade la, stand by me."

We laughed, and warbled two stanzas together. It helped to keep things light, but deep down worry and concern were digging holes in my heart. I needed answers. "Let's go check out that doodlebug thing."

She hooked her arm in mine, and said, "If that's what you want, that's what we'll do."

I changed into more rugged clothes and shoes, while Dale rummaged through the kitchen for food supplies to take with us. Dale pointed to the neatly packed cooler. "We won't starve. Okay if I take the rest of that wine?"

"Sounds perfect." And, of course, we took her truck.

I wasn't as fond of Dale's truck as she was. It was old, noisy and not very comfortable. Someone along its ownership trail had installed a radio-CD player. Dale's CD collection, gleaned from garage sales, filled the glove compartment. Lots of good old stuff. As the passenger, I got to choose the discs. I liked to close my eyes and pick. This time I got bluegrass, *Oh, Brother Where Art Thou.* Rather appropriate until *O Death.* I shut it off. Another half-disc of the Beach Boys and we turned off the highway onto a graveled road. The old truck shimmied and rattled, the noise so bad we shut off the music and just talked over it.

I didn't need a preamble. Dale knew what was on my mind. "That note can be read in lots of different ways. Taken at its simplest, the message was: Max is okay. This Deefy person tried, but help is still needed. Hurry to a doodlebug. At least that's the meaning we've come up with. But if we're right, why did he give the note to me, and not the cops? I wouldn't know a doodlebug from an ant's behind.

"Maybe he was scared of the law, so he came to you instead, knowing you'd tell the cops when he couldn't himself."

"I almost did. I probably will." I just needed time to think about the Deefy connection."

Nothing but flat, dry land stretched in front of us. Scattered within the miles we could see were clumps of greenery. The larger ones, indicating ranches, either current working ranches, or possibly, abandoned old homesteads. One of the larger areas of growth seemed close to a slender butte, hiding it from view now and then. Big or small, water was the key. Wherever water was, for long periods or short, it left its mark. Thirsty soil slurped it up, seeds jumped in, grasping their chance for life. It was one of my favorite things about the dry desert land.

But I couldn't help wondering if this was the wildest of all wild goose chases. We passed occasional broken down wind mills sitting in their own clusters of parched sage, and cactus, all difficult to see through the hazy dust cloud we drove in. I hadn't a clue where we were. Why would Max have been out here? Why would anyone be out here? We seemed to be headed toward a big green clump to the right and above another big one. We could already see thickening clusters of willows and possibly even cottonwood trees.

"Are we getting close? And tell me more about this doodlebug thing, and why you think it might be the doodlebug the note mentioned."

"Shot in the dark. There's all kinds of junk, machinery, you name it, left out here, but something with a fence around it was special. That's why I remembered it."

I agreed about the junk. I'd long thought Wyoming was the land of abandoned stuff, as if the large open spaces fed a need to hang onto crumbling barns, cabins, outdated machinery.

Dale pointed. "See all those willows along the road ahead and that hill up ahead?"

"Only a flat-lander would call that a hill."

"Over the top of that slight rise," she gave me a smile, "is a bend in the road heading to the right. At that point we need to start looking for the creek. Lots of willows surround its path. The creek had water the first time I saw it. That's what caught my attention, but it could be dry now. Also grown over. What we should look for is the trail I found not far from the bend. It might be easier to spot. It's on my side of the road, so keep your eyes out for it."

She slowed to a crawl, rolled down her window and we both squinted diligently at the side of the road, thick with weedy growth. We drove on about half a mile.

"Is that it?" I asked, then answered myself, "No, there's a fence across it."

She rolled her eyes at me, and reversed the truck. "Where?"

"A little farther. There. Does that look like a faint trail?"

"Could be." She stopped, then drove forward.

"Not it?"

"Absolutely it. I'm a little uneasy about parking there, is all. We'll be crossing a fence. It might be private land." Dale shrugged. "I don't know. I don't worry much about it when I'm just looking to see what's out there. If it's worth coming back, then I try to find out if it's private or public land."

She probably didn't try too hard, but who was I to judge?

"I prefer to be as inconspicuous as possible. Some people can be pretty hostile. There's a better parking place a little further on."

We drove on about a quarter mile and saw a wide spot that looked as if it had been used as a turnaround. "This is it." She swung in and off behind a couple of large raggedy bushes. Not really hidden, but less conspicuous. She took a loaded backpack from behind the seat and tossed an empty one to me. I put my water bottle in it and slung it over my shoulders.

It took a while to find the trail again, but find it we did. The barbed wires on the old fence had enough give for easy access. Dale held up the top two strands and stepped on the bottom two to give me space to crawl through, and I did the same for her. The trail was slight, not much more than an animal track in places.

"This is it," Dale crowed. "There's the creek bed. Look how overgrown it is. No wonder it was hard to see." She strode ahead. "Let's go."

The track followed the dry creek bed lazily up over a couple of hillocks and around a cluster of wimpy looking willows. Then there it was, across the creek from us, right on top of the bank. The tall, old-fashioned wrought iron fence with spiked tips leaned a bit here and there, but still marked its spot well, even though surrounded and nearly engulfed by long grass and weeds. It enclosed what looked to be a pile of rotting boards and rusty metal.

We stepped easily across the trickle of water, and climbed up the bank.

"Let's see if there's a gate. Here's the plaque."

I stepped up beside her. Shaped like a shield, the letters on the plaque were barely discernible. I spat on my fingers and rubbed the incised marks. The letters in Doodlebug were quite worn. The miner's best friend, that appeared below, was a bit easier to read.

"I found the gate," Dale hooted. "Simple latch, stuck of course." She grunted, putting all her weight against the bolt.

"The weeds might keep it from opening, too."

"Never fear, my dear." She slung off her backpack and took from it a small hammer and a huge hunting knife. "If this lady wants in, she gets in." Two pounds from the hammer and the latch squealed open. I pushed the gate as far as it would go and she hacked at the weeds with the knife until there was room to squeeze through.

On closer inspection, the doodlebug remains appeared more understandable as something once standing that eventually collapsed on itself. An open-ended square piece of weather-grayed, warped wood that might once have been a cab leaned against a couple of bent and rusted metal wheels. They in turn leaned against a majestic pile of boards, beams, heavy chains, and more miscellaneous rusted metal pieces, all about seven or eight feet long. I couldn't make heads or tails of the thing. Every bit of it enthralled Dale. She knelt and peered, and tried pulling different pieces.

"Look," she said. "This must be part of the drag line. Here," she held up a loose board, "this is part of the box, I can't see any crawlers. Wheels must have been used instead. One's missing. It's really old."

"Where'd the name come from?"

"They crawled, or were pulled, along river beds or creeks, wet or dry, and had a bucket or shovel of some kind that would dig deep down, then throw the dirt on a screen. As it crawled along doing its thing it left piles of discarded dirt behind. Some prospector must have thought it looked like a big bug crawling along leaving dumps behind." She shrugged. "Probably cabin crazy."

She sat back on her heels, and looked around. "I wonder if this could be a ghost town site. Somebody had to put the fence up. There's a town not too far from Garnet Pass that honored an enormous coal tipple in the same way. It's not a ghost town, just a tiny town. You'd like it, maybe you could write an article about it." She hacked at more weeds and pulled them from under the doodlebug. "Too bad nobody's taking care of this place."

All interesting, but my mind was focused on other things. Sooner or later Dale would remember we came here because the note might have meant "doodlebug" to be a destination. I left her to her inspecting.

Obviously, no one had been here for a long time. I

glanced around, remembering my worry about another word in the note. The *hurry* that might have been a *burry*. But if something had been buried here, it hadn't been recently. The area around and behind the doodlebug had been cleared at one time. I walked to where the wild, tangled growth began again and spied a glint among the wildness.

"I'm going to look around a bit," I said and walked toward the spot. Something metal. Some kind of shed, maybe. Bigger than a shed, I thought when I got closer. A small storage unit. Like the doodlebug, it was mostly obscured with weeds and scrub oak.

"Hey, Dale," I called over my shoulder. "I found something."

CHAPTER 5

I brushed aside a clump of tall weeds, baring the shack's flimsy corrugated tin wall, then let the weeds bounce back. Curious, I walked the perimeter, as much as I could, letting my hand trail through the tall grasses, dodging around plants as big as trees. There was a small window without glass. The whole thing was larger than I thought, maybe eight by ten. Most of the riveted seams had burst in places and were rimmed with crumbly rust. I turned the corner and stumbled when another bunch of rabbit brush I touched simply fell over and revealed a partially open door.

"Dale, come here."

"Where are you?"

I stepped away from the building so she could see me. "Over here." She waved and I went back to the door, peering in cautiously before crossing the threshold. Very dark. Basically empty, except for some stuff on the concrete slab floor.

"Well, snort!" Dale said, pushing in beside me. "What kind of place is this?"

"I don't know, a storage shack in its better days, maybe. Not as old as the doodlebug by a long shot, but seriously neglected, anyway."

"I'll get a flashlight. Be right back."

A pile of something—looked like a blanket—was in the far corner. A closer look showed a well-used tarp, covered with dark grease stains. I kicked at it lightly, hoping it wasn't a critter's nest. An empty water bottle rolled out.

"What did you find?" Dale rushed back in, flicking the light's beam all around before settling on the pile at my feet. "Huh. A dirty tarp. I hoped there would be some really old stuff in here. Grab a corner," She did the same and we flipped the tarp over. Three more empty water bottles, and a couple of dirty blankets, one shaped into a pallet.

"Looks like someone's been bedding down."

"And not that long ago," I added. Dale slid the pallet with her foot. There were stains on the floor. She moved the light closer. Dark, black, like those on the tarp. I pulled my water bottle from my backpack and poured some on the floor stain, letting it pool a bit before sliding my foot through. The water spread out on the concrete.

"Holy crap," Dale said, "looks like blood."

My heart began a slow, deep thudding. "You're right. Max?"

"Come on, Thea, don't go all girlie on me. You know it could be anybody's blood."

"But remember why we're here. We were sent by that note. Sure, it could be coincidence, but I think coincidence is telling us that Max was here...and injured. Just like the note said."

"Kinda said. Or it could have been Deefy who bled. He's the one who's dead. And Max is—"

"I know, I know." My voice rose in irritation. "Max is in his pickup driving off into the sunset."

What on earth would Max be doing way out here the evening before the wedding? No matter what the note said or Rhonda said about his being elsewhere. It felt like a mind-blowing game. Some crazy person, messing with my head.

Dale kicked at the pallet again. A shimmer of silver appeared. She flashed the beam on it. I gasped, and snatched it up. A money clip. Silver with an engraved bronze saguaro cactus.

Max's money clip.

Dale read my reaction accurately. "Max's?"

I nodded. "A birthday present. I gave it to him two years ago. He always had it in his pocket."

I closed my hand around it, holding it tightly, the symbol I'd been looking for. Something that spoke of Max's presence. Max *had* been here. I pressed the clip against my cheek. Its coolness spread through me like soothing vindication. Something *had* happened to keep him away from the church. Even if I didn't know what it was, it meant my belief in him was correct. His disappearance wasn't intentional.

"He was here, Dale."

"Yeah, but gone now."

"True." I shuddered. "What a horrible place to find yourself down and out, injured, sick, whatever the case had been. How desperate he must have been." I put Max's clip in my jeans pocket and gave it a pat. My first piece of evidence. "I need to give the note back to Rhonda, Dale. Maybe they'll really start looking for him now."

Dale flashed the light around again, stopping at some empty Vienna sausage cans. "Jeez, a diet of water and

Vienna sausages. If that's Deefy's best, it's a wonder anybody survived. And I'm thinking we should get out of here. Spooky. Whoever's been using it could come back anytime, and I don't think we want to be here."

We left everything where it lay, except for the money clip in my pocket. Quick-stepping to the door, we ducked out and jogged across the creek bed and up on the bank to the path.

A shrill screech stopped us in our tracks. I glanced behind me and saw a wizened old woman with long grey hair hanging past her shoulders. A couple hundred yards away, she was trying to make her way towards us with a walker.

"Stop!" she yelled, stomping the wheeled legs on the ground. "My land! My property!" She reached for something from the walker's basket and raised her arm.

A gun? Not waiting to find out, we ran down the trail. I followed Dale, stumbling on the uneven ground, but not slowing. We scrabbled through the fence, and took off down the dusty road to the pickup. I soon slowed to a half trot and, relieved, collapsed against the truck's bed, gasping for breath while Dale unlocked the cab. Nervous laughter burst from both of us, but Dale lost no time getting the truck started. We blasted off down the road, straight ahead, not back the way we came in.

I don't know what we were so worried about. The old woman couldn't have caught up with us, unless, of course, she had a vehicle close by, and a road, or a short cut. Just in case, I watched carefully, but nothing followed us. We were all alone on the road, leaving an impressive and highly detectable dust trail behind.

"You can slow down now." I dragged out my water bottle and took some great gulps. "We're safe."

She grinned and held out her hand for the water. I gave it to her. We still wore back packs, which were incredibly uncomfortable to lean against. She eased to the side of the road and stopped while we struggled with straps and threw them behind the seat.

"I don't know where this road goes," she said, "but I'm pretty sure it will lead to the highway. Let's go a little farther before we stop. I need a sandwich. That old witch really scared me."

"Me, too. I was afraid she pulled a gun out of her basket. Did she? Did you see one?

"Hell no, I just wanted out of there."

"What was Max doing on her property? Could she have shot him and hidden him in the shack?"

"Why would she shoot him?"

"Because he was trespassing? She certainly didn't like us being there."

"She's using a walker. How'd she get him in the shack? I didn't see any signs of a body having been dragged."

"Maybe she had help. I wouldn't think she'd be living alone out there."

"Deefy must have been with him."

I'd forgotten Deefy. "Yeah. Maybe he lives there, too. Or used to. She could be his mother for all I know."

"Or his girlfriend." We both snickered at that thought.

"Oh, I don't know, Dale. We probably overreacted. She startled us, is all. Maybe we could have gotten some information if we had tried to appease her."

"Ho, ho. You're a brave one suddenly. Don't forget we were on her land where two guys had been holed up, one of whom is now dead."

I hadn't forgotten. One of them murdered, the other possibly headed out of the state. Injured? Or could the writer of the note be the one who bled all over, and his *tried my best* was about what…escaping maybe? He had escaped, or he couldn't have put a message on my door. And why did he supposedly want me to hurry if they were both gone? Max disappeared five days ago.

CHAPTER 6

The constant truck noise was giving me a headache. Now I knew rattletrap was an honest word. We were trapped in the rattle. Difficult to talk, listen, or think.

"You're awfully quiet," Dale said, over the noise.

"Do you know who that old woman is?"

"Hell no. Other than, obviously, the property owner. I'm sure we can find out."

"How?"

"Well, ask around, for one thing. Or you can go to the court house in Green River and look at the plat book. But that takes forever. Your best bet is to ask Rhonda when you drop off the note. If you do, and I think you should. The sheriff's office knows everybody.

"Hey, look at that!" She pointed ahead. "The only real tree we've seen for miles and some wonderful idiot put a picnic table under it."

She gunned the truck, then slid to a stop beside the table. A typical wooden number with attached benches, weathered out of shape, and covered with gouged-in names of numerous happy campers. I was happy too, to jump out, stretch my legs, and relax my ears.

Dale hauled out the ice chest while I stood on the road, gaping at the scenery—or lack of it. We were back in the empty area. This scraggly, gnarled cottonwood was, indeed, a lonely specimen. From here I could see the butte I'd noticed before and the nearby clumps of greenery not too far from where we were. They didn't look as far away now.

"Does this area have a name, Dale?" I asked with a touch of awe.

Sandwich in hand she stood beside me, munching and gazing. "I suppose it could be part of the Red Desert Basin, though I always think of that as being east of here. It's just a big empty area. Don't think it has a name. There are a couple of county roads through here, a few ranches. More unnamed dirt roads, and several creeks, but none go completely through the area."

"There's a refinery back there. We're about forty miles from Rock Springs, less from Garnet Pass, but none of these roads go there. You have to get back on the highway for that." She swallowed the last of the sandwich and brushed her hands off on her jeans. "Come on. Get something to eat."

We went back to the table and I grabbed a sandwich. The sweet smell of baked ham and tangy mustard brought saliva to my dry mouth. Dale produced a frosty bag of grapes. I took the wine bottle from its bed of ice along with a couple of plastic glasses. We put everything on the scarred table and sat down.

"Let's not stay long," I said, even though it all tasted wonderful. "I want to get the note to Rhonda. Tell her what we found. I might even read it to her. Make sure she pays attention."

"Yeah, ask her if she knows the old witch. I'd like to know, too." She took another half sandwich and munched silently for a moment. "I've prowled around out here a bit, but I don't know anyone who lives here. There aren't many. Over there," she gestured with her right arm, "are some sand dunes, and up there," she nodded vaguely with her head in what I assumed was a northwest direction, "are some canyon lands. I'm more familiar with that area, which is closer to South Pass City and the known gold areas than where we are now."

I poured the last of the wine. "Where we were, where the doodlebug is, must be one of the ranches."

"Yeah. There's lots of public land, as well as private. It's hard to tell what's what."

I shook my head, bewildered. "Why would Max be out here with Deefy? How did they meet? Accidently, or on purpose? And why did Deefy get killed?"

There's another possibility we haven't touched on." Dale grimaced and gave an odd smile. "You won't like this, but what if Max, you know, what if they had a fight, or maybe it was an accident, but could Max have killed Deefy?"

"Max? No way! Not possible!"

"To save himself, or someone else?"

I cringed. Unbelievable. Self-defense? "Then why would Deefy say Max was okay?"

"It might have happened later that night, after Deefy left the note."

"Not if Max is driving all across the country." Something else I didn't want to believe.

"He could have turned around and come back to Garnet Pass."

I drained the wine from my glass and began to pack

things up. Dale cocked her head and watched me as I piled everything back in the cooler.

"I shouldn't have brought it up. I just thought we should look into all possibilities."

"Oh, Dale," I sighed. "It's all right, just unbelievable to me. Max wouldn't handle things that way. He's not only big and strong, he's smart. In a bad situation, he'd find a way to overpower the man, tie him up, and haul him off to the cops. Or if he killed someone, accidentally, or intentionally, he'd turn himself in."

I rubbed my temples and began to pace. "We, or maybe just I, assumed from the note that Max had been injured, because that's where I was in my mind. So, *Max ok*, was a huge relief for me. He wasn't dead. And, *I tried my best at doodlebug*, raised the assumption that whoever wrote the note tried to help Max. Going to the doodlebug because *hurry* was in the note was a wild shot on our part, but it actually panned out, and made us believe that Max—because of his money clip—and probably Deefy, had both been there."

"But aren't there now."

"Right. But it's all assumption, Dale. Even the money clip could have been put there by someone else."

"Don't forget the blood. That was real."

"And Rhonda claiming someone reported seeing Max close to Sheridan is also true, I guess." I added glumly, "Even the note's simple statement, 'Max ok', could mean either Max is alive and well, or that Max is an okay guy. The only thing we know for sure is that if the dead Deefy is the Deefy Max and I know, then the note could implicate both Max and me in his murder. Is someone trying to set us up? It's been done before."

"That's ugly."

"Very. We need facts. First I need to know the dead

man's last name. I'm pretty sure I'd recognize it if I heard it."

"The gossips in town probably have that by now."

"Or I could ask Rhonda." I chewed my lip, still trying to straighten things out. "I'm having second thoughts about giving the note back to her. As I said before, if they connect the *deef* in the note with the dead man, both Max and I become tied to the murder. That's bad enough." Might the sheriff, thinking Max was mixed up with Deefy, come up with the same question Dale had?

CHAPTER 7

I t was late afternoon when we drove into Garnet Pass. We were both exhausted. Worn down by the rough ride, constant dust, air conditioning that produced more noise than cool air. Dale's old truck, which she adored with a passion, left much to be desired. Silence had reigned pretty much for the last half hour. My brain was numb.

"I'm pooped," Dale said, and yawned. "What do you want to do now? Want any food?"

"Not yet. Let's stop by the house and unload this stuff. I'll make some coffee and try to decide whether to approach Rhonda or not."

"How about this. I'll drop you off and while you make the coffee—which I'm assuming you'll top off with whisky and whipped cream—I'll check in at the restaurant and see what the good old boys are talking about."

"Sounds perfect. Thanks a bunch. And please bring the whipping cream. I don't have any."

By the time Dale returned, I had showered, changed clothes, made a big pot of coffee, and set out my fanciest mugs, which weren't much. Most of my good stuff was still at Max's house.

Dale had done the same, at least the shower and change bit. "Hey, you're looking good, lady," I told her. Her hair was down, waving softly around her shoulders. She wore a nice pair of slacks and a pale blue lightweight sweater. No hiking boots. I call this her Saturday night look and have only seen it twice, though never on a Saturday night. The first time was at the church, and the second when we drove to Green River to eat in a restaurant she liked. One of her many attempts to get my mind off you know who.

She handed me a covered bowl. "Thanks, and ditto. I even whipped the cream so we could get right down to business."

"And the business is...?" I prepared the mugs with two shots of whisky each and a mountain of cream. We took our mugs and sat on my comfy, lumpy couch in the living room.

"The business is facts." She sipped. "One, at least." She licked the creamy mustache from her lip. "The old guy's name is Hammersmith. Deefy Hammersmith."

"That's him!" I set my mug on the coffee table with a small splash. "That's the name. He's the Deefy I know...or knew. The first time I saw him was at a rodeo in Rawhide."

"Where's that?"

"A tiny town not far from Rawlins. He was dressed as a mountain man and had a pet fox. He was a regular at all the small town rodeos."

"But not a good guy."

"More like one of those unfortunates who are always in the wrong place at the wrong time."

"This evidently was another of those."

"Yeah, a whopper. Did you hear how he died?"

"Somebody said he had a heart attack. Somebody else heard he was beaten to death." She shrugged. "Could be a combination of both. Who knows? Also heard they took the body to Rock Springs, which I assume is true. I suppose that means the county sheriff will take over the case."

I swirled a big gulp of the spiked coffee around my mouth, "Probably. I don't want to get involved with another sheriff. I need to find out exactly when Max was seen driving out of state or close to it. Sheridan's some three hundred miles from here. It would help to know if it was days ago, or recently."

Dale didn't bother answering. How would she know? However, the possibility that Max might have, for whatever reason, come back here was tantalizing. I said, "There's one more thing I could do, or we could do if you're not sick and tired of all this mess. I think you know that Max and I planned to live in his house after we were married, at least until we decided if we wanted to stay here or go somewhere else."

"Yeah, that jazzy straw-bale he had built. Did I ever tell you I took the open house tour during the business fair last year?"

"No, but anyway, I'd already moved some of my things over there. A few days after the wed...well, you know what I mean. I went to the house and picked up some clothes and personal items. It was pretty emotional. I didn't stay long, just grabbed what I wanted and got out. I snooped a bit, of course, checked his closet, you know..." I hesitated, cupped the warm mug in my hands and took a couple more sips. I didn't want to remember the overwhelming surge of aloneness I'd felt in that empty room.

"Tell me. Had he cleared everything out?"

"No. But what I'm trying to get at is I didn't make a real effort to see if there were any...clues, or what have you, as to where he might have gone. I checked his calendar to see if he'd made any notes, and his land-line for messages, but that was about it. I'd like to go back now and look more carefully. Will you go with me, or are you bored with all this?"

"Sure, I'll go. I haven't had this much excitement for a hundred years. I'll even help you pack up some more stuff, if you want."

We drained our coffee.

Max's house was one of only four widely spaced homes in a new housing development about a mile out of town. It had been the showcase for the town's Business Fair last year. Max commissioned the house more as a favor for the mayor and his efforts to bring business to Garnet Pass than as a place to live. He seldom stayed in one place long but followed his oil field business wherever it took him.

The structure's straw bale core lent itself beautifully to the adobe-like appearance of its finish with nice thick weather-wise walls and an overall friendly-to-the-earth feeling. One of the new ecologically sound and energy efficient ideas; it was difficult to realize that the walls were made of forty pound bales of straw encased in mortar, the straw so tightly packed it became more fire resistant than wood.

When Dale turned into the driveway. I noticed that the automatic yard light at the far end of the garage was not working.

"That's weird, the yard light's out." I said. Did that mean Max had been here, trying to hide his presence? Would he be in the house? I hesitated only a moment.

We walked up to the front door. "I don't actually have any rights to the house." I said. "My name's not on the mortgage or anything. All I have is a key." I flashed it, and tried the handle—locked—before using it to open the door.

Hot, musty smelling air of a house closed up too long in the heat enveloped us.

"Ugh," Dale said.

"Let's get some fresh air in here." I went through to the kitchen and opened the windows above the sink, and the door to the patio, letting in a nice rush of cool evening breeze. Then into the bedroom and did the same.

"I'm leaving the front door open." Dale called. "Does the place have air conditioning?"

"Yes, the thermostat's inside the dining area. We'll be gone before it can do much good, but turn it on if you want."

I stood in the bedroom and looked around. Nothing had changed. Everything was as it had been when I last was here. Again, I checked the closet and the bathroom. Everything as usual. I'd noticed then that there was no suitcase packed for a honeymoon. Was that significant? I hadn't known then, I still didn't know.

CHAPTER 8

I f I was going to find anything helpful in Max's house, it
would most likely be in his office. That's where he spent
most of his time.

Dale stood in the middle of the living room gazing at
everything. "This place is really nice. Too bad…" Thankfully, she let the thought go unspoken and followed me into
the office.

A nice room, it looked just as an office should look.
Leather chairs, a big masculine desk, and ranks of book-
cases along the walls. It hadn't been lived in long enough to
have that homey feel; still his touch appeared in a hard hat
and coveralls hanging from a coat rack and several of the
long tubes for core samples leaning against each other in a
corner. I sat at his desk while Dale eyed the contents of the
adjacent bookcase.

His desk was always neater than mine, particularly if I
was writing an article. Still, there were more papers in a
pile on the left than usual, and a paperback on top. I
picked up the book. A simple title: *Gold*. Subtitle in
smaller letters: *A Field Guide for Prospectors and Geologists*. So

he did have some interest in gold. Interesting. I set the book aside and flipped through the rest of the stack. Nothing more about gold. A couple of petroleum journals, papers related to his business, and a copy of *Western True Adventures* that had one of my articles in it. A heart tug.

The telephone sat on the right side of the large desktop with a paper weight shaped like an oil well standing beside it. No messages on the answer machine. A business card poked out from under the paperweight. I snicked it out with a fingernail.

"Hey," Dale said, "he's got some great books."

"There's one on gold here." I handed her the paperback.

"Wow, this is Dan Housel's book." She ruffled through the pages. "His website's the best ever. You should look at it. It'll teach you more about gold than I ever could. I've wanted this book forever. Hmmm. Suppose I could borrow it?"

"He's not here to say no." I held up the business card. Carson A. Olmstead, Bank of America, Palmdale, Florida. "Florida," I said out loud. Did something tug at my memory? "Why Florida?"

"Why not? Sounds good to me." She had her nose stuck in the gold book.

"It just struck me as strange, is all." Of course, she was right. Who doesn't know someone who lives in Florida? I shoved the chair back a bit and opened the top center desk drawer. Pencils, pens, paper clips, a rubber-banded bunch of business cards and an address book. I lifted the cover of the address book and saw a loose piece of note paper with the same person's name as on the card and, apparently, a home address and phone number, also in Florida. Interesting. The card on the desk top hadn't been bundled with the rest, and the home address wasn't something already in the address book.

"These could be new." I showed them to Dale. "I might give him a call." *Or not.* What on earth would I say? I folded the paper around the card and put it in my pocket, anyway. I shut the drawer with a bang, and shoved away from the desk. None of this sat well with me. Snooping through Max's belongings felt terrible. If he were in the area and hiding out, in good shape or not, maybe injured, he'd surely come here, if for nothing else to get a change of clothes. I felt a rush of anger at him, and at me for caring about what he did. What had he got into and why was it shaping into something—.

A clanging crash sounded from the direction of the patio.

"Max!" I yelped.

Dale jumped up, the book tumbling to the floor. I pushed past her and ran toward the noise, shouting, "Max, you son-of-a-bitch!"

I flipped the screen's lock, and stepped out in one motion. A man rose from the tangle of an upset metal chair. He wore a hoodie tied tightly around his face. Dark as it was, I immediately knew the shape didn't belong to Max. I back-tracked, stumbled, fell on the metal table, banging my forehead against the edge. Pain seared across my face. Grabbing a chair back, I twirled it in front of him and bounced back through the door, screaming, "Dale! Watch out!"

I slammed the patio door shut behind me, flicking it locked, and saw Dale kicking and flailing in the rough hold of another man. This one wore a red hoodie. I grabbed the sweatshirt, trying to pull him off her. He gave her a sucker punch to the side of her face that threw her across the room.

"Dale!" I turned loose of the shirt and moved to her, but he grabbed me from behind, twisting my arm up behind my back. I screamed in pain.

Outside a horn honked repeatedly. I yelled for help. Bad move. He hit my face with his fist, and took another punch to my chin.

A groan burst through my throat. I tried to move, but flopped back down. My head smacked the floor. "Ouch!"

"Be still."

My eyes flew open. Dale loomed over me, wiping my face with a sloppy wet cloth. "What are you doing?"

"Duh. What does it feel like?"

She helped pull me to a sitting position. I shook my head and regretted it instantly. "Who were they?" I asked, feeling pretty groggy.

"Haven't the faintest. Are you all right?"

"Did you run after him?"

"No, I didn't," she snapped. "For some silly reason, when the guy ran out, I crawled over there and locked the front door, damn it. He knocked you out!"

We glared at each other for a moment. Then I remembered the punch that sent her flying. "Hey," I said, grinning sheepishly. "Thanks. Are you okay?" I took the wet cloth from her and wiped my face again. "Tell me what happened?" My thoughts were fuzzy little nubbins, bouncing around my skull like jumping beans.

"I was right behind you, trying to stop…Why did you run out there? Did you think it was Max? By the way, SOB is a great new name for him."

"I'd been thinking about him, I guess, none too kindly. I heard the racket, thought…" I shrugged. It sounded stupid to me now. "It wasn't Max. Some man in a black hoodie." Things began to come back to me. "When I realized my mistake, I tried to throw a chair at him and managed to get back in the house."

"Yeah. About the time you yelled a warning, this other guy popped through the front door."

"Did you recognize him?"

"No. I was too scared to pay attention. I don't suppose you got a good look at the one in black?"

I shook my head. "Too dark. He wore a hoodie, too. Well, thanks for trying to get that creep off me."

"A lot of good it did. He hit you a good one. Let me see your face." She turned her face to me and wiggled her jaw. A large red mark crawled from her jaw through her cheek. "It looks awful."

She ran her hand lightly over the bruise. "It's really tender, but I didn't get knocked out like you did. I was up on my knees when the honking began. It must have been his buddy. You know, the guy dragged you to the door, I thought he was going to take you with him, then when the other one started honking again, he just dropped you and ran out.

"When I managed to get up, I called the sheriff's office. Somebody should be here any minute. I was worried you'd been hurt really bad. Your face doesn't look good."

We both still sat on the tile entry floor by the front door. Dale stood, and I rolled onto my hands and knees and rose to my feet. My head pounded, but I wasn't dizzy. We moved slowly into the living room and sat in chairs. "So they both just ran off? Weird."

"What do you suppose they wanted?" Dale eyed her wrist and flexed it. "All the lights were on, so they knew someone was here."

"Home invasion?" I suggested.

"And we scared them off? We were both on the floor."

The front doorbell rang.

"Will it be Rhonda?"

"No," Dale said, going to the door. "Someone else is on duty. What are you going to tell them?"

I grimaced. "The truth, of course."

Dale snorted her disbelief.

CHAPTER 9

Dale opened the door to an elderly man in a tan uniform with a star badge. He nodded to her.

"How are you, Ms. Anders?" Turned to me. "Ms. Barlow?" He smiled. "Remember me?"

"Well, yes," I said, surprised. "You changed the locks on my house for me."

"Yes, Rollie Upton. I'm the acting Deputy Sherriff until the newly appointed one arrives. He'll be here tomorrow. I was at the station when your call came in," he said to Dale.

I nearly collapsed with relief. Rollie was a kind, nice man. A Garnet Pass old-timer, in his sixties, I'd guess. He specialized in finger-printing, or whatever they call all the new processes they use.

Dale claimed her chair again and Rollie perched on a sofa arm. All settled, he eyed us affably, then asked, "What are you doing here?"

"Uh…Well." The simple question strangely flummoxed me. "This is Max Holman's house. We were engaged to be married, but it, uh, fell through."

"Yes. I know about that." He cocked his head, waiting for me to go on.

"I still have some of my things here. I, we," I looked to Dale, "came to get them." For some reason I felt like a kid caught lifting goodies in a candy store. I rushed on, "I was here once before and picked up some of my clothes and books. Max gave me a key." My words sounded defensive even to me.

"Yes, and what happened while you were here?"

"We were starting to gather some of my things—"

"What kind of things?"

"Pots and pans, some dishes I'd brought over. The house was very hot for being locked up so long, so we opened some doors and windows and, as I said, were about to gather some things together when there was a huge crash out on the patio. I went to see what happened, thinking it might be raccoons or something. But some man was there. It looked as if he'd tripped over a chair."

"Can you describe him?"

"He wore a black hoodie and had the hood tied so it covered most of his face. So I can't tell you what his face looked like. Average height, I think, but I don't remember anything else."

"And you, Miss Dale?"

"There were two of them. I had run after Thea, and then this other person just burst through the front door and grabbed me from behind. He knocked me across the room, but really cold-cocked Thea when she tried to help me. I was scared as hell. He dragged her around and then all of a sudden—I guess it was his buddy—started honking his horn outside. I tried to get up because I thought the guy wanted to drag her out with him, but he just dropped her and ran out the front door. As soon as I got to my feet,

I quick as hell locked the door, called you and tried to revive her."

"You did the right thing. What made you think he wanted to take her with him?"

"Well, I'm not sure." She thought a moment. "When he got her to the door, he kind of made a move...bent over a bit, maybe, like he was going to pick her up, or something." She shook her head. "I can't really remember. I was just scared for her."

He rose from the chair and inspected my face. "Are you all right now?" I nodded. "Can you show me where you were?"

"I came to right there." I pointed to the entryway. "But when I first saw him..." I lead the way to the patio. I, too, was curious to see what was out there. Two of the wrought iron chairs were on the patio floor. An oil barrel was on its side not far from the kitchen window.

Rollie inspected everything with a flashlight, including the ground beneath the window. "Looks like he might have been standing on the barrel so he could look in the window. Come inside, now. I want to put some tape out here. We'll check for prints as soon as possible."

Dale and I went back in. He made a short call before following us.

"I hope you'll be more cautious in the future, Miss Thea. This house has been empty for a while; there are always people who like to take advantage of that." He tucked his phone back in its carrier and eyed us. "Both of you should check in with the urgent care clinic. Your bruises need attention.

He looked from Dale to me. "If you like, I'd be glad to help you pack up your things and take them to your home."

I'd forgotten about that. I looked blankly around the

familiar room with its comfy chairs and memories of laughter, love, long talks, and plans for the future. My hunger for Max and the comfort and security of his arms folded around me left a hollow place in my heart.

"No," I said, eyeing the smear of blood on the carpet as if it signified the collapse of all the promises we held dear. "Thank you, but I think we've had enough excitement for one night. I'll do it another time." *Or maybe never.*

"Unless you're a part owner of this house, I think you should let me have your key. I assume that's how you got in?"

I nodded dumbly. Did he think we might have crawled in the window? I pulled the key from my pocket and held it out.

"You can come back anytime to get your belongings, just stop in the office and pick up the key. As I said before, Rusty's replacement will be here tomorrow. His name is Dave Krause. He's from the Rock Springs Department. A good man. We'll fill him in on everything that has happened here."

"I wish you were the new sheriff," I said. The known is always better than the unknown.

"It was offered , but I'm ready to retire. My wife and I want to do some traveling before we get any older."

He smiled nicely at both of us and gestured to the front door. "After you, ladies. I'll see that everything is locked up. Be careful driving home."

"Oh," Dale said. "I have to get my book." She limped into the office and came back hugging the gold book to her chest. Rollie escorted us out to Dale's truck and gave each of us a hand up.

Even with his help, I could feel my bruises as I pulled myself into the old pickup. Dale echoed my groans. We said goodbye, and assured him we would be very careful, and were on our way.

"And now we have a new sheriff," I said. "Dave Krause. I wonder what he'll be like."

"I wish it could have been Rollie, too," Dale said. "Can he do that?"

"What? Take the key? I don't know."

"It just seemed weird to me."

"Me too." I felt like I'd been robbed of my last connection to Max. But then I remembered I had another way into his house. A garage door opener.

As much as I enjoyed Dale's company, it was a pleasure to be dropped off at my house. One glance at the mirror and I knew I'd look like a zombie tomorrow. We probably both would. It didn't hurt much unless I touched it. So I prepped an ice bag, took it, a sandwich, and another Irish coffee topped with a good slug of wilted whipped cream, into the living room and settled on the couch to contemplate. No matter how I tried to sort out today's happenings, and shape them into something coherent, nothing really hung together. On the other hand, some things became clearer. We didn't find any evidence that Max had returned to Garnet Pass, or that he'd done anything else of note.

To hell with logic. Feelings worked better. My heart knew, sappy as that sounded. I grinned. As Dale would say, oh, snort. I was a living soap opera.

The only thing I knew for sure, was that something—most likely bad—had happened to Max to keep him from our wedding. A feeling rather than fact. No one was looking for him except me. Fact. Because of the note, I believed I had knowledge that the sheriff didn't. Most likely a mixture of fact and feeling, depending on a bunch of things. Whether it was harmful to me and Max, or not, I needed to give the note to the Sheriff's Department, which might give them an impetus to look for Max as well. True, true. The inevitable passage of time made all of this scary. Tomorrow would be the seventh day. A week, and closer to the tenth day which loomed like an ultimatum; a dwindling of hope for a solution. A time when people, officials even, think a lost person won't be found, at least alive. A time for the dreaded D word to rear its ugly head. I said *no* to that word. I promised myself not to think of death, only rescue.

CHAPTER 10

I needed a plan. Unfortunately, I couldn't think of anything other than what had served me well in the past: give all the information I had to the authorities who, supposedly, knew what to do with it. *Supposedly*, being the scary part, given my past history with them.

I hedged a bit by calling the authority who wasn't really an authority any more, Rusty Metzger, ex-Deputy Sheriff of Garnet Pass, who now worked in Utah. As a rule, I didn't call people after ten o'clock in the evening, but it was only ten past and I couldn't wait. I refreshed my coffee again before dialing. Maybe not a good idea. But, at least to my mind, false courage was better than none.

Fortunately, he was home, it wasn't too late, and I wasn't too woozy from the hopped up coffee to make sense…I hoped. I began by asking if he'd heard from Max. He hesitated, most likely embarrassed by my eagerness.

"No, Thea, I haven't. I'm sorry. I would have told you if he called."

"That's all right. Just curious." I didn't want his sympathy. "Some strange things have happened today, Rusty, and I'd like your opinion as to how I should handle them."

Without giving him a chance to say no, I unloaded, starting with the note on my door, Deefy's death, our trip to the doodlebug, what we found in the shed, and ended with the weird incident at Max's house.

"Did you get a look at the man?" was his response.

"What man?"

"The one who attacked you."

"No, neither one. They were too hidden by hoodies, and everything happened too fast. It...it wasn't Max. At first I thought he might have come back to his house for something. Did you know that Rollie was the temporary deputy sheriff? He's who came to the house when Dale called for help."

"Yes. And that the new man is Dave Krause. I've met him a time or two. He'll be good for Garnet Pass."

"Rollie took my key to Max's house. Can he do that legally?"

"I'd have to check it out. Look, I'm sorry you and Dale were attacked. It must have scared the hell out of you. You did the right thing to call the sheriff. And you need to give all that information, everything you told me, including the note, to the new sheriff. Everything, Thea. Tell him everything." Cop notes hung heavily on his voice. "What else do you want my opinion on?"

"Could those happenings be tied together, to Max's disappearance?"

"You mean even the mugging, because they happened the same day? I understand how tempting it is to think they could be tied together, but as a lawman I know that's not always the case. My advice, if that's what you want, is to tell the sheriff everything you've told me. You'll be sure to give him the note?"

"I planned to in the morning."

"Why don't you go down there now? Someone will be on duty."

"You don't think Max might be mixed up in it?"

"In what?"

"I don't know. Whatever's going on! The old man's death, thugs breaking into his house."

"I doubt it." He sounded as exasperated as I felt. "Surely you were told that he was—"

"Spotted around Sheridan." That again. "Yes, they told me. Do you know when that happened?"

"A couple of days ago, I don't remember exactly. Whoever stopped him told him to call me, but he hasn't. Who knows what Max has on his mind? If he wants to contact either of us, he will. I know your propensity for wanting to figure things out. But you've been hurt enough already. Leave it alone. I can't emphasize that enough. It's interesting that you found the shed out in the country, but don't try to investigate anything on your own. Give your information to the sheriff. He's a good man. Let him do his job. Don't meddle with this stuff. Okay?"

Easy for him to say. I couldn't let it go. "Do you think it was really Max in that truck?"

He hesitated, maybe a moment longer than necessary. "All evidence points to it." Which wasn't much of an answer.

"It's getting close to ten days, Rusty. Do you think he's dead?"

"No! Ahh, Thea, don't ask me that. He's my friend. I'm pissed that he's done this to both you and me. And no, I don't think he's dead. Sooner or later he'll show up and, to tell the truth, I don't know how I'll react."

That was honest, and comforting in a strange way. And if Rusty didn't think Max was dead, then I wasn't crazy for thinking the same thing. "Thanks, Rusty. I guess that's what I wanted to hear." Eager to be rid of the awkward conversation, I asked, "Is Charlotte there?"

"Sure." I heard the relief in his voice. He, too, was glad the conversation was over. "She's indicating she wants to talk to you."

Once Charlotte got on the line, I barely got a word in edgewise. Unusual for Charlotte who was the essence of politeness and courtesy. "Are you all right?" she asked me for possibly the fourth time.

"Yes, Charlotte, I'm fine. Why do you—"

"I've been thinking about you a lot recently. It would be so much fun if we could get together some time."

"You're not having visions again, are you?"

"It's just that I'm having…"

I broke into her pause. "Is Rusty in the room with you?"

"Yes, yes, that's the problem."

"You want to tell me something you don't want him to hear?"

"Yes, well, not really,"

"Is it about Max?"

"No, no. Nothing about that at all. Worrisome things. Uh, I haven't met many people around here yet, you know how it is when you move to a new place." Her voice was light and happy, and I felt sure she was putting on a show for Rusty's benefit. "But we're invited to a barbeque this weekend, so that should be a lot of fun. Are you working on any new articles?"

"No, I haven't found anything to grab my interest yet."

"Well, it's best to keep busy, isn't it? I'll call sometime soon and we can plan to meet for lunch in Green River, or Rock Springs. I miss you."

"I miss you, too, Charlotte. Let's do that lunch soon. Bye now."

What was that all about? I knew Charlotte's strong psychic tendencies sometimes got her in trouble. She's had the ability to read auras ever since she was a little girl, something her parents discouraged as much as possible, but her abilities only grew. She tried to hide them, afraid that people would think she was weird. Rusty wasn't crazy about her talents either, particularly if they interfered with his criminal investigations. At any rate, I hoped what she didn't want Rusty to hear was more about auras and visions than any problems in their marriage. Their closeness was idyllic to me.

I was too weary to think clearly. Time to get my pajamas on. I went to the bathroom to wash up and nearly jumped out of my skin when I saw my face in the mirror. A lot worse than before. The slash on my forehead had taken on color, and a bruise was forming below it. The flesh around my left eye puffed with shades of yellow and purple. Damn those two jerks!

For a moment, I stared vacantly at my pathetic looking face, thinking both Rollie and Rusty called the two men casual criminals, looters, preying on empty homes. But the house wasn't empty. Dale and I were there. All the lights were on. What if it were the lights that attracted them? What if Dale and I were the ones who surprised them? Had they expected to find Max? Were they looking for Max, too? Or were they a couple of weirdoes? Did red hoodie really want to drag me off with him?

I paced through the house. Stopped in the kitchen, got a glass of water, locked the doors, sat on the edge of the bed, worry, worry, worry, got up and paced some more. Sleep eluded me. I finally sat at my desk and, with a heavy sigh, placed my hand on the pile of reference material.

Okay, maybe now. I opened my computer. It didn't take long for a spark of interest to ignite. Libraries, large and small, were my gold mines, and the dedicated librarians who took pains to archive hand written or spoken memories of insignificant old-timers were my found bits of sparkling color. I revived contacts with some of my favorites, and sent out a variety of queries for a Honeybell Forever or any other person of interest. Once on-line, it was easy to get lost in fascinating stuff. I spent four hours before my eyelids began to droop.

CHAPTER 11

"**W**ow! What happened to you?" Rhonda asked. Obviously, neither last night's late work nor this morning's ice packs and slathered on makeup had done much good.

"Ask the new sheriff." Grumpy, still I was there, note in hand. I couldn't think of anything else to do except follow Rusty Metzger's advice. If I, or Max, wound up getting involved in another murder investigation, Rusty might be our best advocate.

"Sheriff Krause isn't in right now," Rhonda said, rather stiff-lipped. "But I'd be glad to help you." So it was to be formal now, with the new man, everything official. All right by me. I had my story rigged up and it wasn't too far from the truth.

I handed her the note. "I tried to give this to you yesterday, but didn't want to be a bother when you were so busy. After I learned the man found in the park was named Deefy, I decided you people should see it. It might be a stretch, but the note could have been signed by a person named Deefy."

She spread the note out and looked at it briefly.

I pointed out the statement about Max, the misspelled doodlebug word, and told her how Dale and I happened to find one out in the country. I explained about the shack, what was in it, our conclusions, and even told her about the crazy woman, and asked if she knew her. I let out a big breath, and shrugged, not knowing where to go from there.

Rhonda looked at the note, flipped it over, and looked back at me again. No questions, no nothing. Her total indifference rattled my nerves.

"*You* might not think it's important, but *I* think Max's blood was all over that shack. *Please* give the note to the sheriff and let him decide."

"What happened to your face?"

My face? The note was in front of her and she was worried about my face? My voice rose to a higher pitch. "Dale and I went to Max's house last night to pick up some of my things," I snapped. "Two men broke in and roughed us up." She raised her eyebrows.

Didn't Rollie bother to tell her? I sensed questions ready to burst from her mouth. To hell with her. I stomped out.

My bad temper eased on the walk home, and I faced the morning's chores with some kind of equanimity. After a bit of work, I might even be up to searching for a gold-hungry lady of the night deserving an article.

But first the wash. I took clothes from the hamper and emptied pockets before throwing them in the washing machine. I glanced at the business card wrapped in note paper that I took from my jeans. It took a minute to remember where it came from. Max's house. I tossed it on the kitchen counter. Carson A. Olmstead.

I set the machine to wash. Instead of messing with the ice bag, I got a bag of frozen peas from the freezer, picked up the business card, grabbed my phone, and lay down on the sofa, resting the peas on my puffy eye. No thinking, no planning. I dialed the number.

A pleasant voice answered. "Hello, this is Carson Olmstead. How may I help you?"

"This is Thea Barlow, calling from Wyoming. I—"

"Thea?" He laughed. "Great to hear from you. Are you two still on your honeymoon? Tell Max I've been waiting for his call."

I jerked to a sitting position. The peas splatted on the floor. "What...who are you?"

A pause. "Carson Olmstead. I'm sorry. Did I make a mistake? Aren't you the Thea who married Max Holman?

"Yes, I mean no, but...Wait. Let's start over."

"All right." He sounded serious now, his exuberance had disappeared.

"I am that Thea, but we didn't get married. Max is... uh...missing. Why were you expecting him to call? When did you last talk to him?"

"Missing?"

"Yes." Impatience seized me. "He didn't show up for the wedding, "When did you last talk to him?"

"The day before the wedding. Around noon time. I asked him to do something for me. He mentioned he was getting married the next day, but said he had time to take care of it that afternoon."

"Take care of what? Where did he go?"

Another pause. "Look. I don't feel comfortable talking about this. Please tell me what's going on." A polite answer to my snappishness.

"I'm sorry," I said, truly contrite. I took a deep breath. "I'm being terribly rude. This is an unexpected development for me, a welcome one, I think. I'll try to explain, but first a question. How do you know Max?" Some kind of memory niggled in my mind.

"I don't know him well. We met at my grandfather's funeral in Rock Springs?" He ended the sentence with a slight question mark, a touch of humor in his voice. "Gramps left his ranch in the Rock Springs area to me?"

Of course! We'd met after the funeral. Before I could say anything, he cut in, "Enough clues. I'm really teed that you don't remember me. I hoped I made a better impression on you."

"I *do* remember. I didn't go to the funeral, but the next evening the three of us went to dinner."

"Yeah. At that restaurant with the flyswatters. I'll never forget it."

"If you had said 'red hair,' I'd have remembered you instantly."

He groaned. "The bane of my existence. Why couldn't it have been, 'A pleasant looking chap, rather taller than most.'"

"Well, that too, of course." I was always a sucker for red hair though, and his was brilliant.

"My memories are more generous. I still think about that blue dress you wore. A knockout! If Max walked out on you, he's got rocks in his head."

I lapped up the flattery like a starving puppy. Still there were other things. "So what did you ask Max to do? Where did he go?"

"Do you remember at all what we talked about that night in the restaurant?"

I racked my brain. "Some of it. Your grandfather was a geologist and a prospector. I'd never met him, but he was an old acquaintance of Max's, and...and he left his ranch to you. I'm sorry, I don't remember his name."

"Alton Olmstead, and good, you *were* listening. I was

afraid I was boring you, or leaving you out of the conversation. I threw so many questions at Max."

Mostly I remembered a lot of laughter and a strong undertone of excitement between the two of them. Not many details. "Treasure hunts! I remember you telling us that your grandfather used to set up treasure hunts for you when you were young."

"Great fun for a kid. The treasure never amounted to much. Most of the time it was simply a lesson learned, but gold was always the lure."

"Gold?" The subject kept rearing its head.

"Yeah. That was Gramps' specialty. He was considered an expert on South Pass City mining fields and worldwide gold deposits. Did a lot of consulting."

I remembered the book Dale and I found in Max's office. "But what did Max have to do with all this?"

"Gramps left me a box of items that also contained a note saying if I needed help with my inheritance, Max Holman would be a good person to consult."

"Really? I wonder why?" Ooops, that didn't sound right. "I mean, Max isn't a lawyer."

"No, but he's a geologist. That's all that ever counted with my grandfather. The note was out of place with the other items in the box until the contents, including the note, reminded me of the clues my gramps rigged up for treasure hunts. Made me think he left me more than the ranch."

"And that's what you talked to Max about?"

"Yes. From the evidence I gave him, he thought the contents might have something to do with gold. Which wouldn't surprise me either." He laughed. "We were both pretty excited about it. Planned to figure it out when I got my act together and got back to Wyoming again."

A treasure hunt sounded right up Max's alley, which

was fine and dandy, but where was Max now? "And so you wanted him to do something for you the day before the wedding?" I asked, not wanting to entertain thoughts about the possibility of a treasure hunt being more exciting to Max than I was.

"Max was keeping an eye on the place for me, you know, checking to see if there were signs of people breaking into the house, shooting out windows, that kind of thing. He called once. Said it looked as if someone had been nosing around. Nothing serious, but I thought I should get some no trespassing signs posted. That's what I asked him to do. Anyway, he said he could get some up, but urged me to get out there soon. He said he'd call when he finished posting the signs. When I didn't hear from him, I just thought he got caught up in wedding stuff." He paused. "Look, I know I've been negligent. Even if I decide to sell the place, I need to get out there and get it done. I've got things here that have to be tied up, but maybe now's the time. I'll try for next week. How can I reach you?"

I gave him my phone number, then risked sounding like a bitter, jilted woman. *Was I that? Is that why I couldn't let Max go?* I said, "I'm curious to see where Max must have decided there were things more important than getting married. I'd like to drive out to your place. Is it easy to find?"

"It is way out in the country, but easy enough to get to. You can't miss it. There's a big butte on the far end. If you want to go out there, it's fine with me. You can look around if you like. And hey, if you see anything out of order, give me a call. I gave Max a key to the house, but I don't suppose…"

"No, I don't have any of his keys, but I don't need to go into the house. I'll just look around the grounds."

I jotted down the directions he gave me. They were straight-forward enough for me, or certainly for Dale, to manage.

The call had been fun. Exciting. Information that was more solid than a doodlebug in the middle of nowhere.

CHAPTER 12

A s eager as I was to tell Dale about my call with Carson Olmstead, I decided to Google the old geologist's obituary first. I found that Alton Olmstead had been a long-time resident of the Rock Springs area. Eighty-seven years old, graduate of Colorado School of Mines—which Max was also—Korean War vet. Survived by one son, a daughter-in-law, and grandson, Carson, whom I had spoken to. Nothing about a wife who had either survived the old man, or preceded him in death. Interesting. Probably a divorce involved.

Then I called Dale. "What time do you get off work?"

"Noon, today. What's up?"

"If you're not busy, why don't you come over when you're finished? We can grab a sandwich. New developments have occurred." I wanted to tell her about the treasure hunt. She'd jump at something like that, but I wasn't sure if it was privileged information or not. "I called Carson Olmstead."

"Who?"

"The man in Florida. The business card I found at

Max's house. Can you come?"

"Wouldn't miss it. Don't make sandwiches. I'll bring restaurant leftovers."

I groaned. "Oh, yum."

"Don't knock it. Today's Fiesta Day. Tacos, tamales, and decent guac."

"That *is* a yum. I'm game. Bring it along."

The enchiladas were heavenly. Fat and hot, covered with green chili sauce and oozing a rich filling of meat, onions and cheese. We talked while we ate. I told her about my call to Carson Olmstead. "He'll be here—Rock Springs—sometime next week or maybe earlier." I filled her in on our conversation, leaving out the treasure hunt. "So that's where Max went when he disappeared. I'd like to get a look at it."

"Come on, Thea, do me a favor. You know Max didn't disappear."

"Yeah, yeah. He was seen. I can't help feeling there's something fishy about that sighting." I used a finger to wipe up the last glob of guac from my plate.

"You mean you don't want to believe it."

I grinned. "That might be part of it. Let me have my foolish dreams."

She smiled at me and touched my arm. "Okay."

That's what I liked about Dale. "I want to go out there now, this afternoon. Will you go with me?" I handed her the directions Carson gave me. "How far do you think it is?"

She took a last bite of tamale, wiped her hands on a napkin, and picked up the paper. "Hmm. This place might be fairly close to the area we were in yesterday. Doodlebug country. He mentions a butte. I remember seeing a butte not too far from where we were.

"I saw it too. Is that a coincidence or what?"

"Hang on, not so fast. We don't take the same road. It'll be west of where we were, maybe close, maybe not. I'll map it. And of course I'll go with you. This is going to be fun. I still think there might be an overlooked ghost town around there. I'd love to be the first to uncover it. You know, be the first to dig through a forgotten town's dump."

"You and your ghost towns," I said indulgently

"You and your Max. I still worry about you, Thea. I think you're headed for a fall. I hate to say it, but if he's alive and well...and as madly in love as, I admit, he seemed to be...wouldn't he have found some way to contact you?"

"You said it: alive and *well*. What if he isn't? And don't throw that police sighting at me again. There are too many coincidences in the things that have happened in the last couple of days. You know what Einstein said about coincidences."

"Oh snort. No I don't. I don't think I know one word of what Einstein said about anything."

"He said coincidence is God's way of remaining anonymous."

She rolled her eyes at me. "And what's that supposed to mean?"

"To pay attention, that something you think is coincidence might be a message, or something like that."

"Whatever." Unimpressed. "It doesn't matter. I'm with you anyway, Thea, and willing to follow any of these threads you want."

"I truly appreciate that. I assure you, I'm not a weeping willow. If we find a ghost town, I'll be delighted. We'll explore it together. Please don't worry about me. I'm a big girl, I know what the possibilities are and can face them... already have. I just feel I have a responsibility to Max... and maybe to myself."

"Did you give the note to Rhonda?"

"Yes."

"And she said…?"

"Nothing. Not a damn thing. Drove me insane."

"And you did…?"

"Walked out on her. I still don't know if she'll give the note to Rollie. Excuse me, *Sheriff* Krause," I said, remembering Ronda's snooty response when I called him the new man. "Let's go before it gets any later."

As it worked out, we only took the wrong road once and had to backtrack, and this was with the butte in sight. Over the years individuals made their own roads for their own needs, usually to connect with a county road for their convenience. These roads were poorly marked, if at all. The county roads were well marked.

I hadn't a clue what kind of a road we were on now, other than it was heavily wash-boarded, and we were fast approaching a heavy growth area.

A little farther and I said, "What's that up ahead?" On my side of the road. It looked like a rickety goal post in the middle of a bare field. When we got closer, it became a large metal sign similar to those many ranches had. Two metal posts with the cross bar featuring a name cut from metal. The whole thing leaned into the wind, but the name was still readable: Olmstead.

Dale yelped, "We're here! We actually found the place." The Olmstead sign straddled a track twisting through bare dirt towards us, but entry from the road was barred by a metal gate. A crude latch without a padlock indicated easy entrance. There weren't any no trespassing signs. Did that mean that Max hadn't been here, or that he hadn't planned to post them? Did he go through the fence, as we were going to do? Or had he been waylaid by some other event before he got here?

CHAPTER 13

I unlatched the gate and walked it open. Dale drove through over old mud ruts from some long-forgotten rain. I closed the gate—law of the land; open a gate, close it behind you—and got back in the truck. We could see buildings, and yes, some trees and other growing things. The butte wasn't as close as it had appeared to be, maybe a mile or so beyond the house. We passed another less-used road going off to the right that we could explore later if we had time.

I had to smile when the house came in sight. "It's a grandma house." Tall, two stories, white painted clapboard, tatty with age. A couple of dormers broke the roof line, indicating a possible attic.

"What's a grandma house?"

"Oh, you know, the kind of homey, hard-worked country homes so many of us remember visiting when we were kids."

"Huh," Dale said. "I wasn't so lucky. My grandparents had a doublewide trailer home."

"I'm sorry," I said without thinking.

"Don't be." She smiled a no-offense-taken. "Doublewides were hot stuff in those days. It was a palace to me, but before that, they had a small, hand renovated, log cabin. I don't really remember it. It's always broken my heart that they had to work so hard for so long. Then when they were old and worn to a nubbin, during an oil boom, they got a couple oil wells on their property. Not enough for millions, but more than they'd ever seen before. That's when they bought the doublewide. That's all they ever did for themselves. Gave everything else to family, their grandkids, me, my brother and sister.

"I didn't know you had a sister. Was she older or younger?"

"Younger. She's dead. I...I can't talk about it anymore."

I touched her arm. "That's okay. I always remember that when you go back as an adult, you're shocked to find grandma's is just a normal home, not the gigantic building you remembered."

"You're right. I remember that, too."

We parked where the neglected browned grass began and got out. Struggling shrubs that had over-lived their time sat on both sides of the front door. A large add-on poked out of the left side of the building, and there was a second floor sun room that might have been a later addition as well.

The house sadly needed paint, and the siding around the entry begged for repair. I tried the door. Locked, as expected. Old and neglected, still there was a comfortable feel to the place. "In its heyday, I expect it looked quite nice."

"What heyday was that? A hundred years ago?" Dale peered through the large window to the left. I did likewise to the right; a living room with the usual kind of furniture.

"Nothing out of order that I can see," I said, joining Dale.

"Likewise. Looks like a bedroom here, but the window is mighty dirty."

We walked around the side of the house. Tender loving care was needed everywhere. I wondered how long the old prospector had lived alone, and what had happened to his wife; he'd obviously had one.

Off to the side and back of the house stood a large open shed and a metal Quonset building several yards beyond. A jacked-up, wheel-less old Cadillac from the eighties or nineties filled the left side of the shed. Withered, blackened bales of hay, threatening to collapse, filled the other side along with a pile of rusted tools. Dale kicked at the pile, knocking things askew. She squatted and fished through the stuff. "Gold pans." Held another up. "Sieve pan, hole torn in sieve. Rock hammer, broken handle. Just junk. I've got better stuff in my backpack."

I wandered towards the Quonset where there were more piles. "Looks like more gold pans."

"Newer, better design," Dale said, joining me. Two dusty black backpacks lay in the weeds behind the pile.

I wondered why they were just lying around outside. Max had a black backpack, as did probably four hundred others around here. They were as common as hoodies. I picked one and opened the zipper. Gloves, hammer, chisel, couple of bags of gorp, telescoping water cup, wads of plastic bags. I fished through all the compartments, looking for anything that might identify the owner, or an item that I might recognize as belonging to Max.

Dale did the same with the other. Both had maker's logos. I didn't recognize either one. I hadn't paid much attention to his backpack, other than knowing it resided behind the seat in his truck and he seldom used it.

"Just the usual stuff in here." She dropped it on the ground. I snatched it back up and looked through it again, afraid she might have missed something. But no. Nothing.

We went back to the Quonset. The walk-in door on the side of the building was locked, but the full-front roll-up door showed no lock. I tugged on the handle and it slid up easily. A small tractor sat in the far left corner, while miscellaneous tools and equipment littered the rest of the floor.

"This is an oldie," Dale said running her hand along the tractor. "Pops had one like it on the farm. And it was old when he had it."

I walked around the odds and ends of equipment, dodging spots of oil sludge on the cement floor.

"You know, Dale," I said, stepping out of the opening and looking back in. "There could have been other big stuff in here. There are oil stains behind the tractor and one in the space beside it. A truck could have been parked there."

Dale jumped down from the tractor and eyed the spots. "You're right. As a prospector, the old man might have had a digger of some kind, or a dozer." She stuck a finger in one of the puddles. "It's still sticky."

"When I talked to him, Carson said he and his parents came here after the funeral and closed everything up. I can't imagine they left things lying in the open, or unlocked like this."

"Yeah, looks like someone helped himself. This is all useful stuff for gold hunters. A lot of guys I know would be tempted. Hell, I'm tempted!"

Vandals...Or Max? Would he have been tempted? No way. Not his style. "I'm going to look around, see if anything else is disturbed."

A screened-in porch covered the back of the house. The padlock on the handle was intact. Three stately old cottonwood trees shaded the back yard. Two faded green Adirondack chairs sat in the trees' shade, while a large, fenced-in garden plot filled with last year's dead debris, sat out where the sun could get at it, sadly missing its caretaker.

I walked quickly around the far side of the house. The only thing of interest was one of those old-fashioned, slanted cellar doors that sat on the ground. The heavy door would open to stairs leading down to a basement entrance. I remembered being scared to death of one like it at my grandma's house when I was little. A large padlock secured the door to this one, so monsters couldn't jump out of it, as my cousin used to warn me. I smiled at the memory, but knew I'd never open the thing.

When I came around the front of the house, I saw Dale hauling her backpack out of the truck.

"Let's get closer to the butte and that heavy green area. She tossed me a bottle of water. "It can't be more than a mile. We can see if there's a creek, and maybe tell if anyone's been digging around. Grab one of those old pans." She pointed to the pile of junk in the shed as we passed by. If there's water in the creek, I'll show you how to pan." She had a big grin on her face. This was her element. "So let's go."

"Okay," I said, with a twinge of regret. We hadn't found any evidence that Max had been here. Not even a no trespassing sign.

CHAPTER 14

W e took off cross-country, headed toward the butte. "Hey, look at that." Dale pointed to a pond set a short distance behind the Quonset. We walked over. A couple of logs for seats were placed by the edge.

"Lots of pond scum!" But I marveled that the bright green was a nice interruption of the dull brown soil.

"Water's down about three inches from the high mark." Dale squatted at the edge. "Well, hey, water is water. Hand me your pan."

I watched as she skimmed some of the scum away with the pan's edge, then filled it with dingy water. Using some of the water to soften the pond's dirt edge, she broke off a couple clumps and dropped them in the pan. She handed me the pan.

"First lesson. Swirl it around a bit to break up the clumps." She took out two small glass vials from a cargo pant pocket.

Accomplishing a swirl motion without slopping was surprisingly difficult. Both my pant legs were wet. Dale put a hand over mine and gentled the motion so the water barely hit the pan's edge without sloshing out. She emptied the bottle of black stuff into the water. "Black sand." She took the pan and, turning her back to me, shook the contents of the other bottle into it as well. Facing me, still swirling, she smiled with satisfaction. "This is how Walt taught me to pan. He always spiked it. Not to cheat or fool, but to illustrate what you're looking for and how to find it. Panning can be slow and tedious work until you get really good at it. Let's go sit on a log."

We sat. She held the pan between her legs and swirled. "By now all the heavy stuff, the black sand and the gold, if there is any, is on the bottom of the pan. It's time to get rid of at least half the water and as much of the dirt and light stuff as you can. Like this." The swirls became stronger, sloshing water, dirt and pebbles between her feet. "You try."

The motion was still awkward, but I was getting better.

"Good, that's right. It just takes a lot of practice. Here, let me do the rest." She took the pan from me without stopping the swirl. "I really want to get to the butte and see what it's like."

It took merely seconds before the only thing left in the pan was a small pile of black sand spread along the pan's bottom crease barely covered with water. She handed the pan to me.

"Oh, look!" I saw tiny glimmers of color.

"Tilt and move the pan so it all spreads out in the crease. Now tap the edge of the pan. Keep tapping." Gradually the bright bits swam out from under the black sand into a line of tiny gold pieces. I couldn't stop saying, "Oh, oh, oh." A slight movement of the pan slipped sand over the gold again, but tapping brought the bright specks peeking out as if they were live things scrabbling from the darkness. The sight, the brightness gave me a thrill of...

what? Happiness? Delight? Certainly a high of some kind. It felt wonderful. Dale stood behind me, tapped a few more times, then stuck her finger on the line of gold and moved it out of the water. I was speechless, couldn't stop smiling.

Dale got another bottle out of her pants: plastic with a snout. "Snuffer bottle." She put the nozzle to the gold and sucked it into the bottle. Then sucked the black sand in as well. "I'll clean all the gold out of the sand some other time." She packed the bottles away as if there was nothing to it. For the first time, I envied her cargo pants.

Dale grinned. "Close your mouth."

"I can't. I'm blown away."

"I told you it was fun. We can practice with the gold some more until you get comfortable with the action, then we'll get back to the real world of panning: nothing but dirt, mud, and stones for days, months, sometimes years. It's not even easy to find black sand. And that doesn't guarantee there will be gold, just a better chance. You have to use your smarts to find this stuff. That's half the joy."

"How much have you found?"

"Not much. My smarts aren't that smart yet. But I'm getting there. Let's go."

I could hardly wait to tell Max about this...Uh. That thought snapped the gold fever right out of me. An hour, maybe, and I hadn't thought about Max once. Good or bad? I didn't know. I grabbed my water bottle, sloshed some on my hands and face, then took big gulps, and plodded after Dale.

No path. The hike was...well, a hike. Less than a mile, but not much. Rough ground, lots of cactus, rocks, stones, and bristly clumps of growth. The heat didn't help. I wore a pair of light-weight walkers, which were adequate, but not as sturdy as the hiking boots Dale wore most of the time whether she was hiking or not.

Finally the butte rose in front of us, tall and majestic. Soft greenery spread around the bottom slope and lured us to meager shade cast by willows and stunted cottonwoods. We stood on the edge of a creek bed. No water. Dale jumped down and scuffed her feet in the dirt, squatting to look at the stones she'd uncovered. I dropped down beside her. She took a short-handled shovel from her pack and dug deeper.

"What are we looking for?"

"The heavy stuff like black sand which is compatible to gold, or bits of gem stones that are affiliated with gold. Rubies, garnets, sapphires. Take a look at anything sparkly, or that looks different from its surroundings." She handed me a couple of garden tools from her pack. "Here, find a place to dig."

"Are the smarts here?"

"Well, kinda, but not really. We're downhill from South Pass City and Atlantic City, lots of old gold mines there. So there's a chance there could be wash from there. It would be smarter to be much closer. Gold is so heavy it doesn't travel far."

I started scratching with the hand rake to loosen things up.

"Or you could look for a rock that might have stopped rubble traveling in flash floods or heavy rains. Hundreds of years of them.

I spied a rock ahead and went for it, then saw a larger one a few feet ahead. Someone had already dug the area behind it and left a considerable pile of dirt that looked pretty fresh to me. I stood and eyed the length of creek bed, wondering if others had been here before us. Some kind of bag sat on the bank, nearly hidden by a sage brush. It was just another black backpack, but at least it had a red zipper to distinguish it. Maybe we weren't the only ones here.

"Hey, Dale," I said softly, motioning her towards me." Instinctively, I put a finger across my lips to warn her.

A thermos leaned against the pack along with a rock hammer. We walked a few steps farther around a slight bend and saw two men in the distance digging with shovels at the base of the butte. They weren't close enough to distinguish features. One wore jeans and a black muscle tank; the other, cargo pants with a red and black plaid shirt.

"What are they doing? They're trespassing."

"Maybe not. It can be hard to tell a trespasser just by looking."

"This is Olmstead land, isn't it?"

"Yes, but it depends on who owns what. If the government owns the minerals, someone other than the land owner could lease a mining claim from them. If the land owner owns the surface rights, that's the ground you walk on, he can charge a fee for the miner to cross his land to get to his claim. If he—foolishly, in my opinion—sold his surface rights, by law he has to give the miners access to their claim. At least that's the simplified version. But if the Olmsted's own all the rights then, yes, they're trespassing."

As we watched, the man in the tank top backed off from his work, threw his shovel down and wiped his face with his arm. His buddy, the larger man in the loud plaid shirt, looked up and yelled something at him. The sound of his voice drifted our way, but without enough clarity to understand. Their body language spoke for them. Anger, anger and more anger.

Tank top spat on the ground, said something else, and flashed the finger. The bigger man dropped his shovel, strode to the offender and shoved him hard enough in the shoulder to knock him down, all the while shouting and pointing with quick jabs of his arm at the areas they'd been working. He gave a shrug of disgust and went back to work.

Dale and I stood in full view, gawking, but neither of them looked our way.

Whatever was said, black tank top pushed himself to his feet, grabbed his shovel as if it were a baseball bat and took a wild swing at the red and black shirt.

"Watch out!" I yelled automatically. The man jerked around as if he'd heard, or sensed the warning and knocked the shovel askew with his left arm while landing a vicious punch to tank top's stomach.

Dale grabbed my arm. "Let's get out of here. Run!"

We raced back down the creek bed. I snagged the telltale backpack by a strap as we ran, letting it drag in the dirt behind me. We stopped to catch our breath while we still had a bit of cover, and heard the roar of a truck disappearing in the distance. Hoping it meant the men had left, we peeked around our cover of rocks and scrub to scan the terrain.

"All clear," Dale said and we set off at a fast walk to the house and Dale's truck.

CHAPTER 15

W ait a minute," I said, holding an arm out to stop Dale. She stumbled against me. "Isn't that another truck beside yours?" Side by side, the other truck's cab could slightly be seen as a color change above Dale's.

"You're right." As she spoke, a man with a rifle stepped from between the two vehicles and stood there watching us. He held the rifle casually pointed at the ground, still an expressed threat.

"Do you recognize him?" I asked Dale. "Is it anyone you know?"

"Never seen him before." The shed and Quonset were to our left. "Do you have your phone?"

"On my belt." I reached for it.

"Don't. He might think you're reaching for a gun."

"Good grief, Dale!"

"Don't play around when guns are involved. When I say go, we'll run behind the shed. Grab your phone there." The man hadn't moved. He waved us forward with the rifle.

"Now," Dale said, and took off in a fast dash that I imitated. A shot blasted in our ears. We dropped behind the shed. I dragged at my phone and punched 911. No services.

"Get up on your feet," a voice barked.

I whirled. He'd come around the far side of the shed, holding the rife non-aggressively at his hip, none-the-less scary.

Furious, Dale jumped to her feet. "You shot at us!"

"I did not. I shot in the air." As if that made a difference. He was paunchy, mid-fifties, dressed in cowboy boots, jeans, and a well-worn sweatshirt.

"Who are you?" I demanded, surprised by my strong voice. "What are you doing here? You're trespassing."

"You're the trespasser." He stared at me, his eyes traveling over my bruised face. A smirk pulled at his mouth.

"I'm not," I snapped, ready to do battle if he made snarky remarks about my looks. "I'm supposed to be here."

"Who says?" he shot back. We sounded like belligerent teenagers, throwing accusations at each other.

Which didn't stop me. "The owner, Carson Olmstead. I work for him." But my bravado was wearing thin. To my surprise, so was his.

He shuffled his feet and shifted his gaze between the two of us. Then back to me. "So he thinks this is his place, does he?"

Dale stepped up. "Look, why don't you get rid of that rifle?"

He glanced down at the gun, hanging muzzle down from his hand as if he'd forgotten he carried it. He walked to his truck and hung the rifle on a gun rack in the back window.

We stayed where we were. He approached and stood glaring at us aggressively.

"The Olmstead kid doesn't know nothing. The will's being contested."

"By whom?"

"The old man's wife." He lifted his chin, belligerently.

"Who?"

"Yeah, his grandmother. She's got rights to this land. I'm taking care of it for her."

He didn't sound convincing.

Dale barged in with, "You're not doing a very good job of it. Two guys are digging around up there by the butte."

"And about to kill each other," I added.

He looked startled. His lips moved but no words came out. He scratched his jaw. He took a step backwards when he looked beyond me. I turned and saw the big man in the red and black shirt striding purposely toward us.

At first sight, I thought he was the gift shop owner we saw in the restaurant, the one who sold Max our wedding rings. As he came closer I wasn't so sure. Maybe his clothes threw me off; the loud shirt and dirty khakis.

"What's going on, Virgil?" He nodded politely to Dale and me, and then did a double take to check out our bruises. He frowned, and his hand rose as if in concern, but he didn't make any comment. Instead he shook Dale's and my hands rather impatiently, saying, "Richard Townsend here. If you ladies would excuse us, I need to talk privately with Virgil for a moment."

He grabbed the man's arm, none too gently, and pulled him aside; Dale and I walked over to her truck and leaned against the front bumper.

"What was his name?" I asked Dale

"Richard Townsend."

"No, the other one, Virgil. Was his last name mentioned?"

"I don't think so."

"I'll have to call Carson about all of this. Unfortunately, I forgot to put his number in my cell, or I could call him right now."

"No services, remember?" We spoke desultorily while watching the two men. They kept their voices low, so once again it was silent movie time. Obviously, Townsend was chewing out the meeker Virgil. He kept jabbing his arm back at the butte. It didn't take much imagination to know his complaints were about his digging partner.

"Do you know Townsend, Dale?" She shook her head. "He might be the jeweler who sat with your prospector friends in the restaurant yesterday. But I'm not certain."

"This Virgil person obviously knows the other two and what they were doing. And what about the grandmother thing?"

"She must be Alton Olmstead's wife, or ex-wife. Nothing in the obituary mentioned her one way or the other. Carson didn't say anything about a grandmother, either."

The argument between the two men lightened. Townsend stared at the ground, and Virgil picked his nose.

"I'm going to put a stop to this," I said. "Whatever *it* is." I went over to the two of them and addressed Virgil. "I think we better come to an agreement until this legal matter is settled."

"Legal matter! What legal matter?" demanded Townsend. He glared from Virgil to me.

"I'm acting as a legal agent for the man who is the owner of this property, Carson Olmstead," I said, embroidering on my original story a bit.

He drew back, startled by my words.

"I'll be posting no trespassing signs on his orders," I added, cementing my authority, "and protecting his property from vandals. With legal help if necessary. I will call Carson and see if he's aware of the legal action you mentioned."

"Legal action?" Townsend again.

"My aunt has a legal right to this property." Virgil insisted.

His Aunt? "She's the wife of Alton Olmstead?" I asked.

"Ex-wife," he added begrudgingly.

One point solved. "If I may ask, what is her name?" I was quite pleased with myself. I sounded quite lawyerly. I just hoped Dale didn't start to giggle.

"Stella Parker."

So she didn't keep her married name. Probably a contentious divorce. "And yours?"

"Virgil Parker. Yours?"

I hesitated only a moment. What difference did it make? "Thea Barlow."

Virgil Parker's eyes widened in surprise, and then he quickly wiped his face clean of expression. Obviously, he knew my name, but not my face.

I said, "Until we get this settled, I'm asking you not to come on the property. I'll post the no trespassing signs, but won't do anything else until I've talked to Carson Olmstead. Will you agree to that?"

Townsend said nothing during this exchange, but listened intently, eyes fixed on Virgil Parker.

Parker answered my question with a shrug and a casual, "Yeah." The fact that he agreed so easily confirmed my suspicion that he wasn't telling the complete truth.

No one moved. Finally I said, "Why don't you go ahead, we'll follow you out."

Townsend jerked his head at Parker with a sour expression. "Come on, I need a ride," and headed to Parker's truck. A deadly combination. Two angry men and a rifle close at hand. Glad I wasn't their passenger. We watched them drive off.

CHAPTER 16

"Halfway into Dale's Dodge, I stopped. "Wait a minute. I forgot something." I took off cross-country, jogging back toward the creek where, exhausted, I'd dropped the backpack I'd snagged from the bank. Grabbing it, I hurried back. "This could belong to Townsend's digging partner. Maybe his name is in it."

She drove while I unzipped the pack. The inevitable water bottle, tools, and a kit of some kind. Scratches, dents and discoloration scarred the box's lid. I broke a fingernail opening the damned thing.

Dale glanced at it. "What's that?"

"Just stuff." I pulled out a large nail, a piece of glass which could have been from a window pane, a small plastic squeeze bottle.

"Looks like a rock and mineral testing kit."

"Oh, right." I dropped the items back in the box, remembering that Max always kept a big nail in his shirt pocket for a quick scratch test on any interesting rock he happened to find. I peered into the bottom of the bag and ran my hand through the corners.

"Nothing else in here, except some granola bars. No identification. Doesn't anyone around here worry about losing stuff?" I hefted the kit a couple of times in my hand before dropping it back in the red-zippered backpack. My assumption had been that the bag belonged to Townsend or his digging partner. I wondered how long it might have sat there on the side of the creek. Was it not dropped there today? Would this be the kind of thing Max would stow behind the seat of his truck? It certainly looked as if it could have lived in such a place for many years. I had no memories of ever seeing anything like it, but then I'd never inspected all the wonders he had stashed behind the seats in his truck either. I knew somewhere in its depths were the testing items he needed when the nail wasn't enough. I'd seen him fetch them often enough. I'd never seen Max use his backpack, either. His truck was his backpack. Dale was pretty much the same, but she also used backpacks. Could this bag be the thing that tells me Max was here? Or was I grasping at shadows?

"Do most prospectors carry testing kits with them all the time?" I asked.

Dale shrugged. "I have one, but I haven't used it much. I'd think rock hounds would be more likely to need one than gold prospectors.

We drove on silently for awhile. Then Dale leaned over the steering wheel and said, "Look up there, isn't that somebody hitching?"

A man with a sleek, swift stride walked on my side of the road with his thumb held out. He wore a black jacket with red, blue and yellow stripes on the sleeves. "Oh, snort," Dale said. "Jake the snake. I'd recognize that walk anywhere." She sped up, as if she were going to speed right by, but changed her mind and slowed to a stop beside him. I rolled down my window.

Dale leaned across me and barked, "What are you doing out here?"

He looked up, grimaced when he recognized her. "You own the place? What're *you* doing out here?"

"None of your business."

He glared at both of us. "Truck had a flat back at the cross road. Give me a lift?"

"Where you going?"

"You can drop me at North Springs."

I moved over to make room, but Dale put her hand on my leg to stop me, and said, "Jump in the back." He did. We took off.

I shot a sideways glance at her. "Hospitality's low today. You really don't like him, do you?"

"I wouldn't trust him with a rock. And I *do* wonder what he's doing out here. He could be one of those we surprised. We heard a truck leave after the fight."

"The one who tried to wallop Townsend? Black tank top. Would he still be out here?"

She shrugged. "If he had a flat tire."

I stuffed the backpack under the seat so he couldn't see it if he happened to look through the rear window. I moved sideways so I could see him out the back window. He sat on a rolled up tarp and took off the ice chest lid. He saw me watching, grinned and did a wild pantomime, pointing his finger at the cooler's interior, then his mouth, and with a funny twist of his head indicated he was dying from hunger and waved a plastic bag with half a sandwich in front of his face. I laughed and nodded my head.

"What's going on?" Dale said?

"He wanted food from the cooler and I said yes. He's pretty funny."

"Funny? Jake? You're out of your mind."

I glanced out again. He'd devoured the sandwich and

was helping himself to the last of the grapes. The breeze caught the edge of his light-weight jacket and I glimpsed a black tee shirt, but couldn't tell if it was sleeveless or not. Again he caught my eye and began his comedy routine, pointing to my bruised cheek, twisted his mouth down, and indicating tears with his fingers. Then pointed to Dale, making grumpy faces, and amazingly accurate postures and poses of a strong, bossy, crazy woman. I couldn't help my silent laughter, but it wasn't fair to Dale. I shook my head, and firmly turned my back for the rest of the way. He'd be an ace at charades, but I couldn't imagine him playing parlor games.

Dale flew over the wash-boarded road, grinning at the bumpy, dirt filled ride she was giving him. She hit the highway and headed to North Rock Springs.

When she stopped at a gas station, he vaulted from the truck with little more than a brief wave. She blasted off and we headed for home.

"I really do wonder why he was out there, Thea. Green River is his usual stomping grounds. I hadn't seen him for more than a year, then all of a sudden there he is in Garnet Pass, at the restaurant the day Deefy died, and then again today out here when we're checking up on something to do with Max. What's it all about?"

Good question. "If Townsend *is* the jeweler we saw sitting next to your Jake at the restaurant, that indicates there could be a connection."

"Don't call that bastard my Jake!"

"Take it easy. There's another scenario, Dale. It could be a case of him having the hots for you and following us to increase his odds."

"Oh snort, Thea. Get it out of your head. No possibility."

I shrugged. "Your dislike of him might not be mutual."

"Forget it. He's been around here forever. Why, all of a sudden, would he suffer an attack of the heart? No, he's got gold fever. That's what those two are after. They're up to no good. I'd bet my life on it."

"Gold fever! Everything's revolving round gold." An idea slammed me. "That's it, Dale! The article I need to write. Gold fever. I'd bet *Western True Adventures* will eat it up." My mind raced. And surely where there was gold I'd find a prostitute with, of course, a heart of gold.

I worried that stress from the wedding fiasco had dried up my creative juices. Maybe not. I knew Roger, my one-time boss at the WTA magazine, preferred my whorehouse stories, but if I could mix the two together, he'd be hooked. I could use the memorialized doodlebug for a photo and a pull-in for anecdotes about old-time prospectors. I could interview Carson Olmstead about his grandfather, whose story would be a perfect segue into the gold craziness going on today.

Dale broke into my thoughts. "Earth to Thea, earth to Thea."

"Sorry, I'm just organizing my thoughts about this article. I need to bring in some money, and this one will be fun. You can be a source for me, too. I can hardly wait to get started!

"Great. I'm delighted you've finally found something to take your thoughts away from Mr. Perfect."

"Me, too. Heartbreak's not good for the soul." If it pleased Dale to think I could drop my feelings for Max that easily, it was fine with me. Pushing the worry into the background for a while would be a relief. "Drop me off at the post office so I can get my mail. I'll walk home from there. Do you have to work tomorrow?"

"Yes, but I don't have any extra catering jobs for a couple of weeks."

"I want to get a picture of the doodlebug; I'm pretty sure I can find my way back there. If not I'll give you a call. Right now I need to get busy with my notes, before I forget the ideas in my head." I was glittering with gold.

She stopped in front of the post office and I jumped out. "I'll call you tonight. Thanks for the ride, and being my buddy on another adventure."

She laughed. "Any time, but on the next one, *I'm* bringing a gun."

CHAPTER 17

I thumbed through the mail, looking for anything official. Nada. Then checked the phone to see if there were any messages. Nothing. Weird. I'd left the note at the sheriff's office and thoroughly expected to be called in for questioning before this. Had Rhonda even given it to the sheriff? Weren't they the least bit curious? I couldn't believe they weren't going to try to link me to Deefy's death. Or maybe they had to send the note to the Rock Springs office.

I wouldn't push it. I did my duty by turning it in.

I threw the mail on the desk and called Carson. I told him about meeting Virgil Parker on his property. "Do you know him?" I asked.

"I don't think so, but if his last name is Parker, he's probably one of the hundreds of my shirt-tail relatives."

"He accused me of trespassing and I threw the charge back at him. He said his aunt had rights to the property, and the will was being contested. I gathered his aunt is your grandmother."

"Ahh." He paused. "The family secrets are out. I'll tell

you what I know about them when I get to Wyoming. But Parker's lying. Gramps spent a lot of time making sure nothing like that could happen and, in fact, that's what I've been doing here. I've been checking all aspects of the will—everything's tied up tight in a trust. And if the Parkers are nosing around, the first thing I'll attend to when I get there is to check the land boundaries, make sure they're marked and correct. Did Max get any no tres-passing signs up?"

"We didn't see any. But we caught two men digging around the butte."

"We?" A note of hope brightened his question.

I answered quickly. "A friend of mine, Dale Anders, went with me." If he had any thoughts that Max might show up, I wanted to quell them instantly. "She's a gold hunting enthusiast and has heard lots of stories about your grandfather, but never met him. So she was thrilled to see his home. May I tell her about the treasure hunt?

"Sure, as long as she understands a large jackpot is not expected."

"She'll understand. And I'll get signs posted for you, if you like. In fact, I took the liberty of telling Parker that you told me to do so. Do you know a man named Richard Townsend? He was there with Parker, too."

"No, the name doesn't do anything for me."

"He might be a jeweler in Rock Springs."

"A jeweler?"

"I know Townsend is his name, but I'm not positive he's the gift shop owner I'm familiar with."

"A store on a little side street outside of Rock Springs?"

"Yes. Do you know him?'

"No, not really. But it's interesting. Look, it would be great if you could get some signs up for me. And I wish there was some way you could check out the house. I don't trust Parker."

"We did a walk around, and nothing looked out of order with the house. There were some backpacks and tools lying on the ground outside the Quonset. The big roll-up door was closed but not locked. Did you leave it that way?"

"I'm not sure about the door, but I know we didn't leave anything outside. Damn. I should get out there."

"A good idea. I think I scared them off for a while. I told them I was your legal agent assigned to protect your property from vandals. Umm, I hope you don't mind."

"Of course I don't. In fact, thank you, thank you."

"Good."

"There's a house key hidden out there somewhere. I'm not sure where, but it has something to do with an Adirondack chair. Another of Gramps hints that were never easy to unwind. My folks and I tried to find it when we closed up the house after the funeral. No luck. Gramps was a bit eccentric. He liked to be real tricky with his hints. But if you can find it, feel free to go in and look around." He laughed. "And if you do, find the key that is, you'll be crowned High Poohbah and lead hunter for the amazing Olmstead treasure hunt."

I laughed. "A great honor."

"Ah, Thea," he said, going back to serious. "It's rotten of me to ask so much of you. You don't have to do any of it. You know that, don't you?"

"Yes, I do know that, but I have some time on my hands now." Which wasn't exactly true, I did have things to do, but would welcome another chance to see if I could find actual evidence that Max had been at Carson's. If something had happened to him before he got there…well, I wouldn't know where to look next. Depressing thought.

"No problem, Carson, which leads me to another subject. I've decided to write an article about gold fever. I'd like to use information about your grandfather and his work. Would you be willing to be a source for me?"

"Sure. I'd forgotten you were a writer. Is this going to be a book? I've got a lot of granddad's papers. You're welcome to them."

"No, it won't be anything that involved; just a magazine article." Though Carson's idea about a book was enticing. "I'd love to see his papers."

"I'll bring them when I come next week. It will be good to see you again, Thea."

The warm note in his voice ended the call nicely and gave my frazzled self-esteem a considerable boost. Hopefully my black eye would be healed by the time he got here.

I didn't have to force myself to the computer. Gold called and my search for ladies of the night became more focused to the surrounding gold fields. There were a few responses to my earlier queries, but nothing more about Honeybell. I said goodbye to her with no regrets. A real teaser came from a library in Virginia about old family letters from Denver mentioning a Dottie Jacks and, bless my butt, Atlantic City! That was right next door to South Pass City, and close to here, or close as far as Wyoming's concerned, under a hundred miles. More info to come. Another satisfying night.

Restless in the morning, I paced like a caged lion. Well, maybe not a lion, a lesser animal, perhaps, a jittery lemur would be more like it. One way or another, I simply couldn't face sitting at the computer all day doing research. I needed to *do* something and finally decided that getting pictures for the gold article would accomplish several things. First, it would appease my guilt for not working. I'd have to get the pictures, anyway. A good picture of the doodlebug. Why not now? And second, as long as I was out in the wilderness, I could stop at Carson's place for more gold related pictures, and hang some no trespassing signs. All of which would allow a more thorough search for positive traces of Max.

CHAPTER 18

I checked with Dale before I left for the doodlebug and reviewed my memory of the roads we took to get there. She had to work breakfast and lunch shifts.

"You've got it," she said. "Come by the restaurant when you get back and fill me in. Okay? And don't mess around out there, just get the pictures and get out." I knew she was thinking about the old witch.

On my way out of town, I stopped at the Old-Time Emporium, my favorite store, which sold a little bit of absolutely everything. They even had a bathtub for sale, hanging from the ceiling. Johnny Onenote was at the counter, shuffling receipts and making notations on a yellow pad. His hands were basically claws. Arthritis had curved and twisted each finger in an agonizingly different manner. I hated to stare, but loved watching how deftly he handled things. He wrote with the pencil gripped in a way I'd never think possible, but so efficient for him.

Charlotte told me he had once been a concert pianist. Turned to honky-tonk when the rheumatoid arthritis started. That's when he came west, played all over until that became impossible as well. Both Charlotte and I figured he changed his last name somewhere along the line, a fine tradition of the Old West for people who wanted to forget their past. Charlotte didn't know anything else about his background and, of course, was too polite to ask. But I was always curious. Why choose that name? Curiosity was at the top of the list of my abiding bad habits that I was going to do something about…sometime.

Johnny smiled. "Hello pretty lady." Then looked askance at my face. "You all right?"

I just laughed. "Ran into a door." I didn't want him worrying about me.

He frowned and shook his head. Too polite to say anything more about it. "What can I do for you today, honey?"

Dale hated to be called honey or sweetheart, but I didn't mind his old fashioned ways. He reminded me of my grandpa.

"First of all, I need some no trespassing signs. Do you know Carson Olmstead?"

"No. Olmstead? He some relation of Alton?"

"Yes, his grandson."

"Bless me, no. I knew old Alton. We were both Korean War vets. Nice man. I was sorry when he passed. But the rest of the family? Don't have much use for them. His son shucked Wyoming right out of his life."

"Really?" I hoped my verbal question mark would read as *tell me more*. "He didn't ever come back?"

"Not enough. Where were they when he got old and feeble? That's when he needed family. I tried to visit him once a week or so in the past years. He needed company."

"I've spoken with the grandson. He seems like a nice person, but I don't really know much about him. Evidently he inherited the ranch. Max was taking care of it until he could come back here. Max was going to put up signs for him. Did he come in here for signs?"

"No, never for anything like that." He nodded to a woman who came through the door. She headed for the counter. I didn't want to keep him. "Cargo pants?" I asked, backing away. He pointed to an aisle in the back.

They were men's pants. I looked in the women's clothes area, but didn't see any there and went back to the men's area and found a pair of ugly green ones that might fit. Eight pockets! Perfect. I found a gold pan and rock hammer in a different section and went back to the counter. I decided to wear the cargos, tore off the tags and put them with my other purchases, and went to the dressing room. When I got back, Johnny was adding up my loot and gave a little laugh.

"So you got the fever, did you? You be careful now. There are some rough characters out there."

I told him about Dale teaching me how to pan, which reminded me of something else. I went over to the shelves in front with all the rocks and minerals for kids and got three little bottles of gold flakes in water or glycerin; I didn't care what it was. Five bucks apiece. I added them to my pile.

Johnny grimaced. "That's not gold, honey, just flakes. You deserve the real thing."

"That's what *I* have to find, the real stuff. Meanwhile, I like these; Wyoming snow globes."

He went off to the outdoor lumber area and got me the signs and a rentable battery-operated staple gun, and I was ready to head out to the country.

Much to my surprise, I found the trail to the doodlebug with little trouble. I debated whether to park there by the fence, or find the more secluded spot we used before, and chose the latter, even though it gave me a fairly long walk back. I didn't care. A light morning breeze softened the heat, but hadn't the strength to stir up the constant dust. This time I wore gloves and sturdier shoes and had no problems getting through the barbed wire fence on my own.

The lonely monument to doodlebugs still stood sentinel on the creek bank, looking no different than when Dale and I had last seen it. If any deputies had been there, they were certainly careful, but then they might not have been as interested in the doodlebug as the shack. I took several shots of the enclosure and close-ups of the plaque, hoping to catch a sense of its desolate placement.

Even while concentrating on my camera work, I was well aware of the old metal shack not too far behind me. I didn't promise any of the many people who'd told me to keep my nose out of the law's business that I'd actually do so. They weren't, as far as I could tell, doing anything on their own. I found the pull irresistible. I mean, Max had been there. Maybe I missed something. I stashed my camera in a pocket and made my way through the dense weeds. And was glad I did.

Nothing had changed. Everything was exactly like Dale and I had left it. Nothing moved, no yellow tape, no evidence bagged. Water bottles, sausage cans, tarp still scattered on the floor. No sign the cops, or anyone else for that matter, had been there. So much for dear old Rhonda. Obviously there would be no help from that quarter. If I wanted information, I'd have to find it myself.

Thoroughly disgusted, I returned to the trail, looked beyond it, up where it crested the hill, where the old witch had first appeared. If she lived here, there must be a house somewhere not too far. I could be an innocent caller, inquiring about an old doodlebug I'd heard about. All true. And, if by chance, she recognized me from before, I could apologize for trespassing. Maybe sweeten her up a bit. I got along well with old people. In fact I enjoyed them. I'd had a lot of experience with cranky and cantankerous.

Decision made, I followed the path. It widened at the point where we had first seen her. The ground became harder packed, which would have made it easier for her to navigate a walker. And, yes. In the distance stood a doublewide trailer house with an assortment of out-buildings—one obviously a new four bay garage. A neglected wind break with many dead trees stood on the far side of the garage. A thick growth of scrub and crumbling cottonwoods wandered along a large area to the right of the trailer, possibly an irrigated field at one time. The trailer house stood apart from the spots of growth like an abused sore thumb. Antennas bristled from its roof, but nothing softened its bare ugliness.

CHAPTER 19

A young girl appeared from behind the house with a dog bouncing around her feet. They headed toward me but didn't appear to see me yet. Abruptly the dog stopped and began to growl. The girl grabbed its collar and faced me. I hurried my steps toward them.

"Hello," I called out, not wanting to alarm anyone with my presence, or my face. Hopefully, the makeup I'd once again slathered on my bruises rendered me less scary. On the other hand, she looked the right age to appreciate zombies. Purple and green splotches could be a plus.

The dog no longer growled, but pulled taunt at the hold on its collar in a state of full attention. I was very fond of dogs, but as I came up to the girl, I noticed it was a pit bull, and became more conscious of possible danger.

"Sit, Nonnie!" the girl said. The dog obeyed and stared at me with a great lolling tongue and goofy grin.

The girl was young, twelve or thirteen, at a guess. She glanced at my face, letting her eyes slid away.

"Nice dog," I said.

She patted its head, took a leash from her pocket and

snapped it on the dog's collar. "Mostly. I make her obey when I'm here," she said with a shy sense of importance.

"That's a good way to treat a dog. Do you live here?" A pretty little thing, she had a sweet tanned face and a long shiny black ponytail.

"No, I'm just visiting my Auntie for the day."

Was her Auntie the old witch? "And this is her home, her property?" She nodded. "I'm Thea Barlow," I said and held out my hand. At mention of my name, her mouth dropped open in a surprised grin, and she twitched excitedly from foot to foot.

"I know who you are! I know who you are." She dropped the dog's leash and covered her mouth with both hands to stop her giggles. Nonnie, the dog, jumped up on the girl's leg, grabbing her attention. "Down, Nonnie." She took up the leash again and patted the dog's head, looking at me with that shy sweet smile. "Sorry."

She reached her hand to mine and shook it. Her fingers were thin and delicate, but had a nice firm grip. "You write stories for magazines."

Wonder of wonders. "Yes, I do."

"My parents get *Western True Adventures*, and I read all your stories about animals. I loved that last one about sheep dogs the best."

"Well, thank you!" I said, quite delighted with all this. I had a fan.

"You should write more stories about dogs and the funny things they do. They're the best. Sometimes I read the articles about minerals, too. I have an uncle who is kind of famous. He died not too long ago. His name is in some books at school. I went to his funeral. I wasn't supposed to, but I did anyway. I write for my school paper. What happened to your face?"

I laughed. "It looks terrible, doesn't it? I took a tumble

on a rocky path. Don't worry." I reassured her. "It doesn't hurt much. You know, I'm always pleased to meet another writer. And what is your name?"

"Ginny Molina."

"Do you live in Garnet Pass?"

"No. Rock Springs. You know, you could come and talk to my class at school about writing."

I was loving this wonderful disjointed conversation. She was adorable.

"I'd be very pleased to do that. We would have to talk to your teacher, though." Even Nonnie the dog was licking my shoes by now.

"Ginny!" a voice screeched. We both looked at the house. "Who you talking to? Get your butt over here!"

"That's my Auntie Stella. She's old and gets mad a lot. I feel sorry for her and like to come out and help her when I can."

Her Auntie Stella. Where had I heard that before? Virgil Parker? His Aunt Stella. Virgil Parker. Things were beginning to hang together. Had I stumbled on the skeletons in Carson's family closet?

I felt like Alice down the rabbit hole, still puzzled. If I had things right, our old witch was Carson's grandmother, and Virgil Parker's Aunt. Ginny most likely simplified grandaunt, or perhaps even great grandaunt into plain Auntie. Taking it further, Carson's grandfather, Alton Olmstead, the witch's ex, might well be the person who honored the doodlebug. Could I be right?

"I'd like to meet your Aunt, Ginny. The two of you might be able to help me write the story I'm working on."

"Really!" She gave me a big grin and took my hand to lead me to the woman.

I had my eye on the witch, picking her way carefully down a plywood ramp with her walker. She didn't roll the walker as much as bang it on the ground with each step. She wore a longish skirt of what looked like burlap trimmed with yellow and blue rick-rack. A folded sweat band across her forehead held her long stringy, grey-white hair out of her eyes. A hippie of old? Wannabe, or actually was?

I noticed the walker's basket was empty. If there'd been a gun there before, there wasn't one now. She was frail, maybe, but palpable energy fueled her approach. Her face remained screwed into a tight scowl. "Who are you?" she demanded

"It's all right, Auntie. This is Thea Barlow. She's a writer."

"Thea Barlow?" Her face unfolded bit by bit from the scowl. She was very old. My thoughts of her as a villain began to dwindle.

"What are you doing here?" Some of the sharpness disappeared, but not all.

I tried some soothing. "I'm interested in an old piece of mining equipment called a doodlebug. I understand there's one on what I think is your property—on a creek bed."

"How do you know that?" Suspicion and displeasure screwed her face into a knot again.

"I'm writing an article on gold prospecting for a magazine. One of my friends told me about the doodlebug. It's a relic from the early days of gold mining; from the eighteen hundreds. A picture of it would be of interest to my readers."

She shook her head. "I don't know anything about any doodlebug." She looked questioningly at Ginny.

I looked at Ginny, too. "There's a black, wrought iron fence around it." I offered eagerly.

"Oh," Ginny said, "That's down by the creek, Auntie."

She pursed her lips and gave a shiver. "I thought it was an old grave."

The woman scowled and shrugged her shoulders. "I remember now." She shook her finger at me. "I have no information for you. This is private property. You shouldn't be here."

"Oh, Auntie." Embarrassed, Ginny scuffed her shoe in the dirt. "You—"

"I say, no!" She pointed the jabbing finger at Ginny. "Don't get smart with me." She glared from Ginny to me and back again. Dale was right, what a witch.

Something about the light as she turned her head slowly back to me diminished the heavy wrinkles and sagging skin, giving a hint of the good looking woman she might once have been. Too bad there was nothing left but vitriol.

No sooner than the thought crossed my mind, her lips curved into a wicked grin. She pointed to my face "Your old man slug ya a good one?"

Ginny gasped.

I ignored the comment and, deliberately eying her outfit, gave her a grin of my own. "Woodstock?"

"Yeah, I was there." She shook her hair behind her shoulder, in a gesture so common to young women. "Best days of my life, worst days of my life."

"Flower power?"

"I had nothing to do with those fairies. Free love was the name of the game." Her smile widened and her head tilted rather coquettishly, but the sharp, dark eyes remained frosty nails. "Maybe I'll think of something about that doodlebug."

"Oh, thank you, Auntie!" Ginny perked up and kissed the woman's cheek.

She gave no response to Ginny, just addressed me

again, "Get out of here now. I'll let you know when to come back." With a brusque move of her arm, she motioned Ginny to the trailer house.

I, too, was finished with the whole scene. "Thank you," I said, with a nod of deference I didn't think she deserved. "I look forward to seeing you again." I stepped away with a dire sense of reluctance for having to leave the young girl with this woman whose smug smile cast a palpable sense of menace.

With a shiver, I glanced around for an escape route. I didn't want to return via the creek pathway I came in on; that would indicate I'd already seen the doodlebug. Obviously, the old woman wasn't going to move until she saw me gone.

CHAPTER 20

I gave the old witch a nod of dismissal and headed down the only road in sight. It wandered off to my right and appeared to go in the direction of the main road. Hopefully, not far from where I parked my car.

I felt dreadfully exposed. Nothing but bare land lay in front of me with only a few rises and rocky protuberances to break the horizon on my right. At least on the left, tall, shaggy growth lined the side of the road. Probably remnants from a long-past creek, or maybe even bushes and trees purposely planted by a previous owner. I might have been the only person in the world, walking down the middle of a dirt road to nowhere.

I refused the urge to turn and see if she still watched and inched closer to the welcoming growth on my left which would shield me from her eyes once I rounded the curve ahead. I began a slow jog. Light dust drifted lazily into the air above the shrubbery. A dust devil, maybe, or worse, an approaching vehicle. As soon as I thought it, I heard it. Just my luck.

And there it was as I rounded the bend, a large white

pickup. I continued to jog, hoping a slight wave would dismiss my presence. But no. The truck slowed to a stop across my path and the driver-side door opened. I jogged in place, hoping to indicate I wanted to continue my exercise. A man stepped down from the cab and slid around the door to face me.

"Can I help you?" he asked.

"No thanks, I'm just returning to my car." A very handsome man, I thought uneasily, with streaks of white lacing through his black hair in an attractive manner.

"This is a private road. I thought you might be lost." There was a slight high cheek-boned cast to his face, but I didn't like the way his flashing dark eyes traveled over my body, resting on my breasts a moment too long.

"I'm aware of that," I replied testily. "I've been visiting with young Ginny Molina and her Aunt."

He cocked his head with a hint of disbelief. "You know her?"

I cocked mine and answered back, "Yes." In his forties, I guessed, with a strong chiseled face and well-toned body, but something about him raised the hair on my arms—and it wasn't sex. He stepped closer, intentionally invading my space, and held out his hand.

"I'm Quentin Cook."

"Pleased to meet you." Holding my ground, I didn't offer my name, or my hand, but looked at my watch and stepped up the jogging in place again, easing away. "I've got to get going," I said, with a sweet smile.

He took another step toward me. Nearly stumbling, I jumped back and broke my jog. He grinned. "I thought you might recognize my name?"

"And why is that?" I caught a strong whiff of aftershave.

"I've been in a few movies." He shrugged in a failed attempt at self-deprecation.

Oh, no, a Hollywood type. "Sorry, I don't watch many movies, but I'm sure others would have recognized you." I wanted to appease and be on my way. I started jogging steps again.

"And how do you know Stella Parker?"

"I don't. I just met her. Ginny's my friend. I've got to get going," I repeated. "Nice meeting you. And thanks for the offer of help."

He took another step toward me, as if to grab my arm. Fear bounced me away, I jogged off, feeling his sharp eyes pierce my back, but he didn't stop me. I couldn't resist a final glance. He stood still in the road watching me, and then he turned sharply to his truck. I finally heard it roar off. Shreds of fear capped my sense of relief at the sound and I broke into a run. What a pair. A repulsive man and the old witch.

Fortunately, the main road was closer than I could have possibly hoped for. I saw the turn-around where my car was parked off to my right, further away than I could run, maybe, but at least in sight. Puffing like mad, I slowed to a more acceptable pace. Wow. I needed to get back to my tennis playing, or at least a daily run. Grabbing my keys, I jumped in the car, and got the hell out of there.

As Dale had done the other day, I didn't go back the way I'd come, but went straight ahead as fast as the rough road allowed. No vehicles followed me, nor did I meet any on the road. Still, I didn't breathe easy until I reached the highway and could meld into the light traffic. When I turned in the direction to Carson's place I finally relaxed.

I had a lot to think about. Like who was this Quentin Cook? Mr. obnoxious Hollywood. Another of Carson's relatives? His last name wasn't Parker, but that didn't make any difference. And why had he spooked me so badly? Was I being paranoid, skittish because of all the recent events? Or was it just a normal gut reaction?

I needed to find out how Carson was attached to all this; Carson and his grandmother, the old witch, and the shack on her property. Throw in a treasure hunt that both Max and Carson found interesting seemed to make the connection stronger. Virgil Parker said the old woman had rights to the land. Carson said he lied. I still tended to believed Carson. Mostly, I wondered if Carson even knew he had a very respectable relative in sweet Ginny Molina.

I stopped at the gate leading into Carson's place, grabbed a couple of signs and the stapler from the back seat. It took all my strength to operate the heavy stapler, but finally I got a sign on each gate post. Sweat dribbled down my forehead and neck.

I really wanted to talk to Carson. Despite the spotty cell service, my try worked. I made a mental note that this was a good spot for cells. The phone did ring, but that's all. Ring and ring. I left a message asking for a call-back.

Eyeing the large stretch of dry rutted dirt, I ignored the code of the west and decided to leave the gate open enough to get my car through. Nothing wrong with an escape hatch. I drove slowly to the house, watching for signs that others might be around. Only the tall, gracefully shaped butte drew the eye, dominating, dwarfing the land-scape. If Max were here, we'd both want to climb to the top.

No other vehicles visible, I drove around the side of the house and parked next to the back yard fence in the meager shade offered by the old cottonwood trees. Whoever coined the phrase, The Big Lonesome, knew what he was talking about. Getting closer to the house and outbuildings, and the yard and trees, lightened the atmosphere noticeably.

I wondered if there were neighbors. Evidently, Carson's grandfather had been a recluse in his later years, but surely there must be others close by. People who watched out for each other. I thought about the other little-used road that cut off from the one that led to the house. Dale and I never got around to checking it out. Maybe I could explore a bit today if I had time.

I took my camera and a bottle of water from the car and headed to the out buildings. On second thought, the one about getting mugged, I went back and dug out a tire iron from the trunk. But what to do with it? You'd think with eight pockets in my pants, there'd at least be a long narrow one, but then I'd be walking around with a piece of metal slapping my leg. I left it on the front seat of the car. So much for caution. This morning's plan to get pictures for my article felt like a long-ago idea. I tried calling Dale at the restaurant. Good reception from here, too.

"Any change to the time you get off work?" I asked her.

"Still looks noonish. Did you find the doodlebug?"

"Yes, and other stuff as well. I'll tell you all about it. Why don't you come out to Carson's when you get off? I'm taking pictures and need help identifying some of the equipment. And you'll be glad to know I'm ready for some more gold hunting lessons."

"Whoopee. Sounds like a plan. I'll be there."

CHAPTER 21

L uring Dale to Carson's with the idea of gold panning, which was the least of my plans for today, gave me a moment of shame. Surely she had better things to do than follow me around. Yes, I could use her help. What I *needed* was her company. I felt so alone. The two of us had gone quickly from casual acquaintances to being good friends in a short period of time. There were a lot of things I didn't know about her. Vice versa, as well. Was I taking unfair advantage? Had I become a needy little beast? Probably. A disgusting thought.

With a firm grip on my camera, I turned my mind to picture taking. First the hay shed with the old jacked-up Caddie. Dirt covered the license plate. Grabbing a greasy rag from the pile of junk in the corner, I sloshed the plate with water and rubbed the dirt off. Showing the plate's year would make a better picture. I dribbled more water over it, and to my delight found a vanity plate. Just one word. Gold. Of course! What else would the old prospector have used? Perfect for my use, too. A great color shot for the article along with a pile of discarded gold pans.

The sun, filtered lightly with dust motes, shone over my shoulder perfectly for photography. On to the Quonset. Everything, the tools and backpacks, were as we left them the other day. I busied myself making different arrangements of the items, taking shot after shot. It felt good to be back at work.

I kept my eye out for anything I might have missed before, things out of place, things that didn't belong, anything that I could connect to Max. Had he taken the tools from the Quonset? For what purpose? Or were Parker and Townsend the guilty ones, taking advantage of a deserted home, stealing stuff, maybe even prospecting? That kind of thing happens in the country. Did they think the old man had gold on his property? After all, Alton Olmstead specialized in gold. Could Max have caught them doing their dirty work? And they…did what? My mind could go a million places from there. None good. All speculation.

Help me, Max. Even Hansel and Gretel had been clever enough to leave a trail, though bread crumbs hadn't been a good idea. As if I'd be so lucky as to find another item like his money clip. I'd had high hopes for the red-zippered backpack I'd found, but knew it didn't stand up as evidence, just me indulging in a moment of magical thinking.

I only had Carson's word that this had been Max's destination. It would be more logical there'd been an accident on the road somewhere, and Deefy happened to find him and tried to help. *Oh, sure*, the critic on my shoulder snickered, *and took him to a shack miles from here instead of some urgent care.*

Why hadn't Max called me? Even to say, "Well, honey,

let's not get married tomorrow, I have this other thing to do."

"This is stupid!" I threw the words into the vast emptiness surrounding me and stomped off towards the house. Tired of agonizing myself.

Snapping pictures of the house from many angles helped calm me down. I continued on around to the back where the big cottonwoods were, and the neglected garden.

The old green chairs sat forlorn and forgotten, quietly shedding their paint. I'd forgotten about them and the hidden house key. What had Carson said? The hiding place had something to do with the Adirondack chairs. Just the distraction I needed.

Chairs like that had been around summer homes forever. Never my favorite. I sat in one. Dreadfully uncomfortable. Nothing but a bunch of hard wooden planks. I preferred cushy pillows, chairs one could curl up in. I pulled myself out of the deeply slanted-back seat. Both chairs looked alike, a simple design of straight boards. Five made up each chair back, two the arms, with the finished ends pointed. Simple legs. No hiding places.

I sat in the other one, feeling like Goldilocks. Just as uncomfortable. Thinking the sight line might indicate a hiding place, I tried looking out from a seated position in each chair. There was nothing but the Wyoming distance in front of me. Except for the garden.

The garden's brittle plants occupied me for a while, poking around them, kicking some dirt. And if the key were buried in the soil, I wasn't about to spend hours digging. The garden wasn't a logical spot anyway. A person didn't need to sit in a chair to spot the garden; you could see it from many different places. If the chairs were part of the clue, both, or one of them, had to be a crucial element.

But so what. I didn't need the key. I kicked the garden soil from my shoes and brushed it off my hands. I could wait until Carson got here with his own key.

I picked my way through a patch of desiccated tomato plants and looked back at the chairs. From here I got a more distant view of the chair's back. The first one I'd sat in. The tops of the back boards were gradually shaped up from the sides to the middle board, forming a curve. The top end of the middle board slanted to a point, matching the ends of the chair's arms. From here it looked enough like an arrow point that my eyes followed it up into the tree branches. I moved closer, but couldn't see anything other than leaves and branches. The chair's backward slanting seat made it difficult to stand on, so I used the broad arms instead, one foot on each. Nothing caught my eyes as a possible hiding place, but the added height brought me tantalizingly close to a nice thick lower limb.

Crumbling cookies! I hadn't climbed a tree since grade school. The temptation was too strong to resist. I threw an arm around the branch, braced the other hand against the trunk for better purchase and lifted one foot to the top edge of the chair's back. A push of my foot gave enough boost to pull myself up and get straddled on the branch. It also knocked over the chair, which didn't bother me at that victorious moment.

A rich loamy smell of bark filled my head, and I couldn't stop grinning. Limbs, branches, twigs, and stubs provided all kinds of hand and foot holds, and I quickly ascended four levels. The view was astounding and gave me a different perspective of the layout of the land, particularly of the entrance and the other little road that went beyond the house to fields and pastures with hints of more greenery in the distance. I thought we could explore the road later today. Might be interesting.

I inched myself back around and found a comfy seat in a wide fork surrounded by leafy branches. The cottonwood's trunk made a decent backrest.

I gazed up into the height of the tree as a wispy breeze rustled through the leaves, lifting left-over bits of tree cotton to float lazily through the air. All the stress of the last days drifted away with them. I closed my eyes and dreamed that Max was there, sitting in the notch below me. He reached up and held my hand, and we just sat there, enjoying the moment as we had so many other moments, soaking up the sun's heat, breathing in the scents of leaf and loam. My eyes filled with tears.

"I love you," I whispered. *Please, please don't let anything horrible to have happened to you.*

Opening my eyes, I brushed away the tears, but found it difficult to tear my gaze away from the swaying limbs above me, and patches of blue sky, drifting in and out among the branches. My peripheral vision caught something a little different from its surroundings. Twisting, I got a better look. A small nest? Or box? Something sat in a similar, but much smaller fork than the one I sat in. Remembering what had brought me to the tree in the first place, I scrambled to a standing position. Grabbing a branch stub, I stretched up on my toes and worked the object out of its niche. The plain wood box had a tiny gold hook closure, and, sure enough, inside not only one key rested on a puff of cotton material, but three, and an amazing rock of quartz matrix veined with brilliant gold. I lifted a corner of the cotton and gave a hoot of victory. A layer of small gold pebbles covered the bottom. I laughed. I'd told Johnny I had to find my own real gold, and here it was. Of course, I knew it wasn't mine, but I felt sure the container was more than a house key. I figured the gold must make it a clue to Carson's treasure hunt. Not usually competitive, I felt a surge of it now. I was a step up on everybody, including Carson. Woo-hoo on me!

The box must have been up here for a long time. Certainly Alton Olmstead hadn't been in tree climbing shape for many years. Maybe he'd planned this inheritance hunt for a long time. It would certainly be more fun than planning your funeral. I tucked the gold back under the cotton and looked at the keys again. One appeared to be a house key, the other two were smaller. I put the big one in my shirt pocket, snuggled the others down on the cotton and closed the box, pleased to have use for my new cargo pants. Time to get back to earth. I well knew that getting down from the tree would be more difficult than getting up.

The familiar noise of an approaching truck broke the silence. Dale, I thought, checking possible descents. She must have gotten off work early. I clung to the trunk and began to lower myself to the next foothold. The truck rounded the house and squealed to an abrupt halt. Two doors slammed. Not Dale.

CHAPTER 22

I scurried back up to my original perch and peeked through the branches.

Two men stood staring at my car. "Whose car is that?" said the one who had his back to me.

The other one kicked a wheel. "That Barlow woman?"

"Where is she?"

"I'm gonna look." He entered the yard. Virgil Parker. I still couldn't get a good look at the other but guessed it might be Townsend.

"I don't care where she is," the man said. "In fact, I wouldn't mind having another witness."

"Whadda ya mean? Witness."

"I told you, I'm through with the whole thing. I brought you in on this, now I'm kicking you out, shutting it down. You lied to me. I'm taking my stuff, and the two of you—if you can find that Barlow woman—can witness that I only took my own belongings."

He strode to the Quonset, picked up one of the black backpacks and threw in a couple of tools from the pile I'd carefully arranged to photograph. Then he picked up one of the larger pieces—it might have been a small generator of some kind—and brought it back to the truck. Now I saw his face. I was right. Richard Townsend.

He spoke. "You said all this stuff belonged to you. Now I know better. I don't want anything more to do with you. You can keep the money I've put in. You and Novak can do what you want. But I'm out."

Novak. Who was Novak?

"Don't say that," Parker yelped. "You've seen too much. You can't get out."

"Oh, yes I can. You and that cousin of yours, or brother, or whatever he is, better stay clear of me. I don't care what you do, but I'm not having any part of it. You'd be wise if you didn't either, but I don't give you credit for being wise. And I want that power cord of mine, too." He stomped back into the Quonset and returned with a heavy cord coiled on his arm. "Come on," he said to Parker. "Let's get going."

"You'd be a fool to quit. That old man's bound to have left a big stash of gold hidden somewhere. You check the price of gold recently? He screwed us out of everything. Besides, you quit, you'll be dead meat." His voice rose with a tremble as if he were frightened by the possibility as well. My grip on the small branch tightened.

"You watch too much TV." Contempt dripped from Townsend's voice. "Look, I might have seen some activities you didn't want me to see, but I have no idea what they were about and have no interest in finding out. Why would I jeopardize my own interests by poking my nose into something other than this mess you got me into? Think, Parker, think. You're such a butthead."

"I didn't get you into this, *you* came to *me*."

"I know, I know, stupid move on my part. Look, we don't have to be adversaries. All we have to do is quit. You go your way, I'll go mine. But if you or any of your friends or relatives starts messing with me you'll regret it big time."

I couldn't see Townsend now, just Parker's head and torso. He stood not far from the tree, nervously surveying the house and yard as if he expected to find me spying on them.

Townsend must have gone to his truck. I heard the engine start and the tires crunch on the gravel as if he were going to leave without the other. What could he have seen that put him in so much danger. And Max. Had he been here?

The engine revved. Alarm raced through me. *No! Don't leave that man here. Please, please don't.* I must have moved. The leafy twig my hand rested on snapped and drifted down, landing at Parker's feet, a big enough twig to make him look up. I held my breath. I had no idea how well the branches covered me.

"She's there, damn it," Parker yelled. "In the tree!"

Obviously not well enough. Fear shot me up and around to hide behind the tree's trunk.

"What are you talking about?" Townsend must have joined him. I had my face plastered on the trunk's rough bark and couldn't tell where they were.

"The tree. Get out of my way." I heard the scuffle of feet, but could see nothing.

Again I heard scuffling noises and a sharp crack against the tree. A rock. Another good-sized one whizzed past my elbow. I nearly yelped.

Sounding incredulous, Townsend asked, "What are you doing?"

"The tree. She's in the tree."

"You're crazy. I don't see anything."

"I swear I saw a shoe. I'm gonna get her."

"You can stay here throwing rocks at squirrels as long

as you want, but I'm going. If you want a ride, get in the truck."

I sucked in all my body parts and willed myself to become invisible. It must have worked. I heard Parker's grumbled, "All right, all right." Footsteps moved away, two distinct door slams, and the squeal of tires. Gone. I sucked air deep into my lungs.

Thank heaven for Townsend, who would live as a good person in my calculations forever, even though, as Dale and I suspected, he, Parker, and at least one other, were illegally hunting for gold. I wondered how many people Carson had told about his treasure hunt, or was it just because of Alton Olmstead's reputation as a successful gold prospector that people were lured to his property?

I stood there, hanging on to my safe spot, and tried to remember—and make sense of—a conversation that held little substance. Evidently Townsend wanted out of whatever deal he made with Virgil Parker and the other man, whom we still hadn't identified. Dale thought he might be Jake the snake. They mentioned a Novak. Was that Jake's last name? No specifics were mentioned as to what the deal was about, other than gold. Though a logical guess would be some kind of prospecting arrangement.

Virgil Parker's panic about Townsend's having "seen too much" seemed important. Had they actually found something? And who was this brother/cousin? There must be four people in on whatever the project was. Parker, Townsend, Jake, and maybe the brother/cousin.

I eased down to a sitting position on the rough, knobby branch, swinging my legs a bit, seeking courage to begin the descent, my mind still busy with questions. Could Deefy be the possible fourth person? The deal sounded shady enough to have attracted him. The biggest mystery to me was the connection between Max and Deefy. How could that have possibly come about? Max would never, knowingly, team up for anything, even an ice cream cone, with a petty crook like Deefy.

Or did all of this have nothing to do with Max? Rats, here I was again on another merry-go-round of useless speculations. At least I'd found what might be the key to Carson's house. That should be my objective now. If Max had left something in the house, something that would indicate he'd actually gotten to this place the night before the wedding, then maybe I could begin putting pieces together.

CHAPTER 23

I needed to get out of the tree. Trying not to think about the height, I picked my way carefully down from branch to branch until I sat quite comfortably on the nice fat branch where I began my climb. I stared at the ground and the chair tipped on its side. The other chair was too far from the tree to be of any help, while the tipped-over one was now an obstacle, too close to the tree to risk dropping to the ground without crashing on it. I didn't need any more bruises. I was just about to work myself to the other side of the tree where my chances looked better when I heard Dale yelling at me.

"Thea, where are you?" she shouted, rounding the corner of the house.

I yodeled my best Tarzan call, and hollered, "Over here in the tree."

She eyed me, hands on hip. Her frazzled hair wisped around her head like a halo. "*What* are you doing?"

I managed a grin. "Sitting in a tree. Move that chair out of the way and I'll come down."

She moved the chair and eyed the drop with a shake of her head. "You're not going to jump, are you?"

"No. I'm going to try to hang and drop." I landed in a pile at her feet.

She gave me a hand up. "Please, please, tell my why you were up in that tree."

I filled her in on my conversation with Carson about the hidden house key. "I found it. I'm quite proud of myself. He'll be surprised. Anyway, something else happened, Dale. Our two friends from yesterday dropped by while I was in the tree and had something of a fight." I got water from my car, guzzled some, and washed my hands with some more.

"No kidding. Who won?"

"Townsend, I think. Their fight was kind of scary. Townsend wanted to quit whatever deal they had, Parker said he'd be dead meat if he did. Townsend didn't seem worried about it. Oh, and what's Jake's last name?"

"Novak. Why?"

"Then he's our third man. They mentioned that name." I got paper towels from my car and dried my hands. We leaned on the fenders.

"Doesn't surprise me. I told you he was a jerk. Did you tell Carson about our confrontation with them?"

"He said anyone with the last name of Parker was probably one of his relatives. He didn't know Townsend, but when I said he might be a Rock Springs jeweler, he reacted as if that might be of interest, more than the man's name. I didn't press him on it. He also called Parker a liar. Said there's no possibility of anyone contesting the will. It's all in a trust."

She fished a granola bar from one of her pants pockets and broke it in half. "Tarzan want food?" I took the offered half. "What did he want you to do with the house key?"

"He didn't expect me to find it. We were just joshing around, but he mentioned checking the house. He's worried about people breaking in. He doesn't trust Parker. Oh, and another thing. You're going to love this, Dale. We're going on a treasure hunt. And gold is the objective."

"Gold? Where?"

"Right here on Carson's place." I told her his story about the second inheritance his grandfather had left him. "He's letting us help instead of Max. The two of them had planned to look for it together.

She gave me an inquisitive look. "Do you think Max jumped the gun on him and got involved with the guys we caught out here?"

I glared at her. "No, that wasn't exactly *my* first thought."

"Sorry," Dale said, offering a crooked smile.

I came off my high horse. "You don't have to apologize. You have a right to your guesses. I don't even know if he's dead or alive."

"Oh, come on. Don't get morbid on me."

I heaved a sigh. "It doesn't *feel* like he's dead, Dale. Don't you think I'd know if he were? Or is that too high woo-woo? Even Rusty Metzger said, and I quote, 'He'll show up one of these days.' And if he does, I'm likely to bash him in the head. Max, not Rusty."

"Better than throwing your arms around him. Tell me more about this gold hunt."

"Carson said I'd be head Poobah if I could find the house key. Which I did. I don't remember ever winning a treasure hunt as a kid."

"Don't knock it. You found the key, and I can help with the prospecting angle, though I'm no expert."

We walked around to the front of the house. It was good to get my mind back on gold, to think again about something other than Max. "Maybe there's a clue in the other tree? We could check it out."

"With a ladder, please. With a ladder."

"I admit a ladder's a good idea."

"Are you going to do it?"

"What?"

"Check out the house."

"Sure. Why not." We both cast our eyes over the house in front of us.

"I don't know." She wrinkled her nose. "It's kind of spooky. We got ambushed last time we went in somebody's house."

"Yeah. I've got a tire iron we can take with us."

"I've got one in the truck, too." But neither of us moved to get one.

We slugged down more water and rinsed our hands with the rest, "Whoa," she said, eyeing my new cargo pants. "Look at you."

I gave her a pose. "So much better than carrying a handbag."

"You got it."

We approached the house. Looking through the front windows again reassured me. Nothing had changed since our first peek. "Looks okay to me."

"You think clues to the treasure could be in the house?"

"Carson thinks most will be outside on the property, but after finding a key in a tree, I'd think they'd be anywhere. I'd just like to get a look inside. I wonder if Max went in."

"Right. Something tells me you're more interested in finding traces of Max than gold nuggets."

To my surprise, the key worked, I'd pretty much convinced myself that, as a clue, it would be for some other house. The warped door needed butt banging and teasing before it loosened a bit. "Open sesame," I said, with a final successful push.

Dale said with skeptical eyes. "Okay, Aladdin, you go first."

"It was Ali Baba." I opened the door fully, and stepped in.

Dale followed cautiously. "I don't see any piles of gleaming gold."

The first thing that caught my eye was a crumpled paper towel on the floor. I picked it up. A hallway led from the front door to a back area, probably the kitchen. The living room to my right. Dale followed a shorter passage to the left of the front door. "Yeah, this is the bedroom I saw through the window," she called out, and reappeared beside me. A staircase led to the second floor.

A well-worn leather recliner faced a rugged oak table at the far end of the room. A pile of loose cords on the floor suggested it once held a TV.

Dust sparkled on the end tables and an old fashioned standing ash tray with a fancy marble top and lighter. "Grandpa had one of those."

"Yeah, I've seen them before too." She tried the lighter. It didn't work.

I lingered a bit, taking in the wing chairs on either side of the window, the bare, boring view, the table in front, the empty magazine rack, and wondered about the old geologist and how long he'd lived alone.

Outside I'd thought the house homey, comfortable, but inside it reeked of loneliness. He must have missed the spark of youth and commotion.

"Hey, there's a dripping faucet in here," Dale called.

I shook away the daydreams, surprised to see I still held the rumpled paper towel.

I hurried to the kitchen and its eerie drip, drip. Tossing

the paper towel on the counter, I watched as Dale tightened the sink's faucet, ending the drip, then twisted it in the opposite direction. Water rushed out.

"Strange. Carson said he and his folks closed up the house before they left after the funeral. Wouldn't you think they would have shut off the water?"

"Yeah," Dale said, "unless they forgot." She flicked on a light switch by the door. Nothing happened. "Looks like there's no electricity." She flipped several more with the same results.

The trash can was under the sink, as expected. Three Styrofoam cups and a paper plate coated with dried food were in the bottom. "They didn't empty the trash either." I dropped the paper towel on top of them. A half-full roll of the towels lay on its side beside the sink.

"There's a lantern over there." Dale pointed to a small gate-legged table under a window on the far side of the kitchen. "They must have used that for light." She walked over to it. "And, yuck, an ash tray with at least five butts and a ton of ash."

"I have no idea what kind of people Carson and his parents are, but I wouldn't have left things like this if I closed up a house, would you?"

"I don't think so. I might not be as neat as my mother, but I know I wouldn't have left the water on. Geez. It's a wonder the pipes didn't freeze."

It didn't sound like Max, either. And Max quit smoking years ago.

I opened a door across from the sink. "Basement." A cool musty smell filtered through the air. Dale joined me. "Black as sin down there. You going down?"

"Not a chance." I shivered. "I don't do basements. Particularly not old dark mushroomy ones." I slammed the door shut. "Let's look upstairs. Then I'm going to call Carson."

Dale headed out of the kitchen. I did a quick inspection of the cupboards. Dishes, bowls, glasses. No food items. Good.

"Hey, Thea. You got to see this up here!"

I rushed out and up the stairs. Dale stood in the doorway of one of the rooms shaking her head. "Look at this."

CHAPTER 24

The upstairs was a mess. Blankets, towels, sheets were tossed all over the floor in the bedrooms. One bed looked as if a game of football had been held on it, or maybe ten rambunctious kids, human or goat, had slept there. All the covers were untucked and wadded up in wild disarray

"The bathroom's even worse," Dale said. Towels and washcloths were tossed everywhere, on the floor, over the shower curtain rod, in the tub. The medicine cabinet door hung open, but was mostly empty.

I shook my head in disbelief. "Teenagers? Gangs? Squatters?"

"Prospectors? Parker and Townsend?"

"But why just the upstairs?"

"There's no sign of booze, or pot, either. There's stuff in another bedroom but it's not as bad as this."

It wasn't as bad. Still, the bed had been slept in, and paper cups filled with smashed cigarette butts and ashes were everywhere. This wasn't Max's kind of scene. Not obsessive, still he'd lived alone for many years and liked things in their place.

"Another abandoned home, Dale, broken into. Like those guys at Max's house. I thought they might have been looking for Max, but maybe this is the latest country crime fad. The sheriff suggested as much."

Dale shrugged. "Let's get out of here."

"Right. Do you suppose Max busted in on a gang hanging out here, been beat up and left for dead?" Lurid comic book visions raced through my head. Deefy to the rescue, hauling Max to the rusting shack by the doodlebug.

"I'd think it's more likely the work of Parker and Townsend and their buddies. We already know they've been messing around here." Dale looked around. "Could they make this big of a mess?"

"Maybe if it was over several nights. No matter whoever, or whatever; it's disgusting. I'm going to call Carson."

We were down the stairs and out the door in a minute. I locked the door behind us, though obviously this key wasn't the only one around here. Once again both Carson's cell and home number rang and rang. I left messages to call on both of them.

"What I'd really like to do now, Dale, is go look where those two men were digging on the butte. Maybe you can tell if they actually hit pay dirt."

"Hey, you're learning the lingo."

"Doing my research. Let's take the no trespassing signs with us. You probably saw the ones on the entry gate. I want to get more up."

I tacked one on the front door, threw the rest in the truck and we headed off to the butte. Riding was better than hoofing it.

"And you found the doodlebug this morning with no problem?" Dale asked. "Did you get some good pictures?"

"I did. I'll show them to you. Best of all, I scoped out the path where we saw the old witch. There's a big trailer house not far from where we saw her, and I met a delightful young girl who said she was visiting her Auntie. Her great-grandaunt. And guess what? The young girl—whose name is Ginny Molina—is related to Alton Olmstead. He's her famous great-granduncle. She went to his funeral when she wasn't supposed to. She writes for her school paper, and wants me to talk to her class in school."

"What about?"

"Writing! She knew who I was when I introduced myself, had read my stories about dogs. I didn't know I had fans, Dale. What a hoot!"

"What did you do, put needles under her fingernails?"

"It all burst from her in a few minutes. She's absolutely adorable. But that's not the big news. The old witch is Carson's grandmother! What did Virgil Parker say her name was? Stella Parker? She's an old hippie and likes to dress like one. Or at least that's what she likes to think she is, or wants people to think she is." I shook my head. "I don't know. I guess troublemaker is the kindest description I can come up with."

"No kidding. My first impression, witch, was right." She did a power arm pump, then said, "Are you going to do it?"

"Do what?"

"Talk to her class, you fool."

"Oh." The steam whooshed out of me. "Ginny was so excited about the possibility that I'll talk to her teacher. But, you know, they might not want someone who's been involved in a murder case to speak to their students."

"Crap! You're more worried about your reputation than anyone in town is. Your slate is clean."

Easy for her to say. What about this new stuff? What about Deefy? What about the note on my door? "Anyway, I had fun meeting her. I have no idea if I'm right about all the relationships, but I think they're logical deductions. I'm dying of curiosity. I'm even more interested in why Max ended up in a shack on Carson's grandmother's property. That's simply one too many coincidences for me."

As was Carson. I didn't say that. But he could be another coincidence. Where does he fit into this melodrama? Or was he the innocent bystander?

We parked the truck by the dry creek bed where we first stopped to dig yesterday, and hiked to the butte. A considerable gouge had been removed from its side and piled in a large mound of dirt.

Dale knelt to face it. "Looks like they had a dozer or digger to start this hole."

"Or a stick of dynamite?"

She pulled on gloves from a cargo pouch on her pants and ran her hands across the rough surface and through the loose dirt below. "This doesn't look like a good choice for a first dig to me. They were digging into the side of the butte rather than at the base where placer stuff might be caught. I think actual lodes would more likely be in the mountains where you can find ancient Precambrian rock. But what do I know?"

"And lodes are where the gold is in veins within rocks?" I asked, kicking at the pile of dirt.

"Yeah, and that's hard work. You have to follow the vein into the mountain, or wherever in hell it goes. You need lots of heavy equipment. That's why placer deposits are favorites of hobbyists, or even serious gold prospectors who don't want to spend a lot of money. We don't get a lot of rain out here, but when we do, it brings out the gold hunters like fleas on a dog."

"When I first heard about a treasure hunt I thought of buried treasure. You know, like X marks the spot, finding a box filled with gold nuggets. But you, Carson and Max assumed from the beginning that it would be a gold deposit that would have to be mined. Isn't there a chance that I could be right? That it's an object to be found rather than a geological deposit."

"That takes a lot of fun out of it, at least for us who love prospecting puzzles, "Dale said. "Makes it a lot easier, though."

"Why would his grandfather suggest Carson consult Max if he needed help? We all thought it was because Max is a geologist."

"Makes sense to me"

"But he's a petroleum geologist."

"Uh. Should we be looking for a geyser, rather than gold?" She took a couple of snack bars from a pocket. "Here." She threw one to me.

"Thanks."

She tore open the wrapper. "I don't see anything here to get excited about."

"I was thinking about Parker telling Townsend he couldn't quit whatever they had going because he'd 'seen too much.' I thought maybe they'd found gold or something."

"If they did, it wasn't here. And if we're going to do some more panning we should go to a better place than this. Let's get something to eat first."

My phone rang. We both jumped. Reception was so spotty here a call was shocking. I tugged to release the phone from its belt holder. "Must be Carson." I said, "Hello?"

"Hi Thea, this is Charlotte."

"Charlotte?" I echoed, surprised. My best friend, my intended maid of honor.

"I'm on my way to Rock Springs. Can we meet for lunch? Or by the time we get there, it might be happy hour."

"Of course. Where and when?"

"How about that Thai place in the mall?"

"Sounds good." I couldn't wait. "Is it anything about Max?"

"No. I'm sorry. It's just lunch."

"That's perfect. I can hardly wait to see you." A letdown, but not her fault. "Dale Anders is with me. We're out looking for gold panning sites. It'll take us about forty minutes to get there. Is that all right?" I ignored Dale's grimaces and vigorous hand signals.

"Wonderful! I'll get to see both of you. It will probably take me closer to an hour."

"We'll wait for you at the restaurant."

As soon as I hung up, Dale said, "I don't need to barge in on you two."

"You won't be. Charlotte wants to see you, too. I think she's homesick. Besides, this will be a good chance to check out Richard Townsend. We can go by his shop and make sure he's who I think he is. And if he is, maybe I can find out more about the deal he made with Virgil Parker. I'm just going to ask him outright." I wasn't about to bore Dale with the most important part of that question which, of course, will include Max. Did he know Max? Had he seen him? And even, was Max part of the deal?

"But—"

"No buts." I started down the path away from the butte. "You know Charlotte pretty well, don't you?"

"She was the first person I met when I moved here. I

came with three girl friends about five years ago. It was just for the summer; we heard they needed restaurant workers. Charlotte helped us find an apartment. The others left at the end of summer, but I fell in love with the place. I guess I'm a small town person at heart. Everyone in Garnet Pass knows Charlotte.

"We've had coffee several times, and I've helped her with some of her charities, you know, food for the old-timers who hang at the senior center. Things like that. She's one of the kindest people I've ever met."

I agreed. And Dale was right about whom one hangs with. Even in small towns, people tend to run with their own crowds. That was probably why I had so few friends in town. I knew a lot of people well enough to say hi, or chat with, but not as active friends. We, Max and I, spent more time with the country folks.

"I was worried about her the other day when I spoke with her," I said.

"Why?"

"I don't know. She was acting strange, is all."

"That's not difficult for Charlotte. You know that as well as I do."

We both laughed. "Her aura reading can be over-whelming at times."

"Oh snort, I call it mind-reading. Spookeee."

CHAPTER 25

It took less than forty minutes to reach Rock Springs. We drove both vehicles. Dale wanted to check with the Glory Hole after lunch to see if she could maneuver a few days off, and I wanted to chase down Richard Townsend. We had time to check out the jewelry store before meeting Charlotte. Dale followed me as I took a couple of turns to get the few miles outside of Rock Springs city limits where I believed it to be. I wasn't too far off track and found the small clapboard building that had once been a home. Hanging baskets of petunias brightened each side of the door and nicely framed the handcrafted sign above that announced Gems, Minerals, Gifts and Jewelry.

Any store that offered rocks and minerals attracted Max. But the quality of the jewelry had surprised us. We had been immediately drawn to a pair of intricately engraved rings like nothing I'd seen before, the top edges spiked with mountain peaks, pines and antlers. Mine was wrought in yellow gold, Max's in white gold. It was a quick and easy decision for both of us.

Ignoring the red closed sign hung on the door, I pulled into a parking space. Dale followed suit. We jumped out.

"Looks interesting. I've never seen it before."

"Yeah, it's kind of away from everything else. We found it by accident." I looked in the window at the artful display, mindlessly cradling my empty ring finger. *Where were our rings now?*

"It's closed," Dale said needlessly. At least her words brought me back to why we were here.

"No surprise if he was at Carson's earlier." We walked around the side of the building. A one car garage sat close behind the store. No cars, no trucks. "We can check again after lunch. Maybe he'll be open then." I remembered Max chatting with the man while I inspected everything else in the store. Had he made friends with him? Could that be Max's connection to these people? Depression settled heavily on my shoulders.

"I bet Charlotte knows this place," Dale said. "She knows every store for a hundred miles."

"Good thinking. I'll ask her. Mainly I want to know if Townsend and this store owner are one and the same. One question off my mind." We snooped around a bit, then headed to the restaurant.

Seeing Charlotte brightened my day. Her genuine squeals of happiness at sight of us brought smiles all around. She looked like a fresh summer breeze in a bright flowered sun dress, her reddish-gold curly hair pushed up in a wonderfully frowsy topknot. Dale and I made a dusty comparison in our sage-stomping clothes.

Hands on hips, eyes flickering from one of us to the other, she said, "What—I say, *what* did you do to your faces? You two have a fight?"

"Yeah," Dale piped up. "She said something smart-ass and I popped her a good one."

I'd forgotten our banged up faces. "No, don't believe her. Dale and I got mugged by a couple of jerks. I fell into a wrought iron table. She got hit with a fist. I told Rusty about it."

"Mugged! What's happening to the world?" She peered at my face through its inadequate layer of makeup. "Humph, Rusty never tells me anything interesting. Well, I see some green peeking through the purple. That means it's healing. It should be gone in a few days."

We sat at the table and shuffled the menus around. I glanced up from the list of salads and caught Charlotte's gaze drifting between Dale and me, back and forth, her eyes going softly out of focus. A sign I knew well. She was checking our auras.

"Not fair," I said, with a wobbly grin and a dash of fear for what she'd see. "You said you never tried to read your friends."

She laughed. "That's what I always say, but it's a lie. I have no choice. I can't turn it on or off. It's just part of what I see when I look at people." Her eyes slid from me and she leaned toward Dale. "Both of you are doing better than expected."

A relief of sorts, but suspicion dogged me. With the happenings of the last couple of days, my aura must have lost its shine. I didn't want her to worry about me. The intensity of her concern could be daunting.

She covered Dale's hand with hers and said, "You're distressed. Is everything all right at the restaurant?"

To my complete and utter surprise, Dale's face flushed and she burst into tears. I hoped my mouth wasn't hanging open.

Dale covered her face with her hands. "Oh, Charlotte, I made such an ass of myself." Angrily, she brushed the tears away and tried to force a smile.

Charlotte moved her chair closer to Dale and held her hand in both of hers. "Not that gorgeous cook; what's his name, something Ashland?"

All this was news to me. I'd never heard about any Ashland man, or lost love. Here I thought Dale and I were such close friends.

"I told him I'd changed my mind," Dale said between angry sniffles, "that I'd be willing to follow him to Connecticut. You can't believe how fast he dropped the Mr. Nice Guy. He said he wasn't interested. Never had been." She banged her fist on the table. "I was such a fool!"

"I'm so sorry, Dale. He seemed like a good person."

Dale heaved a heavy sigh. "It's okay, Charlotte. It's not your fault. It was just so humiliating."

"Next time—"

"No next time, Charlotte. No more men for me. I should have known better." She pushed away from the table and gave me an apologetic smile. "I'm sorry, Thea. I'm going to wash my face." She hurried off to the washroom.

Charlotte and I watched Dale retreat. "What was that all about?" I asked. "She never said anything to me about a lost love."

"Oh, the usual, I suppose. The Glory Hole advertised for a chef a month or so ago and Gary Ashland showed up. Dale fell hard for him and he reciprocated. A handsome man. But Garnet Pass wasn't what he was looking for. He dumped her fast."

Which could explain Dale's antipathy for Max, and even Jake the snake, for that matter.

"I feel bad about it." Had I been so wrapped up in my feelings about Max that I'd missed signs she might have put out? "It must have been heavy on her mind. I never had a clue."

"She probably didn't want to remind you of your loss."

Loss. I closed my eyes. Yes, that's exactly what it felt like. As if I'd lost a part of me, like an arm or a leg, that I had to find...and reattach, or I wouldn't be able to...to...

The waitress plunked our salads on the table. I snapped my eyes open and stared at the strangely normal looking nest of lettuce, tomatoes and pretty wedges of boiled egg. No. I wasn't going to cry.

CHAPTER 26

Dale slipped quietly back into her chair. She gave us a sheepish grin. "Thank you for listening to all that nonsense. I know he's good riddance. I'm fine, and this salad looks yummy. I'm hungry as an aardvark."

We dug in and the subject was dropped. But I felt rotten. I'd never even asked if she had a special guy. What a needy bitch I'd become, everything me, me, me. Or Max. As if no one else had a life. A wonder she bothered with me.

I soon noticed that Charlotte wasn't eating. She was moving her food around. Her mind was a hundred miles away.

"You're not eating," I said. "It's not good?"

"No, no." She speared a small piece of chicken, eyed it, put it in her mouth and slowly chewed. "It's fine." She took a sip of wine.

Knowing she'd be pleased, I said, "I've started writing again," trying to lighten things up. "I'm doing an article about gold fever that will hopefully incorporate some easy ladies who worked the mining fields. Dale's helping me with the technical stuff. And I'm loving the gold research. There's something about all those nuggets and shimmering piles of flakes that's mesmerizing. I've got a bit of the gold itch myself."

That was true. I would have loved to tell her about the fun of Carson's treasure hunt, and how I found the first clue, but confidentiality reigned. Nor did I want to mention my worries about Max's connection to Carson. Heaven help me from disturbing my aura.

I tried to think of an innocent sounding way to segue into the Richard Townsend problem. Dale, perhaps thinking she was responsible for the dismal cloud drifting around us, raised her glass. The belated toast succeeded in bringing smiles and happy chatter.

Not forgetting my purpose, I slid into a pause with, "What brought you to town today, Charlotte? Shopping?" That sounded stupid.

She gave me a rather blank look. "Shopping? No. I came to see you."

"You did? How sweet of…"

Dale cut in, "Thea showed me a neat little store I'd never seen before," saving me from idiotic platitudes. "It's a little out-of-the way place about a mile outside of town."

"Oh, the gift shop in that cute little house? I do know the store. The owner, Richard Townsend, is interesting. He has great jewelry; I bought a pair of earrings from him not too long ago. I was up here collecting donations for a Girl's Club benefit."

Shocked by the quick result—I mean, how easy was that?—I dropped my fork. Dale stifled a giggle. None of which Charlotte noticed. She was staring at her wine.

"I am glad you're writing again," she said, taking another sip. "Rusty suggested I ask you to stay with us for a while. Now's the perfect time, Thea."

Her voice got all chirpy. "Why don't you stay for a week, or however long you wish? We have a lovely guest room on the lower level. There's even a desk for you to work at. I won't bother you at all. You'll just be able to write, write, write." Way too chirpy.

"How nice of you, Charlotte." And it was, but not very appealing. I couldn't stop my quest for more info about Max. The writing was incidental, as was Carson's treasure hunt.

Max, of course, had been the eight hundred pound gorilla in the room since we got there. And as far as I was concerned, he could stay that way. I wasn't going to pester Charlotte about any kind of second sight, but I couldn't drop my investigations at this point no matter how ridiculous, or harmful, Dale and Charlotte might think they were.

And Rusty? Did he want me to have a baby-sitter? He'd been adamant about me not trying to figure out the meaning of the note, even though it was left on my door. "Give it to the Sheriff," he'd said. "Let the sheriff handle it." Did Rusty know more about Max's disappearance than he was letting on? Did he think I was in danger? My heart began to thud, and I remembered the attack at Max's house and my fear that I'd be kidnapped.

Not wanting Charlotte to notice any building anxiety, I forced the thoughts away and concentrated on my salad. I took a big bite before glancing up again. She was back to moving her food around, making little piles of cucumber and cherry tomatoes. She looked so lonely. Maybe that's what Rusty was worried about, and I was letting paranoia take hold again, thinking only of myself.

"Charlotte, I'd love to come and stay with you, just not right now. Give me a couple of days. I have to finish this first batch of local research for the article. You know, check out, uh, mining equipment, old and new. Let me get the preliminary stuff finished and I'll come over. It will be fun." Hopefully Carson would have arrived by then. I didn't want to miss him.

Charlotte's eyes widened and a little frown line tightened between her eyebrows. She began to nervously rub her arms, her food completely forgotten.

"I have a better idea," she said breathlessly. "I'll stay with you! I'll be able to cook and clean and do all those chores that are so bothersome. It would give you much more time to write. I'd love to do that for you! It would be just like old times."

Preposterous. We'd never had "old times" like that.

"Charlotte, what's the matter? Are you worried about me? Afraid of something?

"No! No, nothing like that."

Dale took hold of one of Charlotte's hands, stopping the constant arm rubbing. "Are you lonely?" She must have read Charlotte the same way I had.

Charlotte's eyes flitted from Dale to me. "Yes, that's it. I'm lonely," she said, too eagerly.

"Then I can come with you." Once again, Dale to the rescue. "Thea's busy, but I can take a couple of days off. I'll follow you home now if you like?"

Charlotte closed her eyes and sank back into her chair. "No, you need to stay here with Thea." She took a deep breath, opened her eyes and smiled at both of us. "I'm sorry. I guess I'm just being my silly self again. I *am* worried. Concerned. Not about you two. About Rusty."

"Rusty! Are you having problems?" None of my business, but I had to ask. Something bad was going on with her. I wished I could read auras.

"No. We're fine," she said in a rather bewildered tone. This time it seemed like an honest answer. "He's been working hard, but that's nothing new. Max's disappearance has really bothered him. He's the first close friend Rusty's had for many years. He won't even talk about him."

Aha! Max had finally been mentioned, and not by me.

"And his hurt has worked into me in some weird way," Charlotte continued. "I dream about Max almost every night. Nothing specific, he's just there. And you're in my mind every day, Thea. I see you running, running, running."

I'd done enough of that, but why would running be what she saw? Prickles rose on my arms. Was there more to come?

"I don't know what to do," Charlotte went on. "When I got here today, I expected you to have a dark, sad aura; that I could help some way. But you're both okay, maybe a bit troubled, but nothing disastrous. Still I feel it." She twisted her head as if her neck had cramped. "I need to protect you, Thea. From what I haven't a clue."

"Please don't worry about me, Charlotte. I'm doing fine. A bit heartbroken, perhaps, but that will pass eventually, too."

Dale was back to rolling her eyes. "I'll take care of Thea, Charlotte. You don't have to worry."

"I'm sorry about Rusty," I said. "He keeps telling me to keep my mind on things other than Max. Maybe you can help him do the same." The words sounded more bitter than I intended, but it was the best I could do.

With that we attacked our salads again and drifted into easy, if somewhat uncomfortable, chat mode. Charlotte wanted news of Garnet Pass, and people she knew. We filled her in, leaving out all the business of Deefy's death, the note I'd received, and anything else that might disturb her. If she was aware of our cleansing, she didn't let us know. Her mind was elsewhere.

We chatted some more. Fortunately, Charlotte said she had some other people in town she wanted to see. And I, without saying so, was eager to see if Townsend had returned to his gift shop.

"You're sure you're all right?" Charlotte asked me again.

"Yes, I'm positive." She gave me a doubtful look. "If I need help with anything you'll be the first person I'll call." Too true. I knew what an unlikely wildcat she could be if the occasion called for it.

We settled the bill, gave parting hugs, and trotted off to our separate vehicles. Before Dale got in her truck, I touched her arm. "Thanks for offering to stay with Charlotte. You're a really good person. I get that you don't want to talk about the subject, but I owe you an apology. I've been so wrapped up in my own misery…all my moaning and whimpering must have been hard to take. I'm sorry."

We finally said our good-byes, had a couple more hugs, and went our separate ways.

CHAPTER 27

L uck was with me when I drove back by the gift store. Townsend's truck was parked in front of the garage, and he was unloading items I'd watched him throw in earlier.

He eyed me warily as I approached. "I'm sorry; the store's closed until tomorrow."

"I don't need the store, Mr. Townsend. Do you remember who I am?"

He stood, one hand bracing his lower back. "Umm."

"We met—"

He smiled. "At the old Olmstead place. Right? Thea Barlow."

"You've a good memory. I'd just like to talk to you for a moment."

A wary look shadowed his eyes. I didn't know where to start, and then decided to go for the gold. "Do you know Max Holman?"

"Max Holman?" He thought a moment, then shook his head. "No, I don't think so. If this has anything to do with the Olmstead place, I want you to know that I've cut all relations with Virgil Parker. I haven't been there since and have no intentions of going there again."

Which wasn't true. Should I mention being in the tree?

"Why do you ask about Holman?"

"I'm trying to track down his whereabouts and wondered if he might have been on the Olmstead land with you and Parker."

"No, I don't know the man. My advice to you is to not have anything to do with Virgil Parker. He's a crook."

"What were you doing with him, then?"

"Look, I have no intention of telling you anything about my dealings with Parker, other than they're over. Now, can I help you with anything else? I really need to get some work done here."

"One more question. Were you ever in the Olmstead house?"

"No!" His face flushed red with anger, and he jabbed a finger at me. "I never was in the house. What are you trying to accuse me of?"

"Nothing," I snapped back. "I'm responsible for the property until the owner returns. You made free use of it before and I'd like to know how far the infringement went. Did you ever see Virgil Parker enter the house?"

"I know nothing about the damned house. And if the landowner has any problems with my being on his property, he can come and speak to me himself."

"I'm sure he will."

I stomped off, thinking, *guilty as hell about the house.* He knew something about it. And Max? Was he lying about not knowing Max, too?

What to do now? I had an unsettled feeling of chasing after things over and over with little or no results. I drove slowly down the streets toward Garnet Pass. But the thought of going back to my little house, with nothing to look forward to, was depressing. The best part of the day had been sitting in that crazy tree, dreaming about Max. I remembered the amazing view of fields along that other road that Dale and I hadn't investigated yet. Was that a road Max had traveled? I hadn't even considered it. How stupid of me. I stepped on the gas. That would be something new to do. There was plenty of daylight left. I'd go back to Carson's.

When I drove through the entrance gate, I took a quick spin by the house and garage to make sure no one else was around before heading up the secondary road. It was a one track path that was pretty rough. There was no evidence that it had ever been graded or graveled, but still looked like a well-used ranch road that veered to the right. I guided my car carefully around the worst ruts, rocks and gullies, thinking the road could lead to another boundary fence. I also wondered about neighbors. Surely someone else must live around here. I traveled about a mile before seeing another fence. It was a sloppy right angle affair, needing a lot of tending. I followed its line straight ahead, wondering if there was a gate, but the fence itself gradually collapsed into a string of posts and wires lying on the ground. No gate needed. The road and fence continued on ahead, but enough vehicles had also turned into the field to make it look like a branch of the road. No way for me to tell if it were a boundary line, a fenced-off pasture, or whether it belonged to Carson, or someone else. I didn't want to drive my car across the supposed boundary, but wouldn't mind walking a bit.

I drove to a place where I could turn around and head the car back the way I came, got out and walked across the downed fence. The posts had been kicked out of the way, and wires cut and thrown aside. I knew some ranchers who could read tire tracks as easily as I could read a book, but I certainly didn't have the knack. Some were obviously old with bone dry, crumbling edges. Others were…well, I just couldn't tell. No way would I know if any were from Max's truck.

I'd just walk a little way to see if there was a house or building that might indicate someone living closer than I had thought. It could be a safety thing if Dale and I were going to spend more time out here before Carson showed up.

The breeze outside was nicer than the air-conditioned car. Fluffy white clouds lazed around in the azure preparation for twilight. I picked up a stick from the dry dusty ground and wished I had a dog to throw it to. Yeah, a dog would be nice. Maybe that's what I needed to get through this rough time in my life.

I could see lots of greenery here; bushes, even trees. All looking wild and thirsty. Ahead and to the left was a stand of trees straggling in somewhat regular rows, as if they had been planted rather than grown on their own, probably an old shelter belt. I walked in that direction. Many of the trees were bare and broken, needing much more water than nature provided.

I wandered down a row or two, then saw a touch of blue through the trees and headed towards it. One of those portable outdoor toilets sat partly hidden in the brush, and beyond it were several more.

What on earth! I counted five, a hodge-podge of different colors, some with doors hanging open, but all old and sagging as if they hadn't been used in years.

None of them were in any condition that made me want to get closer. Maybe this had been a sheep or cattle round-up place for branding or something. Having porta-bles available for a group of workers would be a modern convenience probably greatly appreciated. This was one thing I had no interest investigating. When I talked to Carson, I'd find out whose ranch abutted his place and if there was anyone still living there.

I drove to the entry gate before I pulled out my phone and, with a big grin, called Dale. "Hey," I said. "I found some outhouses for you. Maybe not a ghost town, but I'm sure you'll want some pictures."

"No kidding. Where?"

"Close to Carson's place. Did you get some time off?

"Yes. Nothing's scheduled for a couple of days."

"Good. I'm on my way home now, but I'll take you to them in the morning."

"Come on, tell me more."

"Nope. It'll be a surprise."

CHAPTER 28

We made an early morning of it, loading Dale's cooler with the usual selection of leftovers even though we weren't planning on staying long. She liked to be prepared for anything, particularly if it concerned food. And who knew what we might end up doing.

When I directed her to turn into Carson's gate, she said, "I thought you said it was close to Carson's, not at Carson's."

"Just take that side trail we've neglected."

One look at my smile awakened suspicion. "Okay, Thea. What's the deal?"

I tried for a face of innocence. "I'm not lying! It's outhouses. More than one."

She stepped on the gas. "So you went exploring and found…?"

"Just what I told you. They're old, too."

"Okay. I get it. There's something irregular about them. Right?"

I laughed. "Right as always. They were strange, but

171

you know this country better than I do. I think you'll find them interesting."

"Here," I said, as we reached the downed fence. We got out and walked through. "I have no idea if this is a fenced pasture and belongs to Carson, or if it's some neighbor's land and we're trespassing. So be warned." I led her in the direction of the scraggly trees.

She eyed them eagerly. "Yeah, this could be a ghost town site. That looks like an old, old wind break." She started to jog.

"Watch out, there's a lot of rough places around here."

"Okay." She slowed and pointed when she caught site of the first blue potty. I caught up with her as she passed out of the line of trees and saw the staggered group of toilets, looking as dilapidated and aged as the trees.

She stared, hands on hips. "What on earth…?"

"Yeah, that's what I thought" She went much closer than I had any inclination of doing.

"Whew! Old or not, they still stink! And what's that over there?"

"Where?"

She pointed to what looked like a scattered pile of rocks and other debris that I hadn't paid any attention to. "Let's check it out! It could be a town dump or something. That's where you find the best stuff."

I skirted the potties and followed her. A dump all right, but not big enough to belong to a town. More like the piles of rock one sees on land that's been cleared for planting. Strewn among the rocks were the usual dump objects, broken bed springs, an old mattress spilling its innards, and, just old junk. The pathetic remains of a small travel trailer were tipped over the contents of a large ditch. Beneath it, the tireless wheel of an old truck peeked out from under the tangled trailer. Dale loved nosing around dumps, but I'd exhausted my interest. Actually, it looked as if Dale had grown tired of poking around as well. I picked my way around the junk and found her taking pictures of the potties with her cell phone.

"You about ready…"A flash of movement burst through the trees. A dog, teeth bared, raced toward us. "Watch out," I yelled. Dale raced away, increasing the dog's speed and bringing on a rash of barks. I turned to run. Instant recognition stopped me. I threw my voice out. "Stop, Nonnie! Sit!"

She cocked her head and dropped her ears a bit. I repeated the order; her projectile speed slowed. Still running, the trim dog body wiggled with a more playful exuberance. I heaved a sigh of relief. It *was* Nonnie! She bounced around my feet with a happy, lolling tongue. What was she doing here?

A distant, piercing whistle broke through the air, followed by a harsh bellow. "Nonnie, get back here, you little bitch!" The old witch?

I grabbed the dog, ran around behind the dump, and jumped into the gulch under the trailer, scrabbling behind the protruding truck wheel. I didn't want to meet whoever it was. Snuggling Nonnie closer under my chin, and dodging her dog kisses, I hoped she wouldn't bark. My mind fizzed with curiosity as I wiggled further under the truck's framework. Why was Nonnie here? Or any of the Parkers? Was that who the neighbors were?

I scooched even further under the truck and hoped Dale had found a good hiding place. The footsteps came closer; and I jumped when the male voice spoke very close.

"Stupid dog. Where are you?" Not the old lady. Some man.

Nonnie swung her head around, perked up her ears, and wiggled a bit in my arms. I let her loose to scoot up and out, hoping he'd think she'd been chasing chipmunks or something. I waited for more footsteps, and then heard Dale's voice. Bright and friendly.

"Well, hello!" she said. "Is that your dog? He scared me to death. I'm glad you came for him. Is this—"

"What are you doing here?" Strong and harsh, the voice sounded kind of familiar. Not Virgil Parker, obviously. He would have recognized Dale. But Nonnie…? Could it be that other, man I met at the old witch's place? Mr. Hollywood hotshot?

"'Oh no, am I trespassing?" Dale chirped with performance perfection. "I thought from my map that this would be a school section. I was told there was a recent ghost town around here somewhere, you know, like one from the forties or fifties. Is this the site?"

Good for Dale. Whoever it was, she was snowing him perfectly.

"How'd you get in here?" His throaty growl raised my hackles.

"Through that gate a ways back." She sounded as innocent as a baby. "It wasn't locked. The main road looked as if it might lead to a homestead or something, so I took that barely visible trail instead."

"You missed a ghost town by about thirty miles," he said dryly. "This is private property, and you're trespassing. I'd appreciate you leaving immediately."

"Gee, I'm really sorry. I better go back to the motel and check my maps again. I won't bother you anymore."

"Good."

Her feet scuffed the ground as she trotted off to where she'd parked the truck. I stayed put, sensing the man would wait until he heard her drive off. I was right.

I tried to shrink into my hiding place. The truck lay tilted up on its side. I sat knees to chest, back to the bank, staring at the vehicle's mud-and-gunk coated undercarriage. Boards from the ruined trailer thrown on top of the truck spread out over my head, providing a roof of sorts. I counted nuts and bolts and rods and pipes, anything to keep my mind off the sinus-tickling odors of dust, and filth and noxious fumes. Figuring that at least ten or fifteen minutes must have passed; I wormed my way out from under my truck tent and listened. Nothing.

Slithering further out, I peeked over the edge of the bank. As far as I could tell, all clear. A minute more.

What the hell, I climbed out, running like a deer out and over the fence, hoping Dale would be waiting close enough that I didn't have to walk all the way back to Carson's house.

CHAPTER 29

I spotted Dale's truck parked off the side of the road. Panting, I jumped in.

"All right," Dale demanded before I could even catch my breath. "What the hell's going on?" She sped off as the door swung closed, dodging the worst of the ruts. "Who's that guy, and what's with the dog? You some kind of dog whisperer? A pit bull, no less. What else haven't you been telling me?"

"Give me a chance!" I took a minute to catch my breath. "I've already told you some of it. The big thing is, we've been stupidly direction-challenged! The old witch, Carson's grandmother, must be his neighbor. And that man could be the one I ran into when I was out there taking pictures."

"Black hair, roving eyes, muscle bound and loving it?"

"Yeah, that's him all right. Creepy. And I met Nonnie the dog through sweet little Ginny Molina. I don't know who the dog actually belongs to, but she was taking it for a walk when I met her. The grandmother must own part of

Alton Olmstead's land. A divorce settlement, maybe. What do you think?"

"Well snort…How would that work?" Dale slowed to a crawl, leaned her head against the headrest and gazed glassily out the windshield. "I'm trying to visualize the map. I guess it's possible, depending on how many sections of land are involved. The doodlebug's about twenty miles from here by the road, but as the crow flies…?"

"Evidently the main entrance to the witch's place is on the opposite side of the ranch, closer to where we crossed the fence to the doodlebug. I took that entrance road out the day I met the old lady and Ginny. I didn't notice any sign or mailbox—I was in a hurry," I remembered how badly I'd wanted to get away from Hollywood.

"Anything's possible. I don't know about Carson. Seems like a pretty weird family to me."

I remembered that Johnnie Onenote didn't have a good impression of the old prospector's family. He could be right. I only knew Carson from a few phone calls. He sounded like a nice person, but who knew? If Carson called, he called. If not, did it really matter? The important thing now was knowing that the doodlebug, and consequently, the shack where Max appeared to have been, was very close to Carson's house. And that house was Max's destination on the eve of our wedding that didn't happen.

We took the turn heading to the house, and Dale slammed on the brakes, nearly throwing us both through the windshield. Thank God for seat belts.

"Whoa," she yelped. "Look! What's going on?"

A silver beige SUV stood close to the front door and a man, holding a rifle, watched our approach. What was it with these guys and their guns?

"I'm out of here!" Dale slammed the gear in place and stomped on the gas. The old truck groaned and whined.

The man stepped forward, knocking back a new-looking straw cowboy hat. A glimpse of color appeared. "Wait." Crisp jeans, loafers with no socks, green golf shirt, he obviously wasn't native. His skin was pale and hair blazing red. "I bet it's Carson."

Dale eased the truck closer. He approached as warily. Early thirties, maybe middles. I rolled down the window. "Carson? Carson Olmstead?"

He stepped up to the window, the thatch of brilliant red hair unmistakable.

"Thea?" he said, with a touch of bewilderment.

I suffered a cringe of embarrassment. "Yes, it's me." What must I look like after rolling around in a trash-filled dump, underneath a smelly truck? I ran a hand over my hair which had sprung out of control, and felt pieces of debris stuck in the mess.

He cocked his head at me. "You've been hurt?"

It took a minute to remember my bruised face. "Oh, I'm sorry. Dale and I had a confrontation with a mugger a couple of nights ago."

"Sorry? Why should you be sorry?" He looked across me to Dale. "Don't tell me Wyoming is getting like the dark, desperate, big city streets."

I didn't care to elaborate at this point, so just smiled and said, "This is my friend Dale Anders who I told you about on the phone. Dale, Carson Olmstead." He nodded at her.

"What's with the gun?" she snapped with her usual confrontational approach to male acquaintances old and new. It was becoming a bit tiresome.

"A gift from my grandfather," he shot back, then tightened his lips over any further remarks, and covered his flash of anger with another smile at me.

"I really did just get here," he said, ignoring Dale. "Haven't unloaded all my stuff yet. I heard the truck coming, and wondered who was around and why; particularly since you told me about the people you caught here before. It's not loaded," he added, aiming the words pointedly at Dale. Then back to me. "Why don't you come in? I stopped for groceries in town. At least we can have some coffee, and cinnamon rolls."

"Thanks." I opened the door and jumped out, hungry and eager to get some questions answered.

Dale hesitated for a long minute, then slowly drove the truck to park beside Carson's new car. At least it looked new to me.

Carson and I strolled to the front door. "I've been in the house." I told him. "I found the key."

"You did! Where was it?"

"Up in one of those trees in the backyard."

"Aha!" Carson grinned and picked a twig out of my hair. "A tree. Just like the old man." He laughed. "So that makes you the Grand Poobah of the treasure hunt."

"Yes, and I'm very pleased. But the key was in a little box with two other keys and some other things. I think it's a treasure hunt clue. May I keep it until the hunt? Or would you like it now?"

"You're the poobah, so you might as well save it for the hunt, which I'd like to have as soon as possible."

"I'll guard it with my life. Oh, and I should warn you, it looks as if someone's been staying in the house. The upstairs is a mess. Both water and gas are on, but not the electricity." I shrugged. "I doubt you left it that way."

"Of course not. Might Max...? He had a key."

I shrugged again. "I doubt it. If Max had stayed here,

he wouldn't have made a mess like that. Besides, it looked like more than one person was involved." Which didn't necessarily exclude Max.

He held the front door open for me, glanced back, and waited for Dale, who stalked towards us, still stiff-legged with whatever irritated her about new, or old, male acquaintances. However, she was carrying her ever-ready cooler from the truck.

"We'll share." she said grudgingly, not looking at him.

Carson ignored her, propped the rifle against the wall, and went through to the kitchen. I followed and watched as he checked my information, turning on a faucet and one of the burners on the stove.

"My Dad would never have left the utilities on. The gas is propane from the tank outside. I suppose anyone could turn it on. The water's similar. Our wells are private, drilled and maintained by family since the early days. All it takes is turning a knob in the basement."

He ran his hands across his face and through his hair. His eyes wandered the room.

I eyed the running water in the sink longingly. "Okay if I wash my hands?"

He nodded. "Granddad lived here all his life, as did his parents and his grandparents." He opened and shut a cupboard here, a drawer there, not really looking at the contents. "We got rid of a lot of stuff after the funeral, but there's still a lot here. Things we thought I might use when I came back, or thought I should take more time to look through."

I eyed the bar of soap by the sink. Dirt from the last user still skimmed its surface. I used it anyway, and scrubbed my hands and arms. Carson fished a dish towel from another drawer and tossed it on the counter for me.

"I should have come sooner," he mumbled, and stepped back into the living room.

I splashed the freezing water on my face and attacked it with soapy hands.

"Yuck," Dale said coming in with the hamper. She dropped it on the floor. "Let's eat in the living room. Too much scrubbing needed in here."

I agreed and grabbed the towel to dry my face.

Dale watched, grinning. "That's an improvement. Guess I need some of the same." She grabbed a well-worn dishpan hanging on the wall by the stove. "Might as well heat some water."

I left her to it and followed Carson into the living room. He was contemplating a black smudge on the wood floor in front of the stairs going up.

"Gramps couldn't get around very well the last two or three years. Dad arranged for him to have an electric chair. He parked it here at the foot of the stairs. Called it a piece of shit. Sorry," he said with a grimace and a quick glance at me. "Claimed all he used it for was to get outside to his four-wheeler. Drove that thing all over the place. We took the chair back to the rental place after the funeral. Pretty emotional for all of us. I guess he went downhill fast that last year." He slammed his fist against the stair's newel post. "I should have come sooner." He glanced up the flight. "So there's a mess up there." He spoke more to himself than to me and bounded up two steps at a time.

Dale hauled the hamper in from the kitchen. "What's going on?"

"Melancholy, remorse. Anger, most likely, when he sees upstairs." I shrugged. "Maybe we should just get out of here."

"Food might help."

"Maybe." Food was her answer to any crisis. I wasn't so sure.

Carson clattered down the stairs, raising his arms in a helpless gesture. "You're right; we didn't leave it that way." He loped toward the front door, tossing words behind him as he disappeared. "I'm getting the rest of my stuff. There's a coffee maker in the kitchen somewhere. See if you can find it."

Dale gave me a look, as if to say, "I was right," and opened the hamper's lid. "You take care of this, there's no electricity for a Mr. Coffee. I'll see if there's a cowboy coffee pot." If food could lessen her antipathy, I was all for it.

I moved a large drum-shaped coffee table away from a corner and set it center front. I still held the dish cloth and used it to wipe off the top, then pulled the wing chairs up to it.

I unpacked the cooler and laid out the usual grapes, cheese and crackers, half a container of dip which hope-fully matched the half-bag of chips, and three and a half rather limp sandwiches. A bottle of wine, two plastic wine glasses, and a pile of napkins decorated with hearts and cupids finished the cache.

"Can you find another glass?" I hollered at Dale.

Carson came back in dragging a large duffle and juggling a couple of bags of groceries.

He dropped the duffle beside the door and took the bags to the kitchen. I heard him say, "And thanks for heating some water." The daggers were sheathed on both sides. At least for now.

We gathered around the coffee table. I plopped down in a wing chair which emitted a small puff of dust; Dale chose the floor and used my chair as a back rest.

Carson pulled the other wingback closer and reached

eagerly for the wine bottle. "I hope we're going to drink this." Not waiting for our nods, he pulled a Handy Man from his pocket and opened the cork screw. Our glasses full, he held his up in a salute and gulped down half of it. Sighing heavily he sank back in his chair and closed his eyes. "Thanks, I needed that."

CHAPTER 30

I couldn't help but think what a day Carson must have had. Early flight from Florida. How many hours was that? Arriving here. Two time changes. Renting—or buying, for all I knew—a car, shopping for groceries. No wonder his clock had run out.

He opened his eyes, took another sip of wine, then sat up and reached for the cheese and crackers.

"All right. Tell me about those guys you saw out here. And you said Virgil Parker was one of them?"

"Yes, the first time we were here." I reached for a few grapes. "We saw two men digging around the base of the butte, and there were fresh diggings in the creek bed, too. One of those men was Richard Townsend, a jeweler who has a shop a little way out from Rock Springs."

"Parker was with him?"

"Not exactly." I wanted to get it right. I took a big sip of wine and related what had happened to us that day. "When we came back to the house, Virgil Parker was here—"

"With a gun." Dale added.

That shocked him. "He threatened you?"

"Not really," I said, "but it was scary,"

Dale snorted.

I repeated Parker's claim about our trespassing. "Then Townsend came back from the dig site and got into a heated argument with Parker."

"This Townsend is the jeweler you talked about?"

"Yes."

"I might know him. When I got the box my granddad left me—the one that led me to believe he had a treasure hunt in mind—it contained some rocks, a vial of gold flakes, a considerable pile of transparent colored stones and a fair amount of black sand. I knew enough to think that the stones could be gems, and wondered what they might be worth. I drove around and stopped at the first store advertising gems and minerals to ask the owner what they were. He said pretty much what I expected: some agate, some jasper and quartz, bits of sapphire and peridot. Nothing worth much. He offered to buy the collection for a small amount. I wouldn't have sold it even if the stones had been valuable."

"Did you think he might have been lying?" I asked. "That he might have wanted to buy something valuable for a cheap price?"

"No, I thought he was a nice guy." Carson grabbed another cracker and piece of cheese. "I'd have been suspicious if he upped the offer, or tried to pressure me, but he didn't do anything like that. Besides, I've been around my grandfather for enough of my life for some of his knowledge to rub off on me. Nothing in the box was sizable enough to have a big price. Even the vial of gold flakes was the kind you can buy in any tourist trap for a few bucks. We talked for quite a while. He told me he was fairly new around here, hadn't known my grandfather. You know how those things go."

"Yeah." I pondered a bit, too. "I guess Townsend is nice enough. At least he was more on the up and up than Parker." I remembered when Max and I were in the store the first time; he and Max had talked for quite a while. But then Max was always easy with people. His business took him to new places, meeting new people all the time. I'd been more interested in checking out the jewelry and other things in the store.

"Then later," Carson went on, "after I met Max at the funeral, and I'd had the idea about the box being a clue, Max looked through it. His conclusion was that the stones in the box were those frequently found in gold deposits. Instantly I knew I was right about the treasure hunt. That's exactly the kind of clue Gramps favored. It's not what the objects are, but what they mean when put together. I was to find gold somewhere. Both of us were pretty excited."

"Maybe Townsend came to the same conclusion," Dale said. "If he's much of a gold hunter, he easily could have. He wouldn't have to buy the items. Even I might have figured it out. The black sand would be the big clue. Did you tell him much about your granddad?"

He shrugged. "I don't remember, but most likely. I'm proud of the old guy."

"He could have found out more about him—like where he lived—from anyone in town."

I took some more grapes and passed the bag around. "And if Virgil Parker is a relative, he, too, could be a logical contact."

"So you're thinking that they might have planned some kind of illegal prospecting together?"

"Could they have staked a claim?" asked Dale.

"No. Granddad had all the mineral rights. They've

been in the family since the homesteading days. And they're mine now."

"Wow!" Dale said it, I thought it.

Carson took the last handful of chips and began munching thoughtfully. "And the two of you think this Parker and Townsend are the ones using the house?"

"It's a possibility.

"I think I'm going to have to have a little talk with both of them. Soon. I saw no trespassing signs on the front gate, Thea. Did you put those up? Or were they already there?"

"No. I did it. Nothing was posted when I got out here."

"I hope it's not impolite to ask…but have you found out anything more about Max?"

"No. I haven't heard from him, and I haven't found any evidence yet…that he was here that night, or that he was *not* here. He just hasn't been seen since."

Dale groaned a bit but didn't say anything.

"All I know is he said he'd take care of the signs," Carson said, "and I took him for his word. I had no reason to think otherwise. But then, I don't know him that well, either. I only met him at the funeral, if you remember. Since then, we've exchanged a few phone calls, but that's it. He seemed like a worthy person to me. We really hit it off."

Dale rolled her eyes. I kicked her leg and changed the subject.

"I have a question for you, more a point of curiosity. I gather your grandmother is your next door neighbor?"

"She owns the land, yes, but she's never lived there. They married in the fifties, I think. Were part of the sixties life style for a while, but Gramps didn't take to it much. His wife hated this place. They had one child, my dad. When they divorced, granddad gave her several sections of land as a settlement. That was a long time ago. She left Rock

Springs and has lived in California ever since as far as I know. Hated country life."

"Not anymore," Dale piped in.

"Oh?"

I said, "She has a mobile home, not far from you. It's my understanding, at least Ginny Molina implied it, that she lives there."

"Ginny Molina?"

It was strange that I knew more about his family than he did. "We're talking about someone named Stella Parker. Is that right?" I asked with some confusion. "I assumed from what you told me on the phone, she was your grandmother. Ginny is her great niece, a nice little gal who's about twelve or thirteen years old. I actually met her and her Auntie, as she calls her, on that property twice, so I'm pretty sure Stella Parker is living in the mobile home."

"Then you're one up on me. I've never met my grandmother."

"Your own grandmother?" Dale said.

"Yeah," He wiped his hand wearily over his face. "Wouldn't recognize her if I saw her. They divorced back in the sixties, well before my time. Gramps got custody of my dad." The words were rather offhand and dismissive. I figured he wanted to change the subject, which he did by turning to me.

"Could be…" He rested his head on the chair back. "I've got too much to think about and my brain is turning to mush. It's been a hell of a day. Thanks a lot for the picnic, but…"

I jumped up, aware we'd way overstayed our welcome. "Yes, of course. Dale, it's time we got out of here." He helped us clear off the table, putting everything back in the hamper.

"Oh, and Thea, before you go, any other odd things you noticed in here?"

"Not much beyond the mess upstairs and the remains of a meal in the garbage can. Maybe they can be easily explained away, but…"

He dragged himself out of the comfy chair, stretched and gave a mighty yawn. "You're right. A mess. I'll have to figure it all out. And really, Thea, thanks for all the work you've done around here. You, too, Dale. I appreciate it. If you want to come out again, just call," he said rather pointedly, or was I being too sensitive?

CHAPTER 31

Dale and I bid Carson welcome to Wyoming, and good bye for now. Once outside, I said, "The plot thickens," referring to our crazy day.

"Yeah." Dale shook her head. "I have errands to run and need to check in with the Glory Hole again. But let's talk later; I'd like to hash all this stuff out, particularly the doodlebug location."

When I got home, all I could think of were the many things I wanted to do. Among them, re-establishing my connection with Ginny Molina was a high point, more so now that I knew more about her background.

But first I took a long, hot shower. Scrubbing like mad, I fought the lingering odors that might have been in my mind more than on my body, that noxious mix of gas, oil, dirt, and dump garbage. If I closed my eyes, visions of the old discarded truck's undercarriage appeared, along with the prickles of fear that had held me captive. I washed them all away singing scraps of, "wash that man right out of my hair." Another of Dale's oldies. Fresh clothes and a final look in the mirror that showed lightened bruises, green fading nicely into new sunburn. I swiped on a revitalizing layer of citrusy lotion.

Next I made a phone call to the only Molina number in the phone book. Ginny's mother answered. I introduced myself, told her how I had met Ginny, and her request for me to speak to her class.

"Ginny was so excited to meet you," she said. "She told me all about it. I worked for the school system for many years as a teacher's assistant. I know Ginny's teacher very well. I'm sure she'd be delighted to have you visit the classroom. I'll talk to her myself and let you know."

Her name was Laurel and she sounded like a nice and interesting person. We talked for many minutes about Ginny, and my various stories in *Western True Adventures* magazine. I felt quite amazed and puffed up about now having *two* fans. I gave her my phone number and we set a lunch date for next week to get better acquainted. I couldn't see either Ginny or her mother fitting into Carson's opinions about his notorious relatives.

The next few hours I spent writing down subjects I might talk about to a class of junior high kids. Something I hadn't done for a long time.

In the middle of a research to-do list, the doorbell rang. I jumped a foot. Doorbell! Nobody ever came to my door who wasn't expected. The law! Was the interrogation about to begin? A quick glance out the window showed no cop car or other vehicle, at least that I could see. The bell rang again. Racing to the door, I put my eye to the peek hole. Carson Olmstead! What now?

I opened the door. "Well, hello! We meet again so soon. What brings you to Garnet Pass? Come on in."

He gave me a big smile. "You came to my abode, so I thought I'd check out yours." He stepped in and glanced around. My gaze followed his in a quick mess check. Not too bad for being caught unawares. The desk was the worst, but that just looked like work. "May I get you something to drink? Coffee, beer, wine, ice tea?

"Sure. Coffee would be great."

Thankfully, the pot in the kitchen was relatively fresh. I poured two mugs and we sat in the living room.

He sprawled on the couch and glanced from the desk to me. "Working on your gold fever article?"

"Barely getting started." I wasn't quite ready to tell him about my new relationship with Ginny Molina and her mother.

"I'm sorry I didn't think to bring Granddad's papers in, but with all this crazy stuff going on, I forgot about it. They're somewhere in all that luggage I brought."

He smiled again. Very good looking. Not in a pretty boy way, but in a tall, casual, red haired, freckled face way with sharp, sparkling blue eyes. He must have changed clothes. He looked more Wyoming now than east coast, with worn jeans, hiking boots, and a light denim shirt with the sleeves rolled up.

"Actually, I came to town to get some new door locks, and more cleaning supplies. I called and got the electricity turned on. I'm not going to spend the night in the house until I get new locks. I got a room at the Outlaw Inn in Rock Springs for the night. But I thought I'd check out Garnet Pass on the way. Is there a place here where I can get supplies like that? Might as well do it here if I can."

I told him about Johnny's Emporium where one could find most anything.

"I've pretty much got the kitchen cleaned up, enough to use, anyway, but I'm going to need a hell of a lot more Mr. Clean for the rest of the place." A pause. "I had other reasons, too."

He tossed me a suggestive eye-twinkle. Too charming?

Suspicion popped up. Deservedly, I suppose, considering his weird relations. Or was it my usual lurking paranoia?

As if sensing my unease, he said, "I know I should have called before ringing your bell, but at the last minute I decided to check out that Townsend person while I was in the area and thought you could give me directions."

Logical enough. Maybe I just needed to relax a bit.

"I'd like to talk to Townsend. Also the other one, Virgil Parker? Do you know where he lives?" He gave a little huff of disgust. "I guess it's about time I meet some of these relatives. I don't want to go to the cops before I confront them."

"I don't know where he lives, but I've got a phone book that might help. And, yes, I can tell you where Townsend's store is. It's not too far from here."

"Good. If he and his buddies have been camping out at my place, I want a word with him."

"There's more you should know, as well." I quickly filled him in on the arguments between Parker and Townsend, both the one Dale and I witnessed when we'd caught them digging on his land, and the one I'd observed from the tree. "That fight between them definitely sounded as if they had some kind of a deal together, and Townsend was backing out, shutting it down. Parker got really worked up, and, in my opinion, scared, too," I tried to remember. "He kept saying, 'You can't do it. You can't do it. You've seen too much!' I don't know how that works into anything, but it didn't bother Townsend. He just gathered up his belongings and said he was done."

Carson laughed. "You're turning into quite an advocate, climbing that tree." He gave me one of those appreciative male smiles that made my stomach curl a bit. "I'm thinking Max is a fool."

"Thank you for that." I liked the flattery, and the smiles, but felt a bit uneasy about it as well.

"Gramps might have led me wrong about Max; I don't think they actually knew each other well."

I sighed. "I'll come to Max's defense, at least a little bit. The most upsetting thing for me is that none of what happened is remotely like the Max I know so well. I fully realize I wouldn't be the first woman deluded by a man who claimed to love her, but I keep waiting for a phone call, some kind of notification telling me why he didn't show up at the wedding. That's the Max I know."

A hesitation on my part, a few sips of coffee, then I continued. "The sheriff's office, here in Garnet Pass, received a call from the Sheridan office that Max had been sighted in their area. All authentic. Right papers, right truck. So if he's not dead, why hasn't he called? The law doesn't care. For them, he's no longer missing. That's why I've started looking into all of this myself. I want to know what Max was doing for you, and if he made it to your place or not that afternoon. I'm worried about the man; no one else cares. If that makes me sound like a lovelorn goose honking into the wind, so be it."

Rather embarrassed, I picked up our mugs and took them to the kitchen. He followed. Without asking, I changed them into strong Irish coffees. "I heard this is supposed to be good for you if you think you're having a stroke." I handed his to him.

He gave me a wry grin, and raised his mug. We returned to the living room. I didn't want to tell him about Deefy, or my propensity for being accused of murder, or the strange occurrence at Max's house, or even today's affair at the dump. Not yet. But..."Do you know anything about a doodlebug on your grandmother's property?"

"A doodlebug." He ran his fingers through his hair.

"Yes, I've heard of such a thing. Some kind of a mining tool. Wow, that's been a long time ago. Why do you ask?"

"A friend took me to see one in the country that had been honored with a fenced enclosure. We later discovered it was on your grandmother's property. I just wondered if you ever saw it, or knew anything about its background. I…I might want to write about it sometime."

"No, I don't remember ever seeing it. But that's interesting. As far as I know, I've never been on her property. I guess that's another thing I'll have to find out about."

I didn't want to dwell on it further so changed the subject. "There are a couple of other things you need to know. There is definitely one other person involved. He's the one who had the fight with Townsend at the butte. Dale calls him Jake the snake. His last name is Novak. There might be another man with them, as well." I said, thinking of Hollywood. "Possibly another Parker relative."

"This is starting to sound like a lot of people. Any others?"

"Not that I know of." And if we were both thinking about Max, I wasn't going to mention that either.

He looked thoughtful and drained his mug. "I'm glad I'm here now. I feel guilty for not coming sooner. Before Gramps died, I mean. He called me a couple of times. He was one of those old-timers who could never come right out and ask anyone for something. But he hinted several times that he'd like me to come out. He was getting confused…had some wild tales about people driving around his property, taunting him. Lights at night, that kind of stuff. I didn't take it seriously, I kept putting him off. I was busy, but…"

"What about your Dad? Did he have more free time?"

"Gramps would never call him for help."

That sounded pretty harsh. "They were estranged?" Not that it was any of my business.

"No, no." He chuckled. "Dad and Mom were always trying to get him to either move to Florida and live with them, or get a more convenient place in town. He avoided those conversations like the plague. He wasn't about to leave the Olmstead land. He figured he was born there, he could die there. My dad didn't feel that way. He was raised on the Olmstead place, but like so many teenagers, he couldn't wait to get away. Left for college in Indiana and never came back except for an occasional visit. They—Dad and Gramps—had an understanding a long time ago that I would inherit the ranch. Dad and Mom wanted nothing to do with it. I had—still have—mixed feelings about it. It's a long way from Florida…in many different ways."

"Well, you're here now," I said rather inanely. All this was interesting, but not helping me with the Max problem.

"Yeah, and look what's happened. Maybe Gramps wasn't so confused after all. Maybe this isn't just about my little treasure hunt gig. Maybe it's been going on for a long time."

"Like what? Going on, I mean."

"I don't have an answer for that." He swirled his coffee mug, took what appeared to be the last drop, and appeared to be surprised that it was empty. I took the hint, got the coffee from the kitchen, and gave him another slug, without the booze this time.

"Thanks." He cocked his head and gave me a questioning look. "You've met my grandmother. What's she like?"

How on earth was I supposed to answer that? "Umm," was my first intelligent choice. I topped off my own mug and took the pot to the kitchen to give myself some time.

"I know very little about her," he continued. "Neither Dad nor Granddad wanted to talk about her. If I asked, the only thing Grandfather ever said was, she had a hard life. Mom's told me a few things she gleaned from Dad. That they tried the commune life for a while. Gramps hated it. She, Stella—I have a hard time calling her Grandmother—preferred it. She liked action. I guess one doesn't find much of that in the Wyoming outback. Evidently after the divorce, she spent most of her time in California, chasing one cult after another, loved Hollywood."

That shook me a bit; just the name. I sat back down and he raised a questioning eyebrow. My turn.

"She looks to be very old, which is no wonder, and uses a walker to get around. Likes to dress in hippy remnants, at least the few times I've seen her. She was angry, confrontational, but that could be because I was a stranger." And trespassing. Softening my opinion, I added, "Ginny Molina, her grandniece, feels sorry for her, and likes to visit and help her out. So she can't be that bad. It's probably more like, you know, the Grumpy-Old-Men syndrome."

"She's never wanted anything to do with me, or her son, my dad, either. Granddad got custody after the divorce. I got the feeling that he'd been badly hurt by the break-up."

I could see his thoughts turn inward, and his words, "apparently it's up to me to mend some fences," were spoken more to himself than me.

"Well," he said, jumping up from the couch. "That's enough of my family problems; I hope I haven't bored you to death." He gave me a big grin. "I planned to ask you out to dinner tonight. Is there a better place here than the one with the flyswatters?"

"No, that's about the top of the heap. There's a better selection of restaurants in Rock Springs."

"To tell the truth, I'd rather do dinner another time. I think I need to run down Townsend. How about a rain check?"

"Certainly." I had other things to do today.

CHAPTER 32

Returning the staple gun was next on my to-do list. Now that Carson was here, he could put up his own signs. Someday, today, tomorrow, I should do a grocery run. No hurry for that. I had expected to hear from Rhonda or even the sheriff by now. I gave them the note day before yesterday. There was nothing in yesterday's mail. No messages. I checked my cell phone now. No messages. What was going on? I couldn't believe *someone* in the sheriff's department didn't have *something* to ask about a note put on *my* door that mentioned a missing man, and might have been written by a recently *murdered* man. Didn't they have the least bit of curiosity? Was I completely on my own? What was the matter with the new guy?

No more waiting. This shot to the top of my list. I'd go to the post office and check today's mail. Nothing there, I'd go to the office myself. I grabbed my bag and went out the door. There was nothing in the mail but bills, junk, and some kind of card in a square green envelope. I shoved them in my bag and stomped off to the sheriff's office.

Rhonda sat at her desk, her hair as crisp as her tan shirt. "Hi, Thea. What's new?"

New! "Absolutely nothing!" I slapped my hand on the counter. "I've been waiting days to hear from you about Max" I suppose my voice was booming.

"Max?" She drew her head back in surprise. "What about Max?"

"The note! The note!" I tried to rein in my volume. "I gave you the note that was put on my door. I told you about the shack out in the country with evidence that Max had been there."

"Evidence. What evidence?" She stood. Her wheeled chair shot back to the wall. She was getting a bit heated herself.

"His money clip. It was on the floor along with evidence of food and water, and lots of blood."

"You didn't say anything about a money clip."

I didn't? I pulled the clip from my pocket, its home since I found it, and held it between two fingers in front of her face.

"You took evidence from a crime scene?" She reached for the clip.

I snatched my hand back. "So *now* you're calling it a crime scene?"

"You thought it a crime scene."

"What did you do about it? Did anybody go out to the shack?"

"I can't talk about an ongoing investigation."

"All I want to know is if there's actually an investigation going on!"

"Not about Max." We glared at each other. Rhonda stalked to the water cooler, filled a paper cup, drank deeply, filled another and handed it to me. "I think it's time we both calmed down." She chased her chair and rolled it back in place.

I filled my mouth with the cooling water, swishing it around to douse the dragon fire, and took three deep yoga breaths. "Thanks, Rhonda," I said begrudgingly. "It's been frustrating."

She sat, opened a bottom drawer, and brought out a bag of minis. "Have some chocolate."

We helped ourselves and finally managed weak smiles. I took another deep breath. "Could I talk to Sheriff Krause?"

"He's not here."

"He's never here!" I said. Rhonda tossed a few more candies on the countertop and put the bag away. "When will he be back?"

"Don't know. Some big-ass meeting in Rock Springs."

"I have so many questions."

She leaned back in her chair. Opened a Hershey's Crunch. "Then shoot. I'll do what I can, but I don't get told much around here. Desk Person is my job title."

Right. I chose a dark chocolate. She'd held the job for more than ten years, and I knew as well as anybody that small offices were like small towns: everybody knew everything that happened, even if they weren't supposed to.

"All I know, Thea, is that the officers are busy investigating that old man's death. Deefy Hammersmith. I read the note and gave it to the sheriff. I know he read it, too, because I watched him do it. I also know nobody's actively looking for Max. At least not since they stopped him outside of Sheridan. I mean, why would they? Come on, Thea, I know it hurts to be left so…so publicly; maybe it's time for you to face the hard facts. If Max wants to come back and face the music, he will, but I wouldn't hold my breath."

My face drew into a stiff slab of concrete, hiding my hurt, my anger. I could barely move my lips. "But the note?"

"That's what the note said, isn't it? Max is okay. Maybe he got into some trouble, maybe he was injured, maybe he was in that shack, but he's not there now. He chose to leave us all hanging. Now we have other things to worry about."

"Deefy?"

"You mean did he write the note?" She raised a shoulder. "Who knows, it's an interesting long shot. That's what the department's doing, investigating. They're busy. That's why they're not looking for Max, even if there was a reason to do so. Give the sheriff a chance. He's a smart man."

I really, really knew I didn't want to hear any more of this.

She rose as if to escort me out. "Stop worrying about Max. He doesn't deserve it. Find something to do, get a job. Stop poking your nose around other people's property."

I couldn't get out fast enough.

The walk home helped calm me down, but I wasn't a happy camper. Was Rhonda right? Should I stop trying to find traces of Max? If I found something that indicated he'd been on Carson's land, what difference would it make? I already knew—at least to my satisfaction—that he'd been in the shack on the old witch's place. The two properties had been joined at one time. And Virgil Parker acted as if they still were. The sheriff is looking into Deefy's case, but not for Max. What more could I do? What I really wanted wasn't traces, but the real thing. Max himself.

I threw today's mail on my desk on top of yesterday's, and spotted the green envelope. I didn't much want to open it. I'd received a few others earlier; thinking-of-you messages of commiseration, as if the botched wedding were a death sentence. No return address. Rock Springs cancellation. Oh, well. I ran a finger under the flap and pulled out a folded piece of green stationary.

"Dear Thea Barlow," it began. Surprise. A fan letter of sorts, saying *Western True Adventures* was her favorite magazine. She liked my stories about the old time "Ladies of the Night" and their houses of prostitution. I flipped it to get a quick glance at the signature. Ginny Molina. What?

My eyes whizzed through the rest. She wondered if I had ever heard of Stella Parker, who had worked in a house in Rock Springs. She's old now, but I think she'd be thrilled to be interviewed by you. It was signed, Ginny Molina, and included a phone number where she could be reached if I was interested.

Ginny! That didn't sound like her at all. Was she trying to act like a grownup and solicit an interview for her auntie?

My heart wept. I didn't want my sweet Ginny turning into one of those sophisticated junior high kids who couldn't be shocked by anything. I checked the phone number with the one I'd used to call Ginny's mother. Not the same number. Maybe there was another person with that name.

So, the old witch had been a prostitute. With all my research, how had I missed that little gem? Narrow searching, I supposed. I always specified the 1800's in my queries. I sat at my computer and did a quick general search. It took some looking, but I finally found it. Rock Springs in the wild and howling late sixties. Stella Parker didn't work in a house, she owned it. Her business created an uproar both before and after they ran her out of town.

Carson's family secrets uncovered. No wonder his

father couldn't get out of town fast enough. He must have been a teen at the time, when life could be miserable enough without a family sex scandal thrown in.

I wasn't interested in writing about prostitution in current times, even though the sixties and seventies was a long time ago to many people these days. But I'd welcome a chance to meet with Stella Parker again and see if she knew about Max being in that shack, or if she was an innocent bystander.

The thought that there might be another Ginny Molina eased my worry about the young girl, but the phone book showed only the one Molina. Facebook didn't help either, at least none in Wyoming with the right parameters.

So I called the number given on the card. No answer. I left a message saying I'd received the card and would be interested in an interview.

Expecting another zero, I dialed Ginny's mother's number, and was instantly rewarded.

"Laurel," I exclaimed, experiencing the high of the day. "This is Thea. I'm sorry to bother you again. Is Ginny there?"

"So good to hear from you. No, Ginny's not here. She went to her great auntie's home in the country for the weekend. Did you want her for something?"

"Not really. In fact…I think I'd rather talk to you about it. I received a card in the mail the other day. You know, one of those fan type things. Said they liked the stories about the old time Ladies of the Night etc., and…uh, did I know of a Stella Parker. Thought I might be interested in interviewing her, etc."

"Oh, Thea, you don't have to stumble around about this. As a family, we've lived with Stella's reputation for a long time."

"But the letter was signed, Ginny Molina."

"It is?" She sounded as surprised as I'd been.

"That's what I thought. It didn't sound like your Ginny at all."

"Hmm. I wonder if Stella wrote it herself. Wouldn't put it past her. I'll ask around and see what I can find out. She's getting more and more eccentric as she ages. She's in her late eighties now and insisting she wants to live out in the country when she's never wanted anything to do with it before. I didn't think she'd last this long. She came maybe seven or eight months ago. Not many of us were happy about it. My cousin Virgil has more contact with her than any of the rest of us. Stella is the oldest of twelve children. My mother was the youngest. Several of the siblings live around here, so I have a bunch of cousins. I have a leg problem, so Virgil takes Ginny out there now and then when I can't. Actually, I think she goes more because of Stella's ex-husband than anything else. Alton Olmstead is his name. He was a well-known geologist. Are you familiar with him?"

"Yes, I am. In fact, the article about gold I'm writing will be mostly about him."

"Really. Ginny will be so excited. She is very proud to be able to claim him as a relative. I introduced her to him a while back. Took her out to see him several times before he died. She was thrilled. I'm quite sure Ginny didn't write the letter."

"If you think there's a chance her aunt wrote the letter herself, I'll go out and speak with her, if you don't mind. There's an old gold mining dredge on her property that I took some pictures of for an article I'm working on. Maybe I can find out more about it."

"There is? Well, that's interesting. You'll have to tell me all about it."

We chatted a few moments longer, reaffirming our next week's lunch date, and said goodbye.

Yes, it was interesting, I thought, echoing Laurel's comment, interesting that while I researched prostitutes of yore, there was one of not-so-long-ago-yore right under my nose. Even more interesting that Dale and I had been driving miles out of our way to get from the doodlebug to Carson's when a shortcut was right under our noses. Also interesting that, regardless of what Johnny Onenote thought, I found I really liked Carson Olmstead. I'd witnessed remorse, and to me, that was a good character-building thing.

CHAPTER 33

I still needed to return the staple gun. It was getting late, but there was plenty of time. I walked, thinking the exercise would do me good. When I got there Johnny was arranging small dinosaurs in a display by the cash register.

"Hi, Johnny, I'm returning the stapler."

"Here, young lady, put that heavy thing on the counter." He took it from me.

Something about his kindness triggered my impulsiveness.

"Johnny," I blurted out, "please tell me about your name. Is it something special? What does Onenote mean?" He looked startled for a moment, perhaps by my audacity. But a tiny smile curved his thin lips. He shook his head and closed his eyes. I wanted to sink through the floor. How could I have been so brazen?

"F sharp." His eyes were still closed. "The perfect note. It resonates, brings importance, richness, brilliance to all the other notes. Its pleasures accompany me wherever I go. It beats in my heart, makes these," he raised his crippled hands, "insignificant." He opened his eyes. "I might be a contentious old man, but I did love playing the piano. So what can I do for you today?"

I stumbled to get words out. "Oh, just the stapler, but I always like to look around."

"Then give me a minute, honey, I need to help Martin over there before he pulls all those leather hides down."

I wandered the store, one of my favorite things, but F sharp filled my mind. Who did I know with a piano? I could find Middle C and count the keys to F. That was about all that was left from my childhood piano lessons. And I remembered sharps were usually the black keys to the right of the whites. And a sharp provided a tang of dissonance. Discord. Like my life now. I must have hit a black key somewhere.

I brushed my fingers across the stack of tie-dyed tee shirts, as if it were a keyboard. I'd bought two of them for my trousseau. Max bought a leather vest and two shirts. We had laughed and loved that Johnny's Emporium was our Neiman Marcus.

My mind a million miles away, I bumped into a rack of sunglasses. It rocked. I stumbled. A hand reached past me to catch the rack. Another stopped my fall with a grip on my waist.

"Well hello," a husky male voice spoke in my ear. He laughed. "You must be fall'n for me."

Jake the snake. "Hi." I backed away. His hold clung for a moment, then slid from my waist. The narrow aisle put him right in my face. I managed a couple more steps back. "Thanks," I mumbled.

He flashed a big smile. "Wanna go for coffee?" Brash, sure of himself. I couldn't help remembering how he'd made me laugh in the truck.

His foolishness made me grin. "No thanks."

"Hot fudge sundae? Beer?"

I shook my head again.

"It's Thea Barlow, isn't it?"

I nodded at that.

"I thought so. You're the hottie Max Holman dumped."

A crude snake charmer. "You know Max?"

"Nah, just heard the story around town."

True, or was he lying? Did he know that Dale and I knew he was part of the gold digging clan?

"Ms. Barlow," Johnny called, stepping toward me. "I'm ready now." He picked up the stapler from the counter. There was a crash, and loud voices rang from the back room. He shook his head and looked heavenward. With a light touch on my shoulder, he urged me ahead of him.

I gave Jake a quick nod and hurried along with Johnny towards the wide door to the open lumber area.

"Don't mess with him," he said.

"Who?"

"Jake. He's no good."

Another shout from the back room. "Get out of my way, you son of a bitch!"

"You got no right!"

Other customers raised their heads and followed us, eager for excitement. Johnny took my elbow, putting himself between me and two men arguing over a roll of barbed wire. Parker and Townsend!

Johnny pointed me to the return desk. "If all you guys are going to do is fight, get out of here." He stepped behind the counter and looked back at them. "I mean it. Get out of here."

"Gladly." Townsend stomped away, eyes straight ahead. I don't know if he even saw me. Parker disappeared through the door into the store.

"Bunch of yahoos," Johnny said under his breath while fishing out my rental papers.

"What were they fighting about?"

"Who knows?" He huffed with disgust. "And with another person who already left."

"Who was that?" Jake, maybe?

"Never saw him before." He slid the paper to me, a knuckle pointing to the amount due. "Red hair."

Whoa. Carson. So he had caught up with both of them. I paid my bill, wished Johnny a nice day, and got out of there. If Carson wanted to fight with those two, fine with me. That was his business, not mine. I wanted no part in it. I headed back to the house with a quick pace, back to thinking about my list. Things to do, things to do.

What interested me now was the newly discovered proximity of the old witch and the shack to Carson's land. Maybe that was where I should be looking for more traces of Max. After all, the only solid thing I really knew was that Max—or rather his money clip, if a picky person wanted to make it even more nebulous—had been in the shack on her property, as was the doodlebug, the clue that lead us there. All much closer to Carson's inherited land than we had realized. I needed to go back. A worrisome idea.

The old woman didn't scare me; I could run faster than she could. But I didn't want to run into good old Quentin whatever-his-name-was, Mr. Hollywood. My gut told me, stay away from him, stay away. And why in the world wasn't the law taking care of this? Like a good little girl, I gave them all the information I had. And they'd done nothing? Fat lot of good it would do either Carson or Townsend if they wanted to report their problems. Almost home I heard a voice call out. "Thea? Thea Barlow?"

I snapped my head around. Across the street two houses down stood Townsend. "Yes?"

"May I speak to you for a minute?" Had he followed me from the Emporium? I glanced around the street. I'd have been happier if Emma Colton was out weeding her flowers, but I didn't see anybody. I hesitated a moment, but finally agreed. I met him in the middle of the street.

"Sorry to bother you," he said. "I apologize for that row in the store. I need to warn you about Virgil Parker. He's a dangerous man. And a crook. I know you go out to the Olmstead ranch occasionally. You need to be very careful, even though I understand that the owner is in residence now."

Not exactly. At least not until tonight, or tomorrow. But this man didn't need to know that. "You've met Carson Olmstead?"

"Briefly. This morning in the store. He gave Parker a good chewing out. Told him he'd report him if he ever touched foot on his land again. I told Parker I'd do the same if he didn't stop heckling me."

"How were you involved with Parker?"

His face hardened. "I believe I told you before that it is none of your business. I simply wanted to warn you. I don't know how you're connected with Carson Olmstead, but if he's part of the Parker family, you better watch out. I'd stay away from that place if I were you." He nodded briefly and left.

"Thanks," I said to his back. I hadn't needed the warning, being wary enough of Parker already, and of Townsend himself, for that matter. But Carson? I'd had my worries about him, but all his actions, reactions, everything he'd said about his family and feelings rang true to me. He felt like a friend, not an enemy. Was I a good judge of character? I had wondered this before, but I felt I was right about Carson.

Townsend had his good points, but not enough of them for complete trust. I walked to the end of the street and around the block to make sure he was gone before entering my house. If he didn't know where I lived, I wasn't about to show him. I locked the door behind me, which most people in Garnet Pass didn't bother with. The day was ending as weirdly as it began.

I made myself a quick dinner of an apple, an orange, a perfectly ripe pear, and a bag of microwave popcorn. The old witch kept rearing her head. Meeting with her would be beneficial in several ways. I could ask about the letter, and if she wanted to talk about her career as a madam, I would listen, but I'd also have a chance to get my own questions in. Ginny would be there, too. Her presence seemed to make everything safer. Poor kid.

But even with that, a shot of prudence wouldn't hurt. I wouldn't go to Carson's ranch without Dale, or to the witch's hovel without both Dale and Carson. Tire irons for all. But that was for tomorrow.

I turned on my Mozart play list which was supposed to be good for the brain. Sat down at my computer and got to work. I found a little more about my prospective Soiled Dove, Dottie Jacks, who came to the South Pass City area or, more specifically, to a place called Miners Delight. She came with four girls she called daughters and stayed with a man whose name might have been Hooten or Swallow. She was then visited by a friend, Sylvia Hanover, from Santa Fe who escorted five daughters. This was in a copy of a wonderfully snarky letter written in impeccable hand-writing by a woman to her sister. Unfortunately, it was a single page of what must have been a longer letter. There was some water damage, and faded ink problems, but the meaning became apparent from occasional exclamation marks and the underlining of daughters. After an uncertain period of time, Dottie and Sylvia exchanged daughters and left for places unknown. New names, new places offered more sites to look at. I searched them all.

A couple of hours later, I jerked awake with my head on the keyboard. A frightening dream left me alert and soaked in sweat. I fought to remember hazy visions of knives and guns, me trying to hide among a line of dancing floozies, pushing, shoving, tripping, and grabbing long grey hair. Yuk. I wiped my face with my sleeve and drank stale water from the glass beside me, the ickyness of which aroused a mental picture of a pint of Rum Raisin ice cream in the freezer.

It helped. I stared at my last typed lines now covered with a string of *ys*. I deleted them, made sure my research was saved, licked the spoon, shut down Mozart, and went to bed.

CHAPTER 34

The next morning was a different bag of beans. I wasn't ready for anything until early afternoon. If I was going to interview the old witch, I needed to get going. There might even be time to see Townsend again. He claimed he didn't know Max, and it was possible he might not know him by name, but if I told him Max bought our rings from him, and could describe them well enough, he might remember a customer he'd spoken to at length. Most people remember faces better than names, anyway. Right, and the outrageous price of the sale might have implanted Max's face thoroughly in his mind. If I'd thought of this earlier, I could have saved a lot of time. I wanted to be able to exclude him as a source of info and be done with him.

The old witch was more important than Townsend. Which meant phone calls. I rang the restaurant. Dale wasn't there; they'd sent her off to Rock Springs to get supplies from Walmart. I rang her phone. It rang and rang. I could practically see it dancing on the dash to merry bells. I would catch her there, or if she were on her way back, no way would I miss spotting the rattletrap.

The Walmart parking lot was packed like weenie fish in a can. I finally found a spot in a far, far back corner. I jumped out, scanning the lot for her truck, which I didn't see. Grabbing my cell phone, I headed for the entrance. Mid-stride, the door slid open. Dale appeared. I opened my mouth to yell when a man stepped out from behind her. Tall, big shoulders, black hat. She turned to him, he drew her forward. What? No! Max? He pulled her into a kiss.

Frozen. Mouth agape. I couldn't move, couldn't make a sound. Max! Max and Dale!

Max came up for air, showing his crooked-nose profile. He squeezed her shoulders; she patted his cheek. He snugged his hat back down on his forehead and strode off, hand trailing along the brick wall, a little unsteady, and disappeared around the corner. A bit shaky? Dale loped through the parking lot to her truck and roared off onto the street.

I couldn't erase the vision. No mistake. It *was* Max. I knew the shirt, denim with a print yoke, soft and faded from many washings. I knew the walk. I knew the shape, I knew the feel of his hands on my shoulders, the kiss, the taste. The way he snugged his hat.

Dale's expression—I'd never seen that look on her face before, the openness, the pleasure. How long had this been going on? What a fool. What a fool I'd been! How had she snatched him away from me? When?

I broke away, lurched into a parked car, fell to my knees. My phone dropped, bounced off the corner of the concrete curb. I grabbed it and watched the cracks crawl across the screen. In a fit of fury, I pounded it against the curb's corner until it crumpled into worthlessness. With all my strength I threw it under the cars, listening to it slide like a scrabbling rat through the rows. Hauling myself up, I stumbled like a drunkard back to my car. My mouth felt like a dry creek bed. I sat under the steering wheel, reached for the water bottle and drank half in large gulps.

My mind didn't know where to go; thoughts flew like dark swarms of bats circling a cave. Dale, the bitch. What was her game? Dale found the note on my door...just happened to know about a doodlebug. Tears burned behind my eyes.

And Max. Where had he been all these days? With Dale? In her house while she pretended to help me look for him? Was it all a game to her? What part did he play? Had he been injured, and she found him in the shack, and took him home to heal? Why in the world would she do such a thing? And he had amnesia? *Oh, right. Sure.* This was crazy stuff.

I slammed my hand on the steering wheel and started the engine. One sure thing—I didn't have to look for Max any more. I knew where he was. Right here in Rock Springs. And I now had no friend, no lover. Except maybe Carson, he could be a friend. Could he be trusted? Dale hadn't liked him. She hadn't been happy when he showed up. That's the best thing going for him. I jerked my car into reverse and headed out of the parking lot. Going where? Why? No need to talk to Townsend now. The old witch didn't matter anymore, nor the doodlebug, nor the shack. Nothing mattered.

I could talk to Carson. Ha! He'd be glad Max was back. They could hunt for the gold together. Did he have a part in this wrenched melodrama? Was he still where he'd planned to spend the night? Breaking my phone hadn't been my brightest moment. The Outlaw Inn was close. I drove there. But no, he'd checked out several hours ago. Like a whipped dog, I headed home.

Pulling into the drive, I saw a man lying on his stomach

in the back yard close to the opened alley gate. What now? Asleep? Drunk? It wouldn't be the first drunk sleeping it off in the alley. Could've fallen through the gate. I shook his shoulder. Stiff. My heart began to pound. A slight pressure moved him enough. A scream stuck in my throat. Even without half of his face I recognized Richard Townsend.

I ran to the house, lungs leaking an eerie wail. Thank God for the landline. I punched the number. "Rhonda, there's a body in my yard!" I yelled.

"Hey, hey, calm down. Who is this?"

"It's Thea. Richard Townsend! He's dead. He's dead."

"Someone you know? Thea, what have you done?"

That sobered me quick. "What have I done? Nothing! Nothing. Please send someone."

"Nobody's here except Billy and me. Don't touch anything. I'll be right there."

What was she thinking? Knowing the man made me guilty? Rhonda would keep me forever with questions. Not now. I couldn't bear it. She could grab me later. Or I'd even go find her. Just not now.

Keys still in hand, I raced outside, jumped in my car and drove off. Going where? Carson's? The only place I knew of. Would Rhonda send Billy to find me? That would be even worse. My red car stuck out like a half-mast flag. I'd be spotted in a minute. I needed a different car. I felt like a not-bright con on the run. And geeze, I hadn't thought about Max for at least fif—"Max!" I yelled out loud. That's where I could get another car. Max's house. The garage door opener was in my glove compartment. I flipped a U-ie, and sped down another deserted street back to Max's house.

Where was he? Would he be there? He must have his pickup. I surveyed the place carefully. No obvious signs of anyone being around. And so what if he was there? Fine and dandy by me. He had a lot to answer for.

I fished out the opener and approached the garage. The door slid open, the light went on, and there stood his lovely Rav 4. I drove into the empty spot beside it, and closed the door behind me.

The Rav's keys were kept in the narrow space between a cabinet and the wall. I eased my hand in. Yes! They were still there. Max seldom used the car, so it was much less recognizable than mine. I fumbled a bit starting it, and then almost forgot to open the garage door. Quivering like a downed bird, I knew I shouldn't be driving, but what the hey. I backed out, reclosed the door without mishap, and took the least trafficked way out of town.

Up to eighty-one, old pavement splotches blurred into Townsend's bloody head. I jammed the radio button. Music. Old Town Road. Yeah, Old Town Road, that's what I was on. I shut it off. Where was Mozart when I needed him? Okay. I relaxed a bit. Thoughts took over.

Had Virgil Parker killed Townsend? Every time I'd seen them together, they'd been fighting. He was the obvious killer. Dumping the body in my yard could have been his way of getting back at me. But why kill the man? There had to be a better reason than trespassing on someone's land, or…jumping someone's claim, if that's what they called it.

Oh, lordy, I should have told Rhonda about Parker. They should be looking for him, not me. And why hadn't someone discovered Max if he'd been in Rock Springs all along? Or were there people who knew where he was and didn't want to tell me, because of Dale? Yeah, Dale the bitch; she'd played me like a stringed fiddle. But why? Why didn't they just run off together? Worse, why hadn't I confronted them, one or the other? I banged the wheel again. I couldn't believe I'd just stood there like a gaping idiot. Pathetic! The drive seemed to take forever.

Finally, the sight of Carson's gate brought a sense of sanctuary. I so needed a friend. A light shone in the house. Eagerly, I knocked on the door and rang the bell as well. More than once. Nothing. Then checked the Quonset. No car there or anywhere else.

Disappointment hung heavy. I thought about sitting in the tree until he returned, but this wasn't the time for contemplating my navel. The thoughts raging through my mind weren't friends. I needed to do something to drive them out. A mental spark threw me back to my original plans; plans for talking to the old witch and seeing Ginny. All that seemed like a long time ago, but better than sitting in a stupid tree.

I drove up the east trail towards the witches den. Seeing Ginny, and even Nonnie, again would give me a gentle boost. Either the need to hide, or the fear of being found, made me look for a less blatant place to park than on the road. Not too far from the limp fence marking the woman's land, I found a rocky outcropping covered with a bunch of dried-up tumbleweeds. I parked the Rav behind it. A poor job of concealment, but better than none.

I crossed the downed fence and jogged towards the dump. Soon happy yips greeted my progress. Nonnie ran to greet me. Exactly what I needed. I scooped her up, and let her sloppy kisses melt a bit of the frosty lump in my chest.

CHAPTER 35

"Thea!" I saw Ginny approaching with a heavy bucket. Water apparently, as it slopped when she put it down. She, too, ran to greet me.

"Hello," she said. "What are you doing here?"

"I came to see you and your auntie."

"Awesome! I'm tired of hauling these buckets. I'll take you to the house; just let me get rid of this bucket."

She picked it up and headed for the string of Porta Potties. I followed, frowning. What were they doing? Surely she didn't have to clean one of those babies. Yuk!

"Ginny!" a male voice called. "Who're you talking to?"

Oh, no. Hollywood, lugging an even larger bucket. Ginny paid no attention and disappeared behind a tree. Appearing again, she set her pail beside one of the potties, then skipped toward the man, motioning me to join her.

"Uncle Quentin, this is my friend, Thea Barlow. She's a writer." He dropped the bucket on the ground, flexing his arm.

"He's from California," Ginny went on. "He's been in

some movies. I didn't recognize the names, but I think it's pretty awesome, don't you?"

"Yes, indeed." I gave him a rather weak smile. Still handsome, he looked harried and disheveled in a water-splashed way.

"Thea Barlow. Hmm. I think we've met before." His eyes were hard as stone.

"He's really my cousin, or something, but I call him Uncle, 'cause he's older."

He didn't smile at that, but I did.

"Ginny, go get another bucket. I filled a couple more for you. We need to get this done."

She ran off happily enough with Nonnie racing after her. "I'll be back," she called.

Once again his eyes traveled over me. "What are you doing here?"

I raised an eyebrow at his rudeness.

"We're really busy today. A lot of work to be done." He glanced at the row of ancient johns, as did I. He saw my look and said impatiently, "We're having a party of sorts."

"A party?" The words burst out before I could stop them. What kind of host offered such gross things for the use of guests?

"Family reunion, and my aunt doesn't take party crashers kindly." I could easily believe that. "If you came for a visit," he continued, "I suggest you come back another day." He glanced over his shoulder, and shouted, "Ginny, hurry on back. Don't go anywhere else. I need your help here."

Slave labor. Perverseness struck; a bad habit of mine. "I won't disturb your work. I'll just say hello to your aunt and be on my way. She did ask me out for an interview." Which wasn't exactly true, but close enough for this jerk. With an unfathomable look, he opened his mouth as if to say something, but Ginny was upon us carrying a large pile of towels, or rags.

"I'm going to see your auntie," I told her.

"I'll go with you." She dropped the load of towels.

"Hey!" Hollywood's head snapped to attention. "You have to stay here."

"But I want to go with Thea. I can help her talk to—"

"You have to stick close to me, remember what I said? I need your help."

Whoa! I didn't like the sound of that. What was this guy, some kind of a pervert? I stood my ground. "She's going with me. We'll be back shortly. I'll even help her with *your* chores." That is, if I found this man was harmless, we'd be back. I'd have no problem taking Ginny home to her mother in Rock Springs if I found things were iffy around here. Maybe the old lady had memory problems, had forgotten what a scary world this could be for little girls. At least I'd talk to her. You'd think with her background, she'd be able to smell out creeps like this guy.

"Don't worry, Uncle Quentin," Ginny said, grabbing my hand and pulling me away in a skipping run. "We'll be quick."

Her Aunt Stella sat at the dining table in the doublewide with a cell phone to her ear. At sight of us, she dropped the phone to the table top next to two other phones. She jumped to her feet, grabbing the handles of her walker which stood next to her chair. "You!" she pointed her finger at me. "What are you doing here?"

Ginny dropped my hand and went to her. "It's okay, Auntie. She just came to visit us. It's nice. We can sit and talk. I'll make us some tea." She patted the woman's shoulder, but got her hand roughly pushed away.

I couldn't stand it. "I'm sorry I came without notice. I

received your letter that said you'd like to talk to me, and thought I'd just drop in. I can leave ri—"

"It's all right, Stella. It's all right." Hollywood came through the door in a hurry, obviously having followed us. "I told her we're too busy for company. We're having a party. Relatives coming. A reunion."

"What letter?" Stella's head swung from one of us to the other. "She said a letter. She got a letter."

He grimaced with a raised-handed indication of no knowledge.

"Where's that damn Virgil?" She started banging the walker wheels on the floor and moving forward.

I'd had enough. I raised my arm. "I'm sorry I bothered you today. I'm leaving right now. Ginny, would you see me out the door?" I held my hand out to her and made a quick exit for the door, closing it behind us.

"I'm worried about you." I whispered, not slowing down. "Call your mother. Tell her to come get you. I…" Hollywood burst out the door behind us. He caught up with us quickly and put a hand on Ginny's shoulder.

"Look—" he began.

I cut in. "I don't want to hear anything more from you. I'm out of here." I shook my finger in his face. "And you better watch yourself." I jogged off. The sooner I could reach the car, the better. Carson should be home by now; if not I'd find a phone somewhere and call Ginny's mom myself. Or get help one way or another.

I hit the road and started down to where I left the Rav, then stopped when I saw an approaching silver-black car like Carson's. Great. I ran toward it until it stopped and the door opened. Not Carson. Jake?

"Well, well!" he crowed. "You just can't stay away from me, can you?"

"What are you doing here? Where's Carson?"

"He your new boyfriend? He's up there at the old lady's place. They're having a party. You oughta go. He let out a big gust of laughter.

Another vehicle approached behind Carson's. A white panel van of some kind. Jake motioned it to go around. The rear door swung open, back and forth, enough to glimpse many girls sprawled on benches and the floor. Jake stepped in front of me, barring my vision.

"Relatives," he said, shaking his head. "Don't ask me. There are a lot of them. Some damned kind of reunion."

No way. He couldn't be that dumb. My glimpse was brief, but those girls weren't headed for a party. They were sprawled, looked half-dead. Something was wrong. Pictures filed through my mind, pictures in newspapers, on TV, of vehicles, small and large, packed with dead or near-dead humans hijacked across borders. Trafficking? Here in this wilderness? Ginny! She was up there. In danger? Had she called her mother?

I forced a bland, indifferent expression. "It's not a party I want to crash. Oh, and do you have a phone I could borrow?"

"Why?"

"Why? Don't be so rude." I eased a step away from him. "My friend Laurel's on her way. I want to know how soon she'll be here."

"Laurel who? Where's Dale?"

"At work." Was she part of this? Jake and Dale? Max? Whose game was this? "Why do you want to know?"

He shrugged took a step away to watch a large, dark service truck approach. "You two are always together."

The truck was black with a white sign on the side. Sweeny Electrical Services. Again, Jake motioned it around.

It stopped instead, and the driver, a big, heavy-set man with a wild mustache stepped out and pointed at me.

"Who's that?" he barked.

"A friend," Jake shot back.

"In here." He shoved open a side door. I backed up a step, turned to run, heard Jake say, "No. Not her." Someone grabbed my neck. My knees buckled.

CHAPTER 36

Whispers. Soft little sounds buzzing in my ears. Bees? Words? My arm hurt. Bouncing, moving. Another jolt. My head banged on something hard, but brought me more alert. I was on the floor of a moving truck. Thoughts drizzled in. More buzzing. Not bees. Words…maybe. I couldn't understand.

A startled shout made me knock my head again. I awakened completely and opened my eyes to see nothing but legs and feet, some pushing against me, some resting on my body. The smell was ghastly. I eased my arm out from under me and pushed to a partial sitting position. The shout had been foreign. Yes, all those girls. I was in the truck with them. The shouted words must have been "Shut up," or something like it. The whispers stopped for a moment, then began again more softly.

I joined them. "Anyone speak English?" I whispered.

"Buenos dias." floated softly through the air. "Have a nice day."

That wouldn't help much. I tried another. "Water?"

"All gone." At least there had been some. Empty plastic bottles littered the floor.

Girls everywhere, jammed on three lengthwise benches with others sprawled on the floor like me. My back was killing me. Scooching my butt forward, I squeezed against another sitter who stared at me listlessly with widely dilated eyes. A disorderly mop of dark hair topped her small heart-shaped face. I dislodged her enough so I could lean against the side of the truck, jammed into a corner behind the driver seat. She snuggled her face against my shoulder and softly sang, twinkle, twinkle, little star, but in a language I didn't recognize.

Another bouncing bump. Low groans, including my own, filled the stifling air. A rough male voice. "Damn road needs to be fixed." Peering through the darkness, I could make out the top of the front seat back above the partition.

Another voice. "It'll happen if the money's there." Whiny tones.

"…many girls we got?"

The words were hard to distinguish through the road noise, moans, and groans. One of the girls was vomiting, another shouting a string of nasty swear words, clogging my ears. I leaned as close to the seat as possible. Twinkle's head, still singing, slid down my arm.

"…here? Twenty, maybe."

It felt and smelled like a hundred.

"All told?"

"Thirty some, I think."

The growly voice might be the driver's. Two men, maybe three. Couldn't tell.

"That's big money, isn't it?"

"Okay, I guess…just transporting."

"Money's in the sex."

"…asking for trouble…not selling them, just transporting."

"…might change her mind for a bigger haul."

She? Did he say she, or he? Dale?

"…can't. Deal's made."

A smug laugh. "Wanna bet?"

We began to slow. I stopped listening. Shifting, jostling bodies pushed at me from all directions. I propped Twinkle against my shoulder, trying to keep her upright. An elbow gouged my breast. I shoved back, grabbed hold of Twinkle's shirt, hoping to pull her with me. Everyone wanted out, including me. A push to the back door. Those on benches stepped and fell on top of us on the floor. I fought back, struggling to my knees, lost hold of her shirt. Got one foot on the floor and was moved like a piece of garbage through sludge to the middle of the pack. Had to get out. Fresh air. Hide. A place to hide. The truck stopped, my face jammed against a bony shoulder, a stifling force pressed my back. I gasped for breath. My head began to spin. When the door shoved open we burst out like a bubbling-over pot. A heavenly rush of cool air. Cries and sobs; bodies writhing under me like a nest of snakes. Kicks, hits, hair pulls from those on top. I screamed, with the rest, yelled, swore, and scrabbled under the truck, raking my knees across rough stones and finally curled up against a hot tire.

I lay there, eyes closed, breathing deeply, sucking in the nauseating smell of rubber; my mind wondering blithely if tires were still made of rubber, or was it some other thing?

Noise thundered. Voices, sobs, shouts. Tin doors slamming. Potties? My eyes flew open. Finally, a hint of reality. The outdoor toilets. That's what they were for.

I was caught in the midst of traffickers. Was this what

had happened to Max? Was he part of it…with his new found love?

To hell with him. I had better things to worry about. Like Ginny. And poor little Twinkle.

Ginny! Was she still here with her aunt? I moved carefully through the aroused agonies of my battered body to peek around the tire. I saw the bottom edge of the potties and enough of the girls to tell they were using the potties. My heart ached for them. Where was Twinkle? Some sat on the ground, others lay on it. Many paced. All drinking water, tossing empty bottles. How could I help them? I'd have to help myself first.

Though my mind seemed fuzzy, I knew where I was. The witch's house was not that far. Could I get there? I could battle the old biddy for Ginny, if I had to.

I stretched my neck farther to get a better look, then shot back. Boots stood beside the truck only about a yard away. Another pair approached. Black track shoes, no logo. I tightened my body.

"You find the woman?" The rough voice of the man who drove the truck?

"No." Boots moved away, or out of sight?

"Where is she?"

"Around here somewhere. She can't go far." More shoes. Laced hikers with a blue medallion. "Don't count on it." A pause. "I'm driving one of the trucks."

"Since when?" Blue medallion and black trackers were speaking to each other, but it was difficult telling who said what.

"Since now. I'm leaving this two-bit state, you and your gold's a bunch of crap. I'm going where the money is."

"None of us going nowhere if we don't get our ass in gear. Gotta get in and out fast. Too many things going wrong. Where's Carson?"

Carson! I'd forgotten about Carson. Was he in on this?

"Don't worry. I took care of him."

"Like the old man? Stupid mistake."

"Old fart had it coming. Didn't know my own strength."

Deefy? They must be talking about him. He killed Deefy. I had to remember this. Blue medallion or black track? I could tell their voices apart now, but not which shoes belonged to them.

"You run out of town, everything's gonna fall on me."

"Tough shit."

"Whattaya gonna do with the girl?"

"Miss prissy Barlow? Don't worry. I'll think of something." They both laughed.

My body flushed with fear. They know me. Who were they? Jake? Virgil Parker? Hollywood? Towns—Not Townsend! I'd forgotten about poor Townsend. How could I do that? Rhonda! She was after me. That could be good. We could use some cops about now. Did she know about Carson's return? Did she know I came out here? I didn't know. And where was Hollywood?

More deep breaths. I had to calm down. *Yes, Thea,* I told myself, *calm down for once in your life. Make a plan. Do something. Okay, a reconnaissance of sorts.* The boots were gone, at least as far as I could see. A lot of people moving around. I was pretty close to the doublewide. Could I mingle with the crowd? Could I get to the house? Thoughts of the three cell phones on the table burned holes in my mind. I needed a phone. *Okay, be casual. Act as if you belong.*

CHAPTER 37

How does one crawl casually out from under a truck? Awkwardly. I actually got a few steps onto the ramp leading to the doublewide's door before my arm was caught from behind, then quickly the other, both jerked sharply up. I kicked back and stomped on his feet. Laced shoes, maybe. He laughed, reached around me to open the door, jerking me across the doorway. I thought my arms would break, or my shoulders pop out of their sockets. I wished they would.

"Look what I found," he said.

"You! Here again?" I knew that voice; the old witch. Pressure on my arms bent my head forward and down. All I could see was the floor. I heard the walker banging toward me. Then saw the walker legs, her skirt, and one of her hands holding a syringe

I yelled, "I came for Ginny," hoping she could hear me. "Her mother called me. Wants me to take her home."

"She lies!"

"Get out of here, Ginny! Hide—"

"Take her away!"

"We don't need her now." A softer voice, farther away.

"Out of here, I said!" That was the witch.

Someone else grabbed my wrists with an upward jerk. I screamed, saw the shoes; loafers. Polished. Hollywood! A stabbing jab in my arm.

A deep guttural noise woke me, shooting my eyes open to darkness. I rolled my head. A rattle of pain fell from my mouth like a fistful of shards. The sounds came from me.

I tried to move. Struggled, jerked and tugged; found my hands and legs tied at the ankle and wrists! Nausea stilled me into a pile of misery, but the fuzz in my head began to spread out. As did my eyesight. Where was I? Large shadows loomed beside me. Walls? Yes, but more. Cars, trucks? Big, anyway. I made out a wheel. A large thing, a van of some kind, maybe. I tried to roll a bit. At least my hands were tied in front of me rather than behind. Though useless, it seemed more normal, if anything could. I ran my hands awkwardly over cool, rough, concrete; noticed the rank oily, gassy smell that burned my nose. Garage. I was in the big garage.

Thoughts began to come back. Voices, I'd heard voices. The old witch, Hollywood, other men. They were talking about the girls, those poor girls, and Ginny! I struggled to sit up. How long had I been here? I raised my hands to my mouth, gnawed at the thin, tight rope, twisting my wrists to find a knot. No luck. Leaning through my knees, I grabbed at the twined rope around my ankles. Despite my efforts, nothing loosened.

Blinking and squinting through the darkness, I searched the vicinity through growing nausea, trying to identify things, anything that might help. The closest was an indistinct shape on the floor to my right. Not square, just a spread out pile of stuff. Something that might help, if I could get there. Tools, please, something sharp.

A flashback to the ghastly sight of Townsend made me leery of anonymous piles. And Rhonda! Was she still looking for me? But that would be good now, wouldn't it? Hurry, Rhonda, hurry.

No, hurry, Thea. Scooching proved slow and awkward. So I flopped back down and tried a roll. Agony, but once, twice. Again. I rested on my stomach a moment, my cheek against the cool, bruising cement of the garage floor before turning my head to face my fate.

I saw legs, and snapped my eyes shut. "No!" *Please, don't let it be dead!*

A sound? A movement? "Hey," I croaked, twisting to see if my legs would reach. Barely. I inched forward enough to kick with both feet.

With an unintelligible mutter, the man flopped over on his back, raising his arms enough for me to see he, too, was tied hand and most likely feet, but I couldn't see them.

He turned his head to look at me. I peered at him. Aches kept me from another roll. I stretched as far as possible, squinting. "Max?" A whisper, then much louder, "Max, you bastard!"

"Thea?"

"Yes, it's me, Thea. Your bride to be. Remember?" My voice was weak, pathetic. I tried for fire, but failed miserably. "What are you doing here?"

"Looking...for you."

"Looking for me? All you had to do was go to my house. I've been sitting there for ten damn days. Where in hell were you?"

"Keep...voice down," he gasped. "Whoever...put us here...not friends."

"Don't you lecture me!" Unable to shake my fist at him, I kicked him again. "You have a lot to answer for. Where were you?"

"Not…real clear about that…yet. Except for hospital." His voice was feeble and fading.

Mine was gaining. "Hospital? You've been in the hospital! Where?"

"Rock Springs. Escaped today."

"Escaped? From who."

"Under police protection. Nobody's…supposed to know where I am."

"Police protection!" I sounded like an hysterical parrot.

"Shhh. Please…shhh."

"Don't shush me!"

"To hell with this!" he said, his voice louder than mine. He did two quick body rolls and landed on top of me. His mouth closed over mine. I could hardly breath.

I didn't care. I started to cry.

"Don't cry." He tried to brush the tears away with his cheek.

"You kissed Dale," I wailed, as he used his arms, which he was lying on, as well as mine, to push off me.

"You saw that?"

I nodded.

"Ridiculous…flopping around like…couple of fish. Help me sit up."

My tied ankles were useless, but I worked myself up on my knees and braced his back while he pushed with agonizing gasps of pain to a sitting position. "Sorry… broken ribs. Four of 'em. Give me your hands. We've got to get out of here."

He began to work on the knots. "Yes, I kissed her…on the cheek…first person I saw that I knew…wasn't afraid to talk to." Each phrase was emphasized by a tug and accompanying groan, sometimes from me, too. "Walked from hospital…kept to side streets. Didn't dare hitch. Kid used to work for me…now at Walmart…wanted his truck."

"Where's yours?"

"Don't know. Gone."

His ramblings were easy to follow, except my questions fought each other to find which would burst out first. His hands dropped away.

"Gotta stop. Hurts."

I gave in. "Here, lie back down." I grabbed his arm as best I could, easing him flat.

His moan sounded more like a sigh. "Better." He held up his hands. "Hurry."

His hands were tied with some kind of cording, which might be easier to handle than the thinner rope on mine. My night-sight had improved some, but not enough to figure out knot intricacies. I put my teeth to it.

"Don't stop talking," I demanded between tugs." I want to know more about that kiss. What was that meeting with Dale about?"

"Met by accident. Everyone promised to tell you where…or that I safe…

"Everyone? Who's everyone?"

"Cops, deputies, the sheriff…even Rusty."

"Rusty! He was involved?"

"Yeah, he—"

"They lied to you! And they lied to me! Just wait until I talk to him."

"Afraid of that. Why I snuck out of hospital. Couldn't understand why you hadn't come to see me. Couldn't believe you wouldn't find me."

Right! I thought, unable to trust even a whole sentence. Fueled by anger, I got a finger under a cord and gave a big tug. To my surprise the whole knot unraveled. "Wow, that was too easy. Whoever tied you up didn't know much about knots."

"Some guy. Black hair, works out. Last face I remember."

"Sounds like Hollywood. Quentin somebody; California license plate. Slime bag. Thinks he's God's gift to women. Probably never tied a knot before in his life." I moved beside his feet and made fairly quick work of a similar knot.

"Gotta get out of here." He carefully flexed his arms, and moved his legs with a sigh of relief. "Your turn." He rolled onto his hands and knees and slowly rose to his feet, staggering for balance. He looked around much as I had. Muttered, "Garage. Must be tools." He took off on a Frankenstein walk, stopping every few feet to flex. I'd never seen Max in such a weakened state before. It frightened me. Something was more wrong than broken ribs.

I heard a soft, "Aha." He returned carrying a flashlight; the lens covered with a few fingers to limit the beam, dropped a roll of duct tape, and knelt at my feet. He waggled something else in front of my face. "Box cutter." Whatever bound my feet quickly gave way to the blade. I, too, had to rise from a hands and knees position. Hip, back, butt, everything ached.

"Hurry," he whispered. "What's happening out there?" He held the beam close to floor, flitting it past two parked vans; the closest one marked "Kirby's Jobs Done Right," across to the wall, the side door. Junk in the corner, a carton of water, its plastic covering torn open. We could hear cars moving, running feet, and indistinct voices hollering.

"Trafficking, Max, They're taking a bunch of girls somewhere."

Max nodded. "Like before. Cops think this is tomorrow."

Fluff still lurked in my mind. I tried to remember what I'd heard. "They're arguing. Have to hurry because things are going wrong. That's probably us. It's like they're changing their minds, saying sex brings more money. Whatever. We've got to stop them. And Ginny!" *How could I have forgotten even for a moment?* "Ginny's out there somewhere. She's only twelve."

"Who's that?" He ran the light over the panel trucks again. Old, dirty, well-worn. Crumpled fender. He fiddled with the closest hood and opened it.

"The old woman's grandniece." He sawed at something with the box cutter and closed the hood. It finally clicked with me. Duh…"Yes! That's what we can do. Disable the cars!" I could have thought of that. Why hadn't I?

"It won't go far." He grinned. "Water…get some, okay?"

I was already on my way. I got as many bottles from the carton as I could carry and hurried back to Max. He leaned wearily against the other truck, its gas cap in hand. I poured as much water into the gas tank as possible, took the cap from his hand and screwed it back on. Tucking a bottle in my pants, and one in each of Max's pockets, I said, "Let's go."

CHAPTER 38

Max flashed the light low on the side door. I grabbed his arm and half pulled, half steadied him over to it. Opening it a crack, I put an ear to the fresh air.

Engines rumbled louder. Voices hollered. "Round them up!"

"Over here." Headlights swirled. A yard light lit the darkness. How long had I been in the garage?

I opened the door farther. "They're down by the potties." We both slithered out. I barely got the door snapped shut before the garage bay door rattled opened behind us and an automatic light turned on.

"Damn." A man's voice. The light flicked off. We plastered ourselves against the building, melding into deep shadows, thankful the yard light didn't cast its beam this far. A motor kicked in. No headlights. The bay door closed and the panel truck drove off to the right. If the driver had looked behind, he might have seen us. He either didn't know we'd been thrown in the garage, or didn't care, or notice, that we were no longer there.

I held my breath as the van slid past us. I grabbed

Max's arm with enough force to make him teeter. "He's headed towards Carson's house. I don't know where Ginny is. We have to find her."

"He won't go far." He loosened my grip. "Again, who's Ginny?"

"She's a young girl, twelve, or thirteen; Carson's cousin or something. They're going to kidnap her, unless we can save her. Sell her as a sex slave. We have to find her. Come on!" I slipped away from him and ran a few steps. With a lurch and a groan, he grabbed my shirt and pulled me to him.

"Not yet, careful," his voice rasped into my ear. "You said, Carson. Is he here?"

"Yes, but I don't know what side he's on."

"You know where we are? Can we move without being seen?"

Good point. I must have been suffering from mental issues, too. What had they done to me? I shook my head then, wished I hadn't. "I've a good idea of where we are, have you been here before?"

"Yeah, don't remember much. Got knocked out, filled full of drugs. Think this time, too"

"That's what happened?" I remembered the hypodermic at the witch's house. "I might have gotten some of that, too. Is that why we're so wonky?"

"Maybe. Hope not. Wasn't fun."

"The night before the wedding?"

"Yeah." He wrapped his arms around me. "They promised me, all of them, they would tell you I was all right."

I wanted to hear it, I needed to know more, but it wasn't that easy. Now wasn't the time. That vision, him and Dale, still lurked behind my eyes. I pulled away from him. "We need to hurry. Will you help me?"

"Of course."

My physical condition was a little better than his, but that wasn't saying much. Reluctantly, I left the comfort of his chest and took his hand. "Over there, to the right and ahead of us, is an old wind break. The trees aren't much, but they'll provide more protection than we've got here. I'm just not sure how far away it is."

With our backs to the corrugated wall, we sidled to the rear end of the garage. From there, I could see the faint shadow of the trees. In the distance I heard Nonnie barking again. Other noises, people noises, soft voices, things clattering. Nothing too loud, but nobody afraid of being heard, either. We peered carefully through the darkness.

"What's that?" Max asked, pointing to an odd-shaped shadow behind the garage.

"The remains of a chicken coop, or some kind of animal shelter. I'm going to try to run there. Do you think you can make it?"

He grunted, which I took for affirmative.

"I'll go first. If nobody's roused, follow as quickly as possible. From there we'll try to get to the trees. We have to get to the farthest back rows of trees. If you remember, the string of potties is within the first few rows. I think that's where the people are."

"Mmm. I remember the potties."

"You saw them before?"

"Yeah, that's where I got caught."

"When, tonight?"

"No, the first time."

My mind whirled with more questions, but I couldn't think about that now. Ginny. I had to be sure she was safe. "We'll have to work our way around the potties. Not too far from them is a dump. Another hiding place. We can rest there if we need to."

"You think the girl's at Carson's house? It'll take too long to get there."

"No, your car's hidden not far from the downed fence."

"*My* car? Wha.."

"Not now. I'm going to run for the chicken coop. I'll wait for you."

"Careful!"

I tried the commando squat run, but my legs were too weak. The best I could do was running bent from the waist. Anyone could have seen me, but Lady Luck hovered. I dropped behind the coop, which was nothing more than a pile of boards. I moved for more cover and landed on a pile of crumpled barbed wire. "Ow." Max dropped beside me. "Watch out. barbed wire." I sucked my pierced thumb. Tetanus. That's all I needed. *Discord*, ran through my mind. Black keys.

Max flopped onto his back, hugging his ribs. I heard barks again. Nonnie. Sounded like the other direction, the doublewide.

"I hear Nonnie, maybe Ginny's…

"Nonnie?"

"Dog. I have to go see. Stay here, I'll be right back." I moved carefully away from the jumbled pile of wire and towards the dark shadows behind the garage. From there I could race to the doublewide's ramped porch. A plan, a plan. I felt better. It might have been the fresh air.

Squatting behind the ramp. I listened. Where was the witch? Anyone else in there? Silence. Didn't mean nobody was in there.

The sharp slam of a car door. Running feet. I shot up. Saw a small figure running toward the garage. I couldn't mistake the bright bouncing of her up-do even in dim light. Charlotte? What was she doing here? I called out, but she was gone. I started to run after her. No! Ginny first.

I ran up the ramp and into the house. No one; hurried down the hall where the bedrooms would be. "Ginny, Nonnie." My soft call aroused barking, yipping, door scratching from the end bedroom. I rounded the bed and opened the bathroom door. Nonie flew out, gave me a welcome hit to the knee, and raced away out the open front door. I checked behind the shower curtain, closets and two other bedrooms, but Ginny wasn't in the house, or Nonnie would have gone to her. Back to the living/kitchen area, thinking phones. I glanced at the table where they were earlier. Nothing now.

Then I saw it. The walker on its side behind the dining table. A quick turn. She lay on the floor in front of a buffet, her long grey hair splayed around her. "Are you hurt?" I asked stupidly, kneeling beside her. Her head flopped over. "Here, I'll help you." I straightened her skirt, moved her leg so I could put my hand under her shoulder. Just as quickly I snatched it back, gasping at blood, the amount of it, dripping from my hand and sleeve. She was lying in a puddle of it. Unseeing eyes open now. Dead, not hurt.

I held my arm out, blood dripping from my fingers, my other hand searching for a neck pulse that wasn't there. Choking sobs shook me, tears flooded my eyes. I dropped my forehead to her chest. She was still warm. The sobs turned to dry heaving. Another body. What was I, a child from hell seeking the dead? Struggling to my feet, I stumbled to the kitchen sink and stuck my hand under a gush of water from the faucet. I spat a mouthful of saliva into the blood-splashed sink.

Still, gagging, hand dripping, I ran from the house. Ran blinded by tears, or fear, into the darkness, unable to stop. Someone, also running, grabbed my arm with a steely grip, pulling me with him. The heavy-set man, mustache, driver of the truck…the girls. My feet couldn't keep up with him, I tripped on a rut, started to fall. He jerked me up, growling, "You're coming with me. Where's the gold? Tell me now, bitch, the gold. You know…"

My legs gave out. He dragged me farther, then flung me down, running on, yelling, "Stop! Get away from there. I'll kill you!"

I gasped for breath, pushed up on my hands and knees, sucking up as much air as possible. I had to get away. I saw the heavy-set man take a big jump across something. There was a lantern on the ground. I could make out a fence. The doodlebug! This was the path to the doodlebug. Half of the spiked fence had been torn down. Two men began to fight. I staggered to my feet, and with a limping trot, made for the garage, the dump, anywhere. Someplace to hide. Wondering, gold…at the doodlebug?

I reached the shadows behind the garage and leaned into them until my breathing eased. Max, Max and Dale. But Max was here. I veered toward the chicken coop, caught my foot on a board and fell flat out on a splintery piece of plywood. The shock brought me to my senses. Yes, this was the chicken coop, but Max wasn't there. Had I imagined all that? I sat on my butt, drew my knees up, wrapped my arms around them, and rested my forehead. Five minutes. I'll give myself five minutes. Charlotte! My head shot up. Had I really seen Charlotte? Or was it the drugs? I couldn't remember what was real.

No five minutes. The dump kept rearing its head as a safe place. Probably easiest to get to. More important than a safe place was discovering what was happening.

I went back to the shadows behind the garage, easing

around the corner to the side door where I could get a better look at where the potties were.

Above the constant undercurrent of running engines, noxious fumes rose and drifted through the yard light's hazy glow. Two vans and a panel truck were parked askew, one with its hood up. Screams and high-pitched shrieks came from a gyrating cluster of girls being loaded into the back of the panel truck, some fighting to get in, others fighting to get out and being pulled away to join another cluster of girls huddled by a toilet. A man carrying a red gas can appeared from the trees, running towards the panel truck. Hollywood?

My eyes burned and watered, my head began to spin. I clutched it with both hands.

Amid rumbling bellows of obscenities, a deep voice rose above the others. "Get those bitches loaded. Grab that woman, get her out of here. Move! Move!"

I whirled, thinking he meant me. But no one was behind me. I stepped toward the confusion. Charlotte? I couldn't wrap my head around Charlotte. It had to be someone else.

My eyes were on the women, or rather girls, by the far toilet. Girls by age, made women not by sex but subjugation. A big man pushed through the group, knocking two down. He grabbed one by the arm and threw her in the air to land with a thud even I heard.

The black panel truck thundered from its parked place, sending swearing, howling men out of its path. I, too, jumped away as it sped past me to the exit road by the doublewide.

I ran closer. I had a bad feeling about that woman who flew through the air. I didn't care where the damned truck went. I saw her on the ground, took a roundabout way to her. No one paid attention to me. Two of the girls huddled beside her. One spoke to me in a whirlwind of Spanish I couldn't understand. The other sang a soft sound of twinkle, twinkle. The woman was Charlotte, all right.

She wiggled her shoulders, one hand rubbing her other arm, mumbling, smiling at the girls hovering over her. She turned her head, when my hand touched her.

"Thea! You're here! Thank heavens you came to help me."

"Help you! What are you doing here?"

She struggled. The three of us helped her sit up. She held her left arm close to her chest.

"I might have a broken arm. It hurts, oh, it hurts. Help me get up. We have to get all these girls together and away from the men. I'm not sure what's going on, but I know they're in danger."

I wanted to scream. "How? How did you know? Did Rusty tell you?"

"Rusty? Heavens, no." She pointed to the last potty on the right where two girls were helping another on the ground to drink from a bottle of water, indicating we should move our group there. "He'd kill me if he knew I came out here. Well, he won't really kill me, but he won't be happy."

"He'll be more than unhappy when I get through with him."

"I had to do something, Thea; they can't understand a word I say."

"But how did you know…here?"

"I had a dream or, or a vision. Oh, I don't know, I just saw it." She sounded as frustrated as I was, and motioned to another girl back in the trees to join us.

"But here…how did you know where?"

"I told you I saw it. I know this place. I saw the butte. I

was raised in this area, everyone knows the Olmstead butte. My father was a friend of Alton Olmstead!"

Stunned, I wanted to cry, I wanted to laugh. I should have known. This was Wyoming. Everyone either knew or was related to everyone else.

I was the outsider.

CHAPTER 39

Where was Max? I needed him. He knew this Wyoming thing. As the grandson of an itinerant sheep herder in cattle country, he'd been a cast out of a different sort. I looked around, trying to understand what was happening around us. Men were slamming doors, kicking tires, throwing hoods up and down. They weren't interested in us. Max, wherever he was, must have damaged more vehicles.

Charlotte gathered a group of maybe fifteen girls. Where were all the others? I had heard Twinkle so she was here. But where was the strong one who threw cuss words at her fate? I found Twinkle lying in a fetal position behind one of the potties. I carried her to the group and sat her next to Charlotte.

"Come on, Thea," Charlotte said. "Let's go. Let's take them to the trailer. We can lock ourselves in."

That brought me alive. "No! Not the doublewide. We can't go there. I know a better place to hide. Follow me." The dump. "Wait." I found Cussing Katie, sitting on an empty gas can, her hands shaking. I put my arm around her, ignoring what spewed from her mouth, and took her to Charlotte.

"All of you stay by this woman. She will help you. Help each other." Probably useless.

I led them through the trees toward the big lumpy pile. We could see the shapeless mess of trailer boards thrown on top of the upended pickup. I didn't know how to tell the women to be careful. So I just said it and hoped for the best. "It's a dump, so watch yourself."

I took hold of Charlotte's good arm and helped her slide down behind one of the wheels where I had hidden the first time. Most of the girls caught on right away and found cover. Others stood on the edge holding their noses.

"Thea, is that you?" Max rose up from further under, pushing with his feet. "Charlotte! What…"

"Max!" she practically screamed, swinging her head to me. "You found him?"

"Kind of." Max saved me from explaining by shaking his fist at the truck.

"Thea, this is my damn truck! Look what those bastards did to it." He was furious, kicking at a wheel rim. The Max of old. I almost smiled. At least the anger had revved his energy.

"Shh," Charlotte said. "We're supposed to be hiding." She motioned to two of the girls to conceal themselves better. I ran over and found them a place to scoot under, and spread an old tarp over them. We could hear others moving around in the debris. Another group had pulled a filthy mattress over their heads. I slid back down by Charlotte. She checked that all were safe, then said to Max, in a reassuring voice, "It doesn't look anything like your truck."

"Nobody puts a pickup in a dump." His voice ripened

with indignation. "If it's dead gone you either sell it for junk or park it in a field some place where it can die a natural death. They threw some kind of acid or crap over it that ruined the paint."

"How can you tell it's yours?"

"There's a barb wire fix in the back. I know my work when I see it."

"But Max, where were you?" Enough of the pickup, Charlotte returned to her first question.

It took him a bit to change gears. "I've been keeping an eye on the Olmstead place for Carson. It looked like there'd been stuff going on around the house. He needed signs. No trespassing signs. I came here to do it, ran into the same thing as this." He sat hunched under the truck, arms wrapped around his ribs. "Asian girls that time. Next I knew someone knocked me out, or filled me full of drugs."

His voice was sing-song. His eyes closed. If there had been space, he would have been rocking. He was like a stranger to me.

He went on. "When I came to, some old guy had me in a shed somewhere, said he was supposed to kill me. Instead he dumped me at the hospital. Sicker than a dog. Told the doc to call the sheriff. Told him what happened. Told him call Rusty. He came, then all the law. Planned a sting. Wouldn't let me call Thea. Everything secret. Promised me they'd tell her I was okay. They didn't."

He groaned, tried to stretch his legs out. We couldn't help him. We were closely scrunched in tight spaces sitting on tin cans, broken bottles and who knew what else. If he passed out, at least he'd be hidden.

"Nobody told me anything." I spoke softly, taking over the story for Charlotte's sake. She still held her arm, her head resting on my knee. "Wait, that's not true. Deefy told me. He put a note on my door. Max okay, he said, Max okay. He just waited a long time to do it. I only got the note a couple of days ago."

"Deefy?" Max mumbled. "You said Deefy? So it was him. Thought I was seeing things."

"Someone killed him, Max." And Townsend and the old witch. I began to shake.

A sudden silence outside brought us alert. Charlotte put a finger to her lips. Max craned his neck. Higher than the others, I crept up the edge and peered out from under a board. A string of headlights headed towards us, breaking the silence into pandemonium. Trucks gears screamed as vehicles that could move hit and crashed, one backed and sped in the opposite direction. A shot took out the yard light. Men ran through the trees behind us. Red and blue flashing lights joined the string of headlights. Coming from both directions now. Max slid up beside me, crawled out and helped me to stand beside him. Holding his ribs, he gave Charlotte a hand up.

"Cavalry's here," he said.

Spotlights sprang from the cars, lighting the area like a half-time show. Men popped out like corn from a kettle. Tan deputy shirts, blue police shirts, green park ranger's shirts, everyday volunteer shirts.

"Hands up!"

"Stop where you are!"

"Center front. Hands on your head!"

"Over here, over here!"

They should have sold tickets. A sheriff stepped out of the car in front of us. Rhonda from the other door, and then Dale from the back seat.

Rhonda clutched my arm. "There you are. You're coming with me." But my eyes were on Dale.

She rushed forward, stopped short and cocked her head when she looked at me, the ice maiden.

"I went to your house, looking for you," she said. "Rhonda was there. She wouldn't let me go."

"You knew all along." I threw icicles. "I thought you were my friend. You kissed him. You drew him in. I saw you."

She turned to stone. Jaw tight, eyes blazing.

She looked at Max. "You found her."

He shrugged, as men tend to do. "Yes." He put his arm across my shoulder. I ducked under it, shaking him away. "No time to explain," he said to Dale.

I ignored him. "You played me like a fool."

"That's what you think?"

"I know what I saw."

She stepped closer. Stuck her nose in my face. "Yes, I kissed him. On the mouth. I was happy. Yes, he kissed me. On the cheek. Whispered in my ear, thank you, thank you. Thank you for being her friend, for watching out for her. I told him—"

"Stop!" Max stepped between us. "This isn't the time or place."

"Right," Rhonda said, grabbing my arm again.

Dale glanced from me to Max. "And both of you can go to hell. I'm out of here."

"Oh no you're not." Rhonda grabbed her arm and jerked us both around. "There's a body involved."

Dazed, I stared at the sheriff, who'd closed in on Max. He must be the new man. Krause. "There's another in the trailer house," I said to him.

"What?" he asked.

"Body."

"Body?" The sheriff and Max together.

The lights, the sirens, the people throwing questions at

the sheriff, made my head spin. Chattering girls crowded around us pushing closer.

"Holman, "Sheriff Krause said, "I thought you were in the hospital."

"I was." Max stood behind me, hands lightly on my shoulders. I wanted to lean against him. But couldn't make myself do so.

"I'll need to talk to you," Sheriff Krause said.

"I'm going with Thea."

Charlotte pulled on the sheriff's sleeve. "Dave, please, Dave. I've got to get these girls someplace they can get some food, and rest. There's about fifteen, I think. I've only got my SUV. I need help."

I shouldn't have been surprised that Charlotte was already on a first name basis with the sheriff, but I was.

A passing ranger, green shirt, leaned in. "I can help. I've got a van. Come with me."

"Thanks." Krause motioned her to follow him.

"Is Rusty here?" she asked.

"No. He's rounding up the outliers."

Charlotte pushed past me; put her hand on my cheek. "Wake up. You're all right. Don't fight like a lamb." The girls rushed through us, eager to follow Charlotte, pushing, shoving.

"Watch out, watch out," the sheriff shouted. They piled into our little group with force enough to send us swaying. Max's hand fell from my shoulders. A large girl crashed into his chest head-first. He fell with an agonized cry.

Sheriff Krause jumped aside and grabbed a passing deputy. "Get one of the medics and a gurney if they have one. This guy already has broken ribs. Take him back to the hospital." The man ran off. The sheriff knelt by Max and took his wrist. "He's okay, good pulse, just shouldn't move around much."

Rhonda hadn't lost her grip on either me or Dale. We were caught in a mass of flailing arms and legs. She actually got onto her feet and pulled the two of us up. My eyes were on Max, who didn't look conscious. I tried to shake her off and lost that one, too, surprised by how strong she was.

"No way, you two are coming with me. You're both under house arrest."

"Why me?" Dale whined.

"You were at the house when I got there."

"But I told you, I was looking for her." She put a nasty emphasis on *her*. We exchanged glares. Dale tried to pull from her grip and failed. Good.

"All you two got to do is answer some questions. The easier you make it, the easier it'll be."

"Use my car, "the sheriff called out. "I'll get a ride."

She more or less dragged us there, put Dale in the back seat, me in the front. She slammed the doors and got behind the wheel. "I don't know about you two, but I'm bushed. Look, all I need to get is a report from both of you and you can go home." She started the car.

"What about this house arrest?"

"Just means to stick around a bit till we figure out what's going on."

"What *is* going on?" Dale grumbled from the rear.

Rhonda got in my face. "I'd like to ask you a few questions, too, Thea. What were you doing here? And Max? And Charlotte? You should have stayed at the site of Townsend's death. A murder site. You didn't do that. That's a serious offense."

"You acted like I was guilty. I thought you were going to arrest me again for something I didn't do."

"I should do that now. Only the guilty run."

"I'm not guilty. I wasn't thinking right, either. The sight of…it made me crazy. Virgil Parker is your man." I jerked forward against the seat belt. *Virgil Parker!* "Ginny! I forgot all about her! Oh please Rhonda. Stop. Help me. We have to find Ginny. Stop, please."

"What? Who's Ginny?"

CHAPTER 40

Surely, I've told everyone in my life who Ginny is, but I did it again. This time to Rhonda. "Ginny Molina lives in Rock Springs; she's only twelve or thirteen. She's Stella Parker's grandniece. She was at the house when this happened. I heard them say she'd bring more money than any of the others."

"Who said?"

"I don't know. I don't know. All I saw was shoes. I just heard men talking. I told her to call her mother. Told her to hide if she was scared. They were going to sell her. I didn't tell her that."

"Slow down, slow down."

"Yes. Yes I will." I took some deep breaths. "Do you have any water?" She handed me a bottle. I took several deep swallows. "I'm sorry for the muddle, but I do know some things. Ginny wasn't in the house, she wasn't in the garage, she wasn't in the dump. They might have her. At least two vans got away and there were only a few girls left when you got here."

"I can check that. We have some guys staking the roads."

She stopped the car, took out her phone and punched in some numbers. "We're looking for a young girl, around thirteen years old. She's a local, name Ginny Molina." After many agonizing moments the answer came. "Between them, they seized two vehicles," she repeated. "None had a girl of that description."

"She might be at Carson's. I know she's been there before. She's definitely smart enough to find her way there and find a hiding place. I don't know where Carson is. I don't know if he's part of this gang or an innocent bystander." Another snort from the back seat.

"We need to look. Please, Rhonda. I promise I won't try to get away."

"I'll help, too," came from the back seat. "Just tell me what's going on."

"I don't know everything," Rhonda said, starting down the trail to Carson's. "Stella Parker is getting paid a big price to use her place as a rest stop on a trafficking route. Girls are packed in like cord wood. Something new, we think. We got an informant on the west coast. Two to four vehicles at a time. Bunch of pro pimps across the country, maybe as far as Chicago, exchanging girls, mostly foreign speakers, getting new blood. We call it The Pimp Patrol. Travel the back roads. They've got rest stops, various places, where they can change vehicles; girls get water, food if they're lucky. Probably drug them up again."

Our Stella, like Sylvia, the 1800's prostitute, I thought. Two of a kind. Sylvia and Dottie Jacks exchanging girls. Nothing changes over the centuries. It brought a nasty taste to my mouth.

"Illegal's?" I asked.

"Some, maybe. Mostly runaways, street kids, I suppose."

"Sounds like FBI stuff to me." Again, Dale from the back seat.

"It is. We called them. Yesterday. They'll be here tomorrow, or next day." She gave a smug little laugh. "Little old Garnet Pass has Cheyenne, Rock Springs, and Utah working with them. This is our baby."

"We just have to be sure Ginny's safe," I said. Can you call her mother? See if she's there. If not maybe she could come out to Carson's, too. Help us."

"Look," Rhonda said. "I'll take care of it. I think we've got more than enough people as it is. Don't need any more."

We were traveling quickly down the trail to Carson's house. "Edge to the right here, the house isn't far. You can pull around to the side of the house." She did. As we turned, the headlights flashed across the Quonset's open door. Carson's silver black SUV was there.

So maybe it wasn't the car Jake was driving, or maybe I simply mistook it because it was the same color. Where was Jake now? Caught by the cops? I wasn't even sure he'd been at Stella's. I'd have to check his shoes; so annoying, and I never figured out who belonged to which pair of shoes. Thea the pathetic.

Rhonda parked beside the Quonset. "Okay, women, get out slowly, look around, be sharp." She got a big flashlight from the car and fished two more from the back for Dale and me. Rhonda threw her beam at the garage, "Is that Carson Olmstead's car?"

"Yes, I think so." I said.

"It is," Dale snapped. "I know cars."

"What does he look like?"

"Red hair. You can't mistake him."

"A light's on in the house. Let's go around front," Rhonda said

"The light was on when I got here," I told her, "but the car was gone. I knocked, but no one answered. So I went to Stella's because I knew Ginny was there. I saw her and Stella, and pretty much got thrown out—look, it's a long story, I'm cutting it short—on my way back to Carson's I met Jake in what I thought was Carson's car, but it might have just been another big black car. I'm not good at identification. He said Carson was at Stella's. I didn't see him there, but I didn't see a lot of things."

"Who's Jake?"

"The snake," chimed Dale who had been silent until now.

"Jake Novak," I said. "I don't know what happened to him either. If he was part of the action, or if he left."

"If Jake was here, you can bet he was part of the action."

"He didn't want the big lug who threw me in one of the trucks with the girls to do that, so maybe he wasn't involved. I don't know."

"We can sort that out later. We can see if Carson is home now." Rhonda rang the bell with one hand and banged the door with her other.

Nothing. She tried the knob. Locked.

We went back around the house. "Whoa," Rhonda said. "A dog."

"Nonnie! This is Ginny's dog." Not her exuberant self, she walked to me and sat on my foot. I picked her up. She nuzzled my neck, then wriggled to get down and stood by my feet. "She must have followed Ginny here." I stooped and patted her. "Where's Ginny, Nonnie? Let's go find Ginny." I stepped briskly away, she followed, but stopped when I stopped, waiting for me to signal what to do.

Rhonda stepped forward. "All right, let's do some looking ourselves. I'll take the garage. Dale, you inspect Carson's car."

I took off for the shed. Nonnie ran after me, thinking it was a game maybe. Nothing behind the old bales of hay, under the caddie, or in it. Nonie sniffed through everything as well. We were all calling, "Ginny, Ginny, Ginny." She wasn't here. I ran back to the others, who were finished, as well. Dale said, "Do you still have a key to the house?"

I'd forgotten about it. "Yes, I must." I started patting my legs, "I've got my cargos on," and forgetting myself, I flashed her a smile. She turned away.

I opened a pocket. "Here it is. Can we use it, Rhonda?"

"You have a key to the house? Olmstead's house?" She gave me the raised-eyebrow look and shook her head.

I let her think what she wanted to think. I was sick of explanations. I just wanted to find Ginny. What if she wasn't here?

"I'll call in and find out." Weariness sounded in her voice as she pulled the radio off her belt again. A weariness that I felt throughout my body, as well. All the aches and pains had settled in a dull way I hoped wouldn't be a new normal.

Rhonda's answer came before she even finished the question. No. "He isn't here now, but we'll keep looking. No, we haven't found the girl yet. We're looking."

"His house is evidence," she said. "If we find Carson, he can't go in either." She tried several times before she got the radio hooked back on her belt, muttered to herself. "Okay, one more quick look around and that's it, we're going in."

I was so worried. "If Ginny's not here, it means someone's got her. Do the police know how many cars escaped?

Are there still people at Stella's place? If we can't find Ginny, surely they'll send out a search party. Won't they?"

"Yeah, there are probably guys still working there," Rhonda said. "Let's just go around the house, look in all the bushes, any kind of hiding place."

We crossed to the far side of the house, flashing our lights easily through the scrimpy shrubs.

Rhonda cast her beam farther. "What's that? Ah, a cellar door."

We left the bushes and stood at the door's foot. A good hiding place. The pale moon light gave its weathered boards a Stephen Kingish look even through our dancing beams. Eerie enough to remind me of my silly childhood fears. There had been a padlock on it before. There wasn't one now. Someone...

I threw my flashlight to the ground, and with a yell that would put Godzilla to shame, I grabbed the handle with both hands pulled it up and over to fall to the ground. "Carson!" Dale yelled.

Rhonda ran down the steps with Dale close behind. He laid crumpled at the bottom of the steps tied and gagged, shocks of red hair bright in the light.

Ronda straddled him while Dale untied the gag. "Water," Rhonda yelled. "Get water from the car, Thea."

CHAPTER 41

I ran, going behind the back screened porch, the two green chairs, the big trees. Nonnie stood up from where she watched me from the big tree roots. I didn't stop to pet her, but reminded myself to get her some water after helping Carson. I grabbed three full bottles and one half full from the holders in the car and raced back.

Rhonda was tackling the plastic ties on his feet with a jackknife. His arms were already free. Dale held his head in her lap and motioned for a bottle. I opened one and gave it to her. Then opened a cargo pocket and took out a collapsible cup and a folded square of paper towel, and put them where she could reach them.

She glanced at me and rolled her eyes, then buried her mouth in her arm pit to hide a smile. I almost laughed, but pulled back. Not ready yet.

Carson's legs freed, Rhonda sat on a step and made a man-down call to—I guessed—the workers still at Stella's place.

I took one of the bottles. "I'm going to get the dog some water." They both nodded agreement.

I picked a gold pan from the pile by the garage. Nonnie was still curled up by the tree roots. She stood, stretched, and expectantly eyed the pan. Once the pan was filled with water, she couldn't lap fast enough. Poor baby. I moved one of the green chairs closer and sat to watch for a moment when a thought brought me to my feet. The tree! I jumped up. Nonnie always came back to the tree. I went to where I began my climb. The other chair was there. I moved it away and reached to touch the fat branch that had attracted me.

"Ginny," I called. "Ginny, are you up there?" No response. "It's me, Thea. I'm with Rhonda from the sheriff's office, and my friend Dale. It's just the three of us. It's safe to come down." Silence. A rustle? Could be wind. "We've been looking for you. The police from Rock Springs came. They got all the bad guys. They've been taken to jail. It's safe to come down now. I'll wait right here for you. I promise I'll keep you safe and get you home."

I paused. Nothing. Then added, "I bet Rhonda will let you call your mom on her police radio." A definite rustle. Another. I held my breath. A branch snapped. Finally the glimpse of a leg. Then her face, checking me out. "It's just me, Ginny. Nonnie's here too, waiting for you."

She stepped out on the big branch. I held my arms up.

"No," she said. "Bring the chair back. I can do it." At the sound of her voice, Nonnie burst into a state of dog ecstasy, yipping, barking, and jumping around my feet, in and out among the chair's legs. Ginny laughed. "Oh, Nonnie, you're so cute." She slid down into the chair and jumped to the ground. Nonnie leaped into her arms.

I let them nuzzle a bit, but when she put the dog on the ground, I wrapped my arms around her. "I'm so glad you're safe. We need to call your mother."

She hung on to me, and said, muffled against my shirt,

"I was so scared. I heard you yell at me in Auntie's house. I was already scared. I locked myself in the bathroom. Me and Nonnie. I couldn't find a phone. I looked for Auntie, but couldn't find her. Is she okay?"

Sooner or later she would have to know, but not from me. "It's a long walk to get here. But it was a good choice. You were smart to come here."

"This is my famous uncle's house. I've been here a lot. Just don't tell my auntie. Anyway, I thought this would be a safer place to hide."

"The lost is found," Dale said, appearing out of the dark. "You must be Ginny, I'm Dale. Rhonda sent me to see what the commotion was about."

"I was hiding in the tree."

"Ah, another tree climber," Dale said without looking at me. "That's a good hiding place. Did you hear us calling for you?"

"Yes, but I wasn't sure who it was, or if there were any of those men with you. And then I heard a loud noise."

Must have been the cellar door, and me yelling. "Or, did you hear it just now, or much earlier?"

"A little bit ago. I thought something bad happened." She took my hand and held it tight. "It scared me again."

"Rhonda will want to see you. She's taking care of a man who got hurt. He's your famous uncle's grandson."

"Then he's my relative, too."

"Yes, he is."

She pulled me to a stop. "What were all those people doing? At Auntie's. Do you know...did it have something to do with gold? My uncle's gold?"

Gold! Again king Midas reared his head. I'd forgotten about the doodlebug. Possible gold at the doodlebug. Question marks swirled in my mind. "I don't know, honey, but why do you think it might?"

"Well, I…He used to talk a lot about gold, and he…"

"Come over here, Ginny," Dale called. "Ronda wants to congratulate you for picking such a good hiding place."

Rhonda and Carson sat on the stairwell's top step. She had her arm around his slumped shoulders. He straightened a little when he heard us. "Thea, is that you?"

"Yes. How are you?"

"I don't know yet, but certainly better than I was."

Ginny and I sat on the cellar door near him. Nonnie ran up and down the cellar stairs, then joined us. "Carson," I said. "I want you to meet your relative, Ginny Molina."

"Hello," she said with a shy smile. "You're my famous uncle's grandson?"

"Yes, I am. My head is a bit wobbly, but this is a mysterious meeting in the dark of night. You must be a princess!"

Ginny giggled. It was a lovely bit of foolishness for a strange night.

What happened to you, Carson?" I asked.

Rhonda answered for him. "He got ambushed while working in the garage. No apparent injuries other than those to be expected from being knocked out, thrown down the stairs and shut in for hours, tied and gagged."

We all saw the lights of two cars approaching. Rhonda waved her flashlight to show where we were.

Sheriff Krause stepped out of a Rock Springs police car. A ranger from a Jeep. The sheriff nodded to us and spoke to Rhonda. "Our EMT van is busy elsewhere. This is Mike; he's a ranger with EMT knowledge. He has strict instructions of how to care for the injured man, and he will transport him to the Rock Springs hospital."

Carson struggled to stand, but the ranger said, "No, sit

still. I have to get some braces and support on you before we get you in the back seat."

I waved to Carson. "Tell them to put you in the room with Max."

"What? Max is here? Will wonders never cease."

"And you, young lady," the sheriff said to Ginny, "Rhonda and I will drive you home right now. We've already talked to your mother. She'll be waiting for you."

Ginny picked up the dog. "I'm taking Nonnie with me. Are we going in the police car? Can we use the siren?"

"Yes, to everything." He said with a smile

"And you two." He looked at me. "I'm Deputy Sheriff Dave Krause." He held out his hand.

I shook it. "I'm Thea Barlow."

"I thought so." He smiled. "I've heard a lot about you."

"I can imagine."

"Do you and Dale have a way to get home? If not, we'll take you, but you'll have to go with us to Rock Springs first."

"Thanks, Sheriff."

"Call me Dave, everybody else does."

I tossed Rhonda a smug smile. "I have a car here. It's closer to the other house. And it might have been found or damaged by one of those men, but if you'll take us to it, and it starts and everything, I can take Dale and me home."

"All right, we'll see if it's still safe. The two of you can go to your homes now, but don't go anywhere else. We need to talk to everybody. Rhonda will call in the morning and tell you where and when. We expect you both to be there."

CHAPTER 42

Max's RAV was right where I left it. Knowing what Max had been able to do to those other vehicles made me worry about what might have been done to this. The keys were in my pants pocket. The sheriff waited patiently while I got the engine purring, and the lights on, and checked the gas gage. Only time would tell now. As I moved to the track, the sheriff took off ahead of us.

Dale had been quiet for a long time. "Do you have a phone?" I asked.

"Yes."

"We'll need it if somebody tried to monkey with the car."

The silence grew heavy. I didn't know what I thought about anything. Thinking had been a luxury; no time for it. "Look, I haven't had a chance to talk to Max about—"

"Max! You don't have to talk to Max," she exploded. "*I* told you what happened, but, oh no, you can't believe me! I thought we were friends. You only have faith in him, never a doubt, never a question, but for me not a damn drop."

"But I saw you." The car slid off the road, I jerked it back. "You came out the door, your arm hooked in his. The look on your face was something I'd never seen before. I thought you'd been together all this time."

"Oh, thanks, thanks a lot. I was happy, happy for you. For the first time in my life, I saw a guy who wasn't a self-serving bastard, who deserved all the faith you gave him. I believed I could help. And you thought the worst of me.

"But he kissed you! I saw it!"

"ON THE CHEEK! What are you, some kind of puritan?" Off the road again. I stopped, slammed on the brakes. We could finish this here.

"What did you see?" She pounded the dash. "Tell me, what did you see? I thought I could save you from one more jackass that treats women like garbage. Not like my sister."

"Your sister?"

She shoved the door open, got out, and leaned on the car beside it, her back to me.

"We loved her so much," she said. "Younger than me, so beautiful, so kind, so happy. I loved taking care of her." The tears started; I heard them in her voice.

"She was born on Memorial Day. When she was just a toddler, we told her the parade was for her. Her birthday. She was so proud. Daddy said she had to share her good fortune with all the folks in uniform. One year the parade director let her lead."

Her words were wet; her voice rocking with wet sobs and shameless slobbers. I closed my eyes and let them fill.

"She rode her tricycle in front of the high school band, decked out with flags, saluting every uniform. Years later, we threw a family party, full of laughter when, as Prom Queen, she got to ride in the parade again."

She bent over, wiped her face with her shirt tail; dug out a worn tissue from somewhere and blew her nose. "I loved her so much."

She stood away from the car, stretched her back, and faced the interior, arm on the open door.

"She married at nineteen; the biggest asshole in the world. Oh, but he was so nice to *me*, sucked up to *me* like a power hose. He brought *her* flowers, he brought *me* flowers. Told me how much he loved her. Showered me with all the wonderful things they were going to do together.

"She wasn't sure, but I...I convinced her. To me, he was the most awesome man in the world. He would be so good to her. She shouldn't miss the chance." She stopped, looked up at the dark sky before speaking again. "He moved her to Alaska the day after the ceremony. We never saw her again. Only letters. She never complained." Again, for a moment, the sky. "She killed herself a year and a half later. Even the coroner contacted us, shocked by the bruises, signs of older bone breakages. Some protector I was."

I got out of the car and put my arm around her shoulders. "Thank you for telling me. It must hurt like hell."

She wiped her face again, mumbling, "Sorry." We each sat on a fender and looked to the stars. A beautiful sight here with no city or town to dim the sky. And I remembered her tears in the restaurant. How tough it must have been, daring to let her defenses down, only to unmask another asshole. The breeze was cool and filled with the secret sounds of insects and animals.

She spoke into the silence again. "I was so shocked to see Max in Walmart. He asked where you were. I said either at home or at Carson's. That worried him. He said some kind of police thing was going to happen there. Tomorrow, he thought. He didn't want you to be caught in it. We decided I'd go to your house and pick you up if you were there. He wanted to go to Carson's right away, in case that's where you were. I forgot the supplies I had to get for the restaurant. Had to go back for them. When I got to your house, Rhonda was there."

"I think Max got to Carson's before I did," I said. "Or rather to Stella Parker's property. At least, he was thrown into the garage before I was. Umm...that doesn't necessarily jibe. I was unconscious, so he could have come any time. I guess it doesn't matter."

"Unconscious? You were thrown in where?"

"The old witch's big garage. She appeared to be running the show. That's where I found Max. Like Carson, we were tied hand and foot, but thankfully, no gags. They shot us up with some kind of drugs, so we were pretty wonky. He has broken ribs, too. We helped each other get untied. Then we had to escape. I had to find Ginny." I stopped, trying to collect myself, to remember.

"Dale, the old witch is dead. I found her, the old witch, her body, all that blood. Everything was crazy. And somebody tore the doodlebug apart, looking for gold. I was crazy, too, but I couldn't forget that kiss."

"Not again. Tell me, please, what did you see?"

The picture was there behind my eyes, indelible as it had been, on and off, all day. His head bent down over her shoulder like you see in so many movies. My mouth opened, words I didn't want to speak, hanging from my lips. But out they dropped. "I saw the back of his hat."

Any other day, any other time, we might have laughed. This time, we exchanged feeble smiles.

Dale said, "We've both had bad days. Yours tops mine. We can't sit here all night, or what's left of it. Let me drive. You've had enough for one day."

It wasn't true, her catharsis was wringing, but there was

no fight left in me. We changed seats. "One more thing," I said. "Max told me the same thing you did. And if it makes you feel better, I didn't believe him, either."

CHAPTER 43

The insistent alarm awoke me. The following jingle of the phone opened my eyes. For that I had to get out of bed. I struggled from the covers and stumped to the living room. It was Rhonda. Yesterday flashed through my mind as if I were on my deathbed. I groaned.

"You're required to meet with the County Sheriff, and Deputy Sheriff Dave Krause, and Rusty Metzger. One o'clock sharp at the Rock Springs Hospital conference room. It's an official wrap-up. Don't miss it. Don't be late." A pause. "How ya doing, girl? You get some sleep?"

"Until you called."

"Sorry."

"Ginny okay?"

"Yeah. She took us through the ropes. Checked out all our equipment and what it's for. Ran the lights, siren, and spoke on the radio. Says she's going to write an article about it for the school paper. Smart kid."

"Good. She's not traumatized."

"Hardly. See you later."

A shower helped. Long, hot, and loaded with suds. I

abandoned my precious cargo pants to the washing machine, the contents neatly lined up on the dryer. I shook up the three bottles of gold flakes so the bright bits would float like a Christmas snow globe.

Again the phone. Max. His voice gave my heart a little leap, the call I'd waited for so long, but now didn't need. I knew where he was, and all the joy and exhilaration I'd looked forward to was doused by that first sight. The kiss I'd missed. The kiss that should have been mine. Doused by my imagination, rage, sorrow, jealousy, so powerful it destroyed something within me.

"Hi," I said, forcing a lilt to my voice. "How are the ribs?"

"Much better. They've got me wrapped like a mummy."

"Good." I didn't know what to say. "Oh, how's the floating one?"

"I don't know what they did to it, but they're not worried about it anymore." A pause. "Thea? You'll be here at one?"

"Yes"

"They dismissed me from the hospital this morning. I'm here. I'm waiting for you." His tone was solemn. "I need to see you."

He knew. I heard it in his voice. He knew, just as I did, that something was missing. All I could manage was an empty, "I'll be there."

My face didn't look real. Close scrutiny revealed a need for makeup, which I applied. The old bruises were about gone, now I covered the new red scrapes of varying depths. The cargoes had protected my legs, but my arms looked like an abstract artist had used them for practice. I popped a couple of Tylenol for the kinks and aches, and wondered what a person could take for the heart.

Max met me at the hospital door, and did nothing other than take my hand and give me that full blown smile that weakened my knees.

"Hello. You're here." He looked me over head to toe. "You look good." He touched my face with a finger, running it lightly over the biggest bruise. "This way," he said, still holding my hand, and led me down the corridor. I watched him with sideways glances. He was different from the Max of yesterday. The long easy stride was back. His voice strong and deep. I did notice when he turned sideways to speak to a passing aide that his arm went up to his chest, but no other sign of pain.

He opened the meeting room door, and motioned me in without turning loose of my hand. Rhonda, Sheriff Krause, Rusty, and someone I didn't know, who must've been the county sheriff, were at the long table at the far end of the room. A curved row of chairs sat in front of the table. Dale was in one of them with Carson, in a wheelchair, next to her. We waved a greeting. Rusty rose and came over to us. He wore casual dress, not the uniform of his new job.

"Thea, it's good to see you. I owe you many apologies, and I know you have no use for them. I've already faced the wrath of Max, so have at me."

I looked him in the eye, unable to smile. "I will, but I'm going to practice with my boxing gloves first. The time will come."

"I'm truly sorry. It's my fault. I thought this thing would be over in a couple of days, and we did believe Max was in danger. Deefy's death confirmed it, along with the two that followed. But that's what we're here for. We should get on with this. Have a seat." And he took one at the head table.

Of course, the county sheriff was the big cheese. In

Garnet Pass we always called our man Sheriff, but he was, in reality, a deputy. Our new man, Sheriff Krause, stood, introduced the county sheriff, Jud somebody, whose last name I immediately forgot. He made a quick statement. "All of you were intertwined in yesterday's events. By bringing you together we believe we can get a better idea of the interactions, and perhaps more information that would be useful. Rusty, you wanted to say something first."

He stood. "Yes. I'm sure some of you are curious as to why and how I got mixed up with this. I was as puzzled as everyone else when Max didn't appear at the wedding, and as you know, my wife Charlotte and I had to leave the next day for Utah and my new position in their Sheriff's Department.

"Max was in very bad shape when he was found outside the Rock Springs hospital on Monday night. When he was able to communicate with the doctors, all he could, or would, say was, 'get the sheriff.' Which they did."

He gestured to the county sheriff at the table, who nodded in return and said, "Max wasn't very lucid, but kept repeating the word, trafficking, and call Rusty. We had a few tips previously about trafficking through Wyoming so were immediately interested. Rusty and I have worked together for a long time. I called him and he came as soon as he could. Max was able to tell him that he was at the Olmstead ranch when he was attacked."

Rusty picked up the story again. "We both had been informed when Stella Parker came back to the county a couple of months before your grandfather died, Carson. We were aware of her background and reputation in Rock Springs, but there were no other records in her past that were bothersome. As an eighty-seven-year-old woman, she drew no special attention from us. Until now. When I contacted my new boss in Utah to report in, I discovered they too, had received trafficking tips that appeared to be connected with Wyoming, and were interested in working together."

The county sheriff took over. "We contacted the informant, who was a relative of Stella Parker, and he agreed to help us. The most important thing he did was to convince the Parkers to do another trafficking run so soon after the one Max had discovered."

I couldn't stand it anymore, and just hollered out the question, "What about that sighting of Max driving out of Sheridan? That was a fake, wasn't it?"

"Yes," Rusty answered. "It was a set up. I did it and I'm sorry, Thea. But I thought it would stop you from looking for Max. We thought it would be dangerous for you if the Parkers thought you were spying on them. And at least you'd know Max wasn't dead."

Max looked at me. "You didn't believe them did you? That I'd be out driving around without telling you?"

I opened my mouth, remembering vacillation, but Dale bounced up. "No, she didn't, she never believed any damn thing against you."

"All right, all right, everyone," the county sheriff said. "Let's all calm down and get this over with. Rusty, are you finished?"

"Not quite. Thea, Max was adamant that you be told he was all right. I gave him a reassuring story to calm him down. Told the others," he motioned at those sitting with him, "that I'd taken care of things. Then I had to go back to Utah. A couple of days ago I was sent back here to help with the process. The job's over now. I'm due back in Utah tomorrow."

"You could have just told me." I said.

"And if I had," he answered with a smile, "both you

and I know you would not have stayed in your home, twiddling your thumbs."

I huffed a bit, but wasn't going to argue with him. He was still on my list.

Rusty rose, motioned again to his friends at the table. "A pleasure to work with you. We'll keep in touch." He left, saying, "Later," to Max as he passed.

Jud, the county sheriff took over. "We weren't happy with his methods, but we've hashed it over enough among us. Let's start now with you, Max. Yesterday you left the hospital without permission."

"I'd had enough of the hospital. I was worried about Thea. Nobody would tell me anything. I borrowed a truck from a kid who used to work for me. I saw Dale at Walmart. She told me that Carson Olmstead had returned to Wyoming, that Thea might be at Carson's. That scared me. I knew the sting was supposed to happen soon. So I drove to Carson's property. When he wasn't there, I went to Stella Parker's land. I'm embarrassed to admit I stepped right in the middle of things, much the same as happened the first time. Whoever their watch dog was, he's damn good." He shook his head. "When I woke up, I was on the floor of the garage. That's where I found Thea. The only other person I saw was the one Thea called Hollywood. I believe he's who tied me up and drugged me." The sheriff and Dave exchanged looks at the name, Hollywood, and made notes.

"Can you identify anyone else you saw there?"

"No."

"What about you, Ms. Barlow? Why were you at the Stella Parker ranch?"

I left out the mind-numbing sighting of Max and Dale, the shock of finding Townsend's body, the fear of Rhonda questioning me for hours. My state of mind didn't matter to them.

"I had a variety of reasons to see Stella Parker. She sent me a letter indicating she wanted me to interview her about prostitution in the sixties. She later denied sending it, but I have it if you want to see it. I also wanted to get more information about the old doodlebug dredge on her property for an article I'm writing."

At the mention of the doodlebug the sheriff threw a glance at Rhonda.

"Yes," he said. "We'll be talking more about that later."

CHAPTER 44

A nd so the questions began. Mostly for Dale and me. How were we acquainted with Virgil Parker, Richard Townsend, Jake the snake Novak, Stella Parker, and even little Ginny Molina. Who did we see when, what were they doing, why were we there, and what were we doing. They seldom asked about Hollywood, but I threw his name in wherever I could. I didn't want him to get away with anything. The questions were persistent, repetitious, boring, and sometimes confusing, but always they came back to the murders.

"Tell us again, exactly, how you found Stella Parker's body."

I told them in great detail about my futile search for Ginny in the doublewide and finding Stella on the floor in the dining area, leaving out only my tears and craziness. Max put his arm around me.

Jud, the county sheriff, took over the questions. "You also found the body of Richard Townsend. Is that correct?"

"Yes. Or, I was the first to report it." Rhonda's pencil

flew through all my answers. I was getting a bit belligerent. "Anyone could have come down the alley and seen him. Just because I reported him, I get special attention?" All I got was a slight smile and another question.

"The body was in your back yard. Is that correct?"

"Yes."

"You told Rhonda that Virgil Parker killed Townsend. Why did you say that?"

"I *assumed* that because every time I saw them together, they were fighting or arguing. I even heard Parker making a direct threat to him. He said if Townsend quit the deal they had going, he'd be dead meat."

"And that deal was?"

Carson jumped in, telling about his earlier connection with Richard Townsend and the box he'd received from his grandfather. "It was a couple of days after my grandfather's funeral. I took the box to Townsend's store, and he identified the contents for me. Later Max told me everything in the box was related to gold. My assumption now is that Townsend, with his knowledge of gems and minerals, would have noticed that, as well. Why else would he be found digging on my property?"

"After I spoke with Thea and Dale, we put our heads together and decided that Townsend made acquaintance with Virgil Parker, who claimed to own the land. They made a partnership. One or the other of them brought in Jake Novak. When Townsend discovered Parker didn't own the land or minerals rights, he wanted out. At least that's what we surmised their deal might have been. Who knows? It could be."

"And when I overheard Virgil Parker threaten Townsend," I offered, "he said he couldn't quit because he had seen too much. I thought they had found some gold, but now I think it might have been because Townsend saw some of the trafficking business, and Parker and his aunt were afraid he'd report them."

"Interesting," the county sheriff said. "We have Virgil Parker in custody now and he corroborates much of what you've said. We were surprised to find that rumors of gold hidden on Stella Parker's property had distracted Virgil and some of his buddies from the trafficking business at hand.

We thank you, Max, for disabling four of the vehicles that could have been used by the drivers. The resulting chaos helped us immensely. Two vans loaded with girls got away, but we caught them on the road. All of the girls have been taken to a safe house in Cheyenne."

He rustled through his pile of papers and turned over the questioning to Sheriff Krause, who said, "Next up is Deefy Hammersmith and the doodlebug."

All eyes turned to me. "Yes, Thea, we did read the note left on your door, and knew you were looking for Max. We were worried that you had so quickly found the doodlebug and had spoken to Stella Parker. The attack on you and Dale was committed by Virgil Parker and Jake Novak. We feared you were in danger and tried to discourage you from any more sleuthing. Evidently Stella Parker encouraged them to capture you, thinking you would lead them to Max. The card you mentioned earlier was written by Stella as a lure to get you back on her property.

"Deefy worked for Stella Parker. He serviced the portable toilets and, according to Virgil Parker, she told Deefy to 'get rid of' Max. Max, you affirmed that by saying that Deefy told you he was supposed to kill you."

I spoke out, perhaps louder than I intended. "Deefy's the only one of all of you who kept his promise to tell me Max was all right. I just wish he had done it earlier."

Sheriff Krause ignored my nudging of the old sore. "At

this point, we're assuming he was killed because he failed to kill you, Max. Again from Virgil, we know they were worried that Max was on the loose and would expose the trafficking scheme."

"Wait!" I said. "There were several occasions when I overheard some of the men talking. One was when I was in the back of the truck with the girls. The other was when I was hiding under the truck. In the truck, it was the driver and either one or two others.

"One man said to the other that killing the old man was stupid. I figured he meant Deefy. The other laughed and said something like he didn't know his own strength. The same man said he'd taken care of Carson. Another time, they were talking about the trafficking and money. One said they were just transporting, the other that they'd make more money selling the girls. He wanted to change her mind. Would the 'her' be the old woman?"

"Yes," Jud said, "Stella was the master-mind of the whole business. What else did you hear?"

I wasn't eager to go into the shoe business, it sounded so stupid, but I thought it best. "When I was under the truck, all I could see were shoes. Two men were talking. One wore hiking shoes with a small blue medallion, the other just plain dirty black track shoes. No logo. One said he was going to drive one of the trucks, which evidently wasn't in the plans. He thought he could make more money selling the girls than hunting for gold."

Dale raised her hand. "That sounds like Jake the snake. Excuse me, Jake Novak. He's a lazy gold hunter. He doesn't think a person should have to do hard work to find it."

"Anyway," I continued, "the other man didn't like his change of plans. Later, in the doublewide, I saw another pair of shoes, polished loafers. I knew they had to belong to Hollywood, or, sorry, Quentin somebody. So he was definitely there. He's the one who threw me in the garage."

I whispered to Max, "You're hurting my hand." His face was grim. He loosened his grip, but didn't drop my hand.

"We've already heard your story, Max. Have you had any more memories about your time with Deefy?"

"No, it's still pretty much a blank. I remember, begging him to tell Thea where I was." He shook his head in bewilderment. "He kept feeding me things…"

"Vienna Sausages! Urp." Dale sang out and got a laugh.

"And way too many cannabis edibles as well," Sheriff Krause added. "Neither mixed well with the sodium pentothal and other drugs you'd been shot up with. To say nothing about unsterile needles. The docs were trying to save you from a bunch of overdoses. We found Deefy's truck in town the other day. He had a stash of edibles in there, too."

At least he saved Max. I closed my eyes and remembered Deefy as I'd first seen him at a rodeo, dressed in deer skins and a raccoon hat. He sat a gorgeous chestnut horse and held a dignified pet fox across his lap. I was among a bunch of kids surrounding him, waiting to pet that arrogant animal. I decided that would be the way I would remember him.

All heads turned at the sound of the door opening.

Hollywood! I jumped up

The sheriff smiled. "Hi, Quentin. Come on in. Folks, this is Quentin Cook, our informant."

Informant! The sleaze-bag? I couldn't believe it. I dropped back down in my chair.

"Quentin wanted a chance to make apologies to some

of you," the sheriff said. "He played a good part for us in a difficult situation."

He made the most of his entrance. A queen's wave, a nod of acquaintance to Max and me, and took center stage. "My aunt, Stella Parker lived in California for many years; she knew all kinds of people, many of them unsavory. But it wasn't until one of her many relatives approached her about using her abandoned Wyoming property for a trafficking stage stop that she became interested in one last money-making prospect.

"As most people know, there are few secrets in a family of many cousins. When I heard what was up, I knew I didn't want anything like that in my background. I believe they tried to convince Stella that it was all legal. Just people paying for rides from one location to another. She didn't care where they came from or where they were going. I knew it couldn't end well."

He was enjoying his star turn.

"When the sheriff's department contacted me, I told them all I knew about the scheme. When they asked if I'd be willing to help them, of course I agreed. Stella welcomed me into her little gang of thieves, and I offered the Parkers to do some of the dirty work, hoping to prevent damage, and to keep the police informed.

"It wasn't as easy as I thought it would be. I had to be pretty rough when someone was watching. I swear I didn't shoot anybody up with drugs; that was all Stella. And if on occasion I was too rough, I apologize. I tried not to tie you up too tight. I tried to stay close to Ginny. I didn't want her running around when all the cars started coming. I was glad when she locked herself in the bathroom, and I thank you, Ms. Barlow, for helping her." He gave a big smile, spread his arms out and dropped his head. I was afraid he was going to curtsy, but he didn't, just said, "That's about it, folks, I'm on my way back to California. The name's Quentin Cook. Be sure to look for me in the movies." With another wave to the law, he left.

We were stunned, slack-jawed. At least I was. Talk about not being a good judge of character. But it wasn't that. He *was* a conceited sleazebag, just not a criminal or worse. I'd have to accept that.

The sheriff laughed and shook his head. "He actually did do a decent job for us. But back to business." He glanced at all of us then focused on me.

"Virgil Parker and Jake Novak assumed that the only reason you and Dale were on Carson's land was for the gold. Consequently, when they heard from Stella that you were asking about the doodlebug, they thought there must be gold there, too."

"So that's why that man was dragging me down there," I yelped. I told them what had happened. "He was one of the drivers. Big man with a mustache; kept yelling at me to tell him where the gold was. Then he ran off. There was another man at the doodlebug. They started to fight, and I got out of there."

"Yes, that's where we found Virgil. He'd been badly beaten. We've not found the other man, but we have his name."

Rhonda got up and passed out small bottles of water. Sheriff Jud gulped down half, grinned, and pointed to Carson. "What about it? Any truth to any of this?"

Carson laughed. "It's hard to believe that little box of scraps Gramps gave me could lead to all this craziness. No, I can't imagine he hid gold all over his ex-wife's property. Or even his own, for that matter. The box is just another kids' treasure hunt, the goal a lesson learned, a reminder of the fun we had together years ago."

"Sounds special."

"Yeah, it is." He cocked his head, eyes on Jud. "You a gold man?"

"Not really, but my nephew is hot about it. He gave me this for a Christmas present. I carry it as a good luck charm." He drew a vial of gold from a pocket. "He's at the School of Mines now."

Dale and I both jumped up for a closer look. Max followed me. Carson struggled out of his wheelchair. We converged on the table. The vial was impressive. Mine were flakes that floated. His were pebbles clinging to the vial's bottom, making a nice pile. Dale and I exchanged looks of envy.

"Do you know where he found them?" Dale asked.

"Some place here in Wyoming. I know he's mentioned Rattlesnake Hills."

"Rattlesnake Hills! Gramps took me there when I was a kid. I was more interested in rattlesnakes then than gold. I've never forgotten the name. Used to brag about having been there to all my school buddies."

Dale was practically glowing with excitement. "I hear it's a big commercial gold site now. I'd love to go there."

"Me too," Carson said.

I glanced at Max. He was smiling. "What's stopping us? Why don't we all go?"

Rhonda leaned back in her chair, rolling her eyes.

Sheriff Krause, said, "Ah, folks, we better get on with this."

The county sheriff gave him a big grin. "You're right, Deputy. Sorry about that." They shuffled their papers and offered more water in an effort to get back to business.

The rest of us weren't quite with it yet. At least I wasn't. I whispered to Max as we took our seats again. "Dale showed me how to pan for gold. It was amazing!"

"You found gold?"

"No, no. She spiked the pan, but it was so much fun, Max. I have to show you, or rather Dale will show you, I'm just learning, we can…" And all of a sudden I was back. Out of that dark abyss. This was Max. We were together again. A golden moment.

I put my hand on his cheek. "Hi. I'm glad you found me." Each word felt bright with wonder, like those bits of gold, sneaking out from layers of black sand to welcome the sun. "I have so much to tell you."

"Thank God." He cupped my face with his hands. "I thought I'd lost you."

CHAPTER 45

The room was still, all eyes were on Max and me. Smug little smiles nearly brought a flush to my face. But nothing could still my happiness. Sheriff Krause coughed and cleared his throat; brought us back to attention.

"Ms. Barlow, do you have any idea why Richard Townsend's body was in your yard?"

Max, his arm still around me, sat forward on his chair. "Was he killed there, or elsewhere?"

"Please let Ms Barlow speak for herself."

I knew Max thought the sheriff was picking on me, and put my hand on his leg to calm him. But it was an interesting question. "I hadn't thought about it before. Was he killed there? I remember thinking that Virgil Parker must have put him in my yard to get back at me, but why kill him? Their arguments seemed petty to me. If he was killed in my yard, would that put a different spin on it?"

"Maybe it was a warning," Max said to me. Once again it was Max and me, thinking a problem through, like old times. The sheriff interrupted.

"As yet, we don't know where he was killed. We may need to call you in for further questioning, Ms. Barlow. We'll let you know. I believe that's it for now. Thank you all for your patience."

Sheriff Krause stood. "One last thing before we finish. We're very seriously looking for Jake Novak. As we said earlier, Virgil Parker is in custody, as well as many others, but Virgil has been helpful, perhaps not offering information, but at least answering questions. To give him credit, he has regrets for getting involved with his aunt. He was through with her when he saw she was willing to give Ginny to the traffickers. How much he did to protect Ginny we don't know. We do know from both Rhonda and Quentin that the credit for that belongs to you, Thea.

"But Jake Novak is a major suspect. Wanted for suspicion of murder. We consider him dangerous. Please keep your eyes open. Let us know immediately if you see him, or know his whereabouts. Be on the lookout.

"Carson, we're still searching your house for evidence. Virgil has admitted that it was used for overnight stays by the traffickers at least once. We understand you will be released from the hospital in the morning. We'll finish with your house tonight, so it will be available to you then. However, our teams will still be working on Stella Parker's property tonight and tomorrow. Thank you for coming here."

We all rose, stretched, and said our goodbyes.

Dale wheeled Carson out of the row of chairs. He was dragging his feet. It looked as if an argument was brewing. We walked over and heard Carson. "I do not need this damn wheelchair!"

Dale had a restraining hand on his shoulder. "I *know* you don't *need* it, but Nurse Betty upstairs said you have to use it. If you don't, she will be angry. If you want to be released early in the morning, as you were told, instead of the middle of tomorrow night, you should not make her angry."

Carson looked pleadingly to Max. "I'm perfectly fine."

"They're keeping you another night?"

"Yeah, some kind of concussion."

"And a severe case of dehydration," Dale added.

"Let me at least walk to the elevator so I can have some pride."

"You have no pride left," Dale said, "wearing that hospital outfit and cute little socks."

Max laughed. "She speaks the truth."

Dale rolled her eyes, and I stifled a laugh.

"I even offered to go out to his place and get him some clean clothes for tomorrow, and this is the thanks I get."

"She's an angel in disguise," Max said. "You better do what she says."

"Oh, all right," he grumbled. "Some friends you are."

Dale grinned at us and shot off, giving him a wild ride to the elevator. Shreds of laughter drifted back to us.

Max shook his head. "I'll be damned, that looks like it might be a good match."

"I'm totally amazed. I never would have believed it." I silently wished her well.

Max grabbed my hand again. "Come on, let's go." We waved goodbye to the few left. Out on the sidewalk he raised our clasped hands. "I'm afraid to turn you loose. I don't want to risk losing you again."

CHAPTER 46

"I drove your car here," I told Max. I loved looking at him. His eyebrows were shaggier than before. His face more thin. He had lost weight during his extended ordeal.

"Good, we'll use it. You're coming with me."

"I am? Where?" His eyes were flittering, uncertain. Max was never uncertain.

"Errands. First." We got in the Rav and drove off. His hands were white-knuckled on the steering wheel, eyeing the street as if he were in a foreign country. His face grim.

"Max," I said. "Your hat. You're not wearing your hat." That's what was different. "Where is it?"

He touched his head. "You're right. I don't know where it is. Maybe the hospital." His smile was more like a grimace. I had a flash of worry about all those drugs.

He found a parking place in front of the courthouse and pulled in. I watched as he opened the door for me and saw him physically pull himself together. He took a big breath, straightened, chin in, head high. He put his hands on my shoulders and looked down at me.

"Thea, we're getting married."

"Yes? Good."

"I mean now. Right now. Here. Justice of the peace. Everything's planned."

"But…" I had on khakis and one of my tie-dyed tee shirts from the Emporium. "I can't like this…what about the license?"

"Right here in my pocket."

"I don't understand. I mean…how? What about the rings?"

"I've got them. They were in my damn truck. I'd hidden them in one of those things you use for a spare key."

My head was spinning, thoughts jumping here, there. "I didn't see it," I said, "I stared at the undercarriage of that truck for what felt like hours."

"You're not supposed to see it. I know how to hide them. None of that matters. Will you marry me?"

"Yes, but…" I looked at the courthouse; saw Charlotte! Charlotte, standing by the door holding a large bouquet. She waved excitedly, arm in a sling, pointing at the flowers, then at me. I started to laugh, and grabbed Max's hand. "You're on!"

"If you want another church ceremony, we can have one. But I have an uneasy feeling that this madness we've been through isn't over yet. I don't want anything to happen to you. I can't wait and risk having you disappear again."

"I didn't disappear, you did."

"Whatever. We're getting attached now." We ran up the steps.

Rusty stood inside the door. I jerked back.

"Yes, I'm here, too, a humbled man, loaded with more

apologies." He bowed us through the door and into the vestibule. "We're ready again to be your best man and woman. If you can't stand the sight of me, Charlotte can do it by herself." He waggled his eyebrows at me.

Happiness can do wonders for a bad attitude. I shook my head, grinned. and said, "Of course I want both of you."

Charlotte gave a happy yip, and began pulling things out of the big plastic bag at her feet.

Rusty presented an envelope to Max.

"We have for you, two bottles of Champagne, a specially made and delivered dinner of your choice from the best restaurant in town, and, ta-da, the Bridal Suite at the Outlaw Inn. All on me." He held up his hand to stop Max's complaints. "Redemption time, no thanks needed."

"For that, I'll take it." They laughed and slapped each other's backs.

Max said to me, "I called him this morning to help me set this up, but he wasn't supposed to do all this other stuff."

Rusty added, "And Charlotte picked up a small wedding cake from Cheyenne's most famous bakery."

Charlotte had her arm out of the sling now, and a comb in her hand. She began fussing with my hair.

"I thought you were in Cheyenne," I said.

"I was. I got a ride back on the police helicopter. Hold still now while I make you beautiful."

"The girls, are they all right?"

"Yes, they are in the hands of the most amazing woman in the world, Consuelo Brown. She speaks flawless Spanish, English, German, and French, as well as several variations of those along with slang and swear words in all. She's devoted her life and fortune to helping sexually abused children and young people. No matter how long they stay, or how well they do in the future, the girls will benefit from knowing her. Twinkle, twinkle sensed it right away, took one look at her and buried her head in her shoulder."

"How about Cussin' Katie?"

Charlotte laughed. "Even her. At least, I think it was approval. She gave Connie a once over, threw her backpack in a corner, and snarled, 'Where are the beds?'"

I was relieved, and should have known that Charlotte could handle anything that came her way. Even that.

She fiddled a bit more with my hair, produced a pearl headband from the bag and a lovely white lace shawl to throw over my tee shirt.

She gave Rusty a rose to pin on Max's denim shirt and said, "You're just lucky nobody is taking pictures. Come on, the judge awaits."

And so we were married. It was wonderful.

In the morning we got a call from Carson. He said he was sure there was nothing we'd rather do on the first day of our honeymoon than come to his house for a party. It was to be a Welcome Home party for him, a Happy Honeymoon party for us, and the first official day of the Alton Olmsted Treasure Hunt. Bring work clothes. He'd just purchased a DIY gazebo, and a bunch of other stuff that was in the back of Dale's truck. She would take care of the food.

It sounded perfect to us. We had talked and talked most of the evening and made no further plans for today. Carson assured me that Dale would bring her gold panning things. I was so excited to show Max the beauty of tiny bits of gold escaping from black sand. That reminded me of other gold.

"Oh! Max, I forgot to tell you that I found one of the treasure hunt clues. I told Carson about it, but not what was in it. I wanted to surprise him." A wee bit of one-upmanship on my part. Which reminded me of something else. "The other night when we found Ginny at Carson's, she was worried about Alton's gold. I can't remember exactly what she said, but she knew something about his gold, or wanted advice about it. I think I should tell Carson."

When I called him, he said, "Why don't you see if she and her mother want to come out for the hunt? The more the merrier. I need to get better acquainted with some of these relatives anyway." A good idea, I wanted Max to meet them as well.

Laurel was delighted by the invitation. I asked her if Ginny knew about her auntie's death. "Yes she does, and about her Uncle Virgil. We've spent a lot of time talking about how people you love can get caught up in bad things, the consequences, and so on. Perhaps we've talked too much. She's been quite melancholy. I think a picnic in the country might be very good for her."

"She won't mind going back to a place where she was so frightened?"

"Hang on, I'll ask her." She came back quickly enough, and with a laugh. "She'd love to go. The answer was a strong yes when she heard you'd be there."

"I feel it's quite safe now. There will be six of us, and the sheriff's crew will be working all day at Stella's place."

"Yes, I've spoken to Sheriff Jud several times, and he assured me they have a handle on things. The only unfinished item is finding Jake Novak, and they've got a lot of people looking for him. So I'm not worried about that part. I'll bring a big appetizer plate."

We bade farewell to the Bridal Suite, drove to Garnet Pass and my house first so I could change clothes. I urged Max to park in front instead of the driveway. I didn't want to see the spot where Townsend had been. Not today. There would be plenty of time to rid ourselves of inner devils.

Max stood quietly inside the front door, looking around at the familiar surroundings. Then he walked slowly, touching the desk, messy with research, ran his hand across the back of a chair, the couch. "It seems like I've been gone for months. I was so confused for so long, my mind a raging kaleidoscope. And I couldn't find you."

I threw my arms around him, held him close. "Yes. I know. I know exactly how that felt." We rocked a moment, then he pulled away, saying, "I'm still worried about my mind, my memory, how much damage the drugs might have done. The docs are encouraging, but they never commit themselves."

"But it's over now. You're on the mend. And we're together."

He shook off his moment of gloom and gave me a wicked smile. "Right! And as soon as Carson's treasure hunt is finished, we're off for as many weeks as we wish, doing whatever we want, wherever we feel like going. Hurry up."

I quickly changed my clothes. Max had difficulty restraining his amusement at me in my cargo pants but helped to fill the pockets judiciously. We were eager for laughter, hungry for fun. Finally, I dug out the box I'd found in the tree from its hiding place under my dresser.

Max wanted to see it, but I said, "No way." He'd have

to wait for the hunt, too. I tucked the box in another pocket.

"As the Grand Poobah of the treasure hunt, I'll be able to make a grand presentation." For some reason, this set us off on another round of idiotic laughter, and hugs, and kisses while we staggered out to the car.

CHAPTER 47

W e were the last to arrive at Carson's. Dale's truck was parked in back of the Quonset by the pond, and it looked as if she and Carson were unloading items into separate piles on the ground.

Ginny was arranging six canvas folding chairs closer to a large table set in the empty area to the left. Dale's blue cooler sat by one table leg along with a big basket most likely containing the usual picnic supplies. Ginny ran to meet us.

"This is the third time we've moved the truck," she said. "We're trying to find the best place for the gazebo."

When I introduced her to Max, she held her hand out and gave him her shy smile. He nodded at the truck, "Is that the best place for the gazebo?"

"Yes, The other spots were too bland," she said in her twenty-year-old persona. "You can see the butte from here and the pond, too. This has my vote and I think you should vote for it too."

She ran back to the truck shouting, "I have two more votes, so I win."

"No way. No way," Carson shouted back, "I might change mine." Obviously an ongoing game between them.

Eager to meet Laurel, Max and I went directly to the woman sitting in one of the chairs with her right leg stretched out wearing one of those awful medical boots on her foot. "That's right," I said, "you told me you had an ankle problem. No, no, don't get up. We can share hugs another time. I'm Thea, as I'm sure you must have guessed."

She took both of my hands. "It's a pleasure to finally meet you and your friends."

"And new husband." Ginny pointed to Max, "And new relative." She cocked her thumb over her shoulder at Carson." She sat on the knee scooter beside her mother's chair.

I sat in the chair beside her. "And how is the ankle?"

Dale and Carson joined us, drawing up chairs.

"It's doing okay. I've got two more weeks of this," she waggled the boot, "but it's the second time around."

Ginny put one knee on the scooter seat and took off on a wild circular drive.

Max watched with a big grin. "That's some machine. Look at those tires. Who's the maker, Cadillac?"

Laurel's laugh was low and genuine. "Not quite. It's all-terrain. We do a lot of outdoor exploring and hiking. It's been a lifesaver for me."

"Hey you," Carson yelled at Ginny, "come back here, I want to ride."

"Ho, ho, I bet you can't." She swung the scooter around and stopped in front of him, skidding her heel in the dirt, more for show than to help the brake.

"Mom's a terror on this; I bet you can't do as well as she does. She chases me all over the house with it."

That gave us a laugh. Laurel shook her head, "You have to have *some* fun. She's better going uphill than I am."

Of course, we all had to try it, ending with Max and Carson checking all the adjustments and how everything was put together.

Then it was time to sit and relax; time to raid the cooler, and lift the screen cover from the appetizer plate. Max reached for my hand. We exchanged smiles, wordlessly acknowledging that this was exactly what we needed after the past week.

Dale briefed Laurel about Carson's role in the events and how he ended up in the hospital.

"I was so shocked when I heard what happened," Laurel said. "Trafficking here in our small community. One thinks that's only in big cities. Then to find members of your own family are involved, and that I unwittingly put my daughter in danger." She shivered and took another sip of ice tea. "Virgil's in custody. I've talked to the sheriff several times. I've told him as much as I know about him and Stella. Thea, I can't tell you how much I appreciate what you did to protect my daughter."

"Please don't thank me. I never thought I was doing enough."

"What about those poor girls? Where are they?"

I told her about Charlotte, and Consuela Brown's home for girls.

"I know Charlotte!" Laurel smiled. "That makes me feel better."

Ginny ran past us to the big basket. "I'm going to catch some pond bugs."

Carson stood. "On that happy thought, I'll tell you that there are parts missing from the gazebo. So that project will be tackled another day." He rubbed his hands together. "Let's get on with the treasure hunt." He moved the ice tea jug and appetizer plate to one end of the table. "Okay, Thea it's up to you."

I stood behind the table and announced the Olmstead Official Treasure Hunt now open . "As Grand Poobah, I declare there are two rules of the game. Number one is that all present get a turn to hunt for clues, the rules of which we will make up as we go along. The second is that anything found, either clue or treasure, belongs to Carson Olmstead as part of his inheritance from his grandfather."

Formalities over, I opened the top pocket of my cargo pants, took out the box, and placed it on the table.

"For those of you who might not know, I was awarded my Poobah title for finding a hidden house key. Carson's parents had been told of it. They in turn told Carson, who told me. The only clue they had was that the hiding place had something to do with the Adirondack chairs in the back yard by the cottonwood trees."

Ginny was back with us and my audience, listening indulgently. "Because it looked as if the back of the chair might be pointing up to the tree, but mostly because I just wanted to, I climbed the tree and found this." Ginny bounced from foot to foot. I made a grand gesture of opening the box's lid. "Because there was more than a house key in it, I think this box was the first clue of Carson's hunt."

"I did it!" Ginny jumped in circles, waving her small net. "I did it. I hid the box for Uncle Alton. That's how I knew I could hide in the tree."

"You did!" her mother said. "When?"

"I don't know. Not the first time you brought me out here, but one of the times." She was so excited she couldn't stand still. "I was so worried when I hid up there and the box was gone. Uncle Alton said it was a present for his grandson. And I asked him if he'd be able to find it. He just laughed and said if he couldn't, I could tell him." In one of her shy moments she looked at Carson. "I thought his grandson would be a kid like me. When I met you last night, I didn't know if you were telling the truth."

"I was a kid once, but now you have an old guy relative. You can call me uncle, or cousin, whatever you like, but I want to see what's in that box. Do you know?"

"No, he didn't tell me, he just wanted me to hide it for him. Cousin." Carson grabbed her hand and everyone crowded around the table.

I placed the three keys in a row on the table. "This looked like a house key, and it opened the door to your house, Carson." The glistening quartz and gold specimen, sparkling in the sun, came next. Carson whistled, and picked it up.

"That's spectacular," Max said. "Anyone have a magnifier?"

"I do." Dale unzipped a pocket. We grinned at each other. She handed him a jeweler's loupe.

Max put it to his eye and loomed over Carson's hand. "Wow. Look at the thickness of that gold vein." He handed the loupe to Carson. Then we all took turns.

Finally, I removed the bottom piece of cotton and rolled the pebbles around. "There's more." I tilted the box so Dale could see.

"Whoa. That's my kind of stuff." Dale waggled her hand at Carson, wanting the loupe.

Once again everyone got inspection time.

Laurel handed the box back to me. "I've never seen anything like this. I'm amazed."

The pebbles were kept in the box, and the box lined up on the table with the other things.

"So, Max." Carson eyed them. "Off the top of your head, what's the value? Is there any?"

"I'm not up on values, and there are a lot of variables. But a specimen like that could go for maybe five hundred bucks."

"What!" I yelped, feeling weak in the knees. If I'd any idea it was worth that much, I wouldn't have kept it from you, Carson. I'm so sorry, and....embarrassed."

"Don't be. It's only money, my dear." The chuckles helped.

"It's not a sure thing," Max said A lot of value is tied up in provenance. So if you don't know where it came from, it won't be worth as much. Knowing Alton for the man he was, he might have that stuff catalogued somewhere."

"Now it's up to you, Carson," I said. "Tell us what this means. Is it all one clue, or is each item a clue in itself?"

"You know, I was a teenager the last time I did one of these hunts. They were all a little different. Like the box that started this event, everything in it was related to gold prospecting, which told me it was a treasure hunt. But it wasn't always that way. For instance the house key," he put his finger on it and moved it away from the others, "might mean that there was something in the house." We were all studying the objects more carefully now. Thinking.

"Ah." Carson put his finger on the smallest key. "This looks like it could be a journal key, or diary key. I'm going to take this. I've got tons of Gramps papers that I haven't gone through yet. Maybe there's a journal, like you were speaking of, Max, a list of specimens and their provenance. I'll have to look."

"And this," Max put his finger on the quartz and gold specimen, "could indicate a lode; gold imbedded in rock formations."

"And this," Dale pointed to the pebbles, "placer gold."

I couldn't fathom it. "You mean there might be all of that here on this piece of land?"

"Well, maybe not." Carson was as stunned as we were. "Could just be related to it…I don't know."

Max pointed to the quartz. "I'm interested in the lode idea. I'd like to investigate that if it's all right with you, Carson."

"Of course. That's the whole point of this."

"And me the placer." Carson gave Dale a deep bow. "Be my guest." She rolled her eyes.

I smiled to myself. There was something in that exchange that made me think their friendship was moving apace. I hoped she'd give it a chance. She hadn't dressed for anything special. Just her usual untidy pony tail and cargos.

I picked up the house key. "Laurel, would you like to join me in this search?"

"Of course."

"I should go with you two," Dale said. "I did some cleaning in there and can at least tell you where it probably isn't.

Ginny was bouncing around again. "I've got one. I've got one. I think I know where a clue is."

CHAPTER 48

Ginny's mother was dubious. "Where did you find a clue?"

"Come on, I'll show you. Ginny ran off toward the old shed.

"Does she ever walk?"

Seldom." We all chuckled and followed more sedately

I asked Laurel if she wanted her cart, but she said no. It did her good to walk.

Ginny was standing by the old Caddie doing a few cheerleading twirls.

"Okay, Squirt, whatcha got?" Carson said.

She stepped back and pointed at the license plate. GOLD. He stared at it, then dropped to his knees laughing. "Laurel, you have a brilliant daughter, and we are the imbeciles of the world."

We groaned in agreement. I'd even taken pictures of the vanity plate.

Ginny gripped its top edge. "I tried to see if there was anything behind it, but it wouldn't budge."

Carson held an open hand in front of Dale. "Screwdriver."

"Yes, Doctor."Opening a pocket, she flipped one into his hand.

The plate was quickly loosened, and much to all of our surprise, there actually was something behind it. An envelope. Carson read what was on it. "'To whoever wants to steal this license plate: Please give this letter to Carson Olmstead, or to the Sweetwater County Sheriff.'"

Ginny jumped and giggled. "Open it, open it."

He unfolded a single sheet of paper, glanced at it and began to read out loud. "Carson, I hope it is you reading this now. Curiosity is the seed that feeds the mind. I hope it means you've come to Wyoming and are, at least, thinking about living on the land your family has owned for so long.

"This might be old news by the time you read this, but I wanted to warn you that your grandmother has moved back to the land I gave her. Since then, I have been harassed on my property, mostly by cars driving around my house and on the road to her place. I don't know if there is a purpose to it, or if it's to get back at me, or even if it is real. My mind isn't what it used to be. I have done my share of spying on them. Virgil Parker and a young man named Jake Novak are the only names I have for you. I miss you, dear boy and....look to the heights. Your grandfather, Alton Olmstead."

Even Ginny was quiet.

He showed us the face of the letter. "The rest is for the sheriff, and repeats what he told me, a bit more garbled, but I'll show it to him." He put the letter back in the envelope, folded it in half and stuck it in his shirt pocket. "He told me about the night lights around the house. I listened, but didn't do anything about it. I thought he was probably confused. He was always about lessons learned, and I guess I'm still learning."

Laurel hobbled over to the Caddie and patted the hood as if it were a puppy. "My grandpa had one of these, too. It was always a dream of his to own a Cadillac." She peered in the windows, opened the passenger door. She thumbed the glove compartment button with no result. Looked at it again, stood, and gave Carson a grin. "My turn. I could be crazy, but…" She pointed at the button's keyhole."

Max was quick. "The other key? I'll get it for you." Ginny ran with him.

Amazingly, the key fit. Too hard for Laurel to turn, but Max fiddled, banged, and teased until the door fell open. You might know, the first thing we saw was a squished water bottle. It looked like the beer cans guys like to smash into tiny accordions. Max flipped it out onto the driver seat, and then moved so Laurel could sit in front of the glove box. Next came a crumpled piece of paper. She moved to toss it next to the bottle, stopped, and smoothed it out instead. *Look to the heights*, she read. That phrase was used in the letter, wasn't it?"

"Yeah." Carson whipped the letter out again, "and I think it was underlined." And it was. "Aha. Another clue."

Laurel still poked around in the glove compartment, "This doesn't feel right." She looked up at Max. "See what you think." They exchanged places.

"You're right. Feels like a false backing." He banged and pulled, then fell back in the seat, groaning, hand to chest. "I don't have the strength of a kitten. Thea, you have smaller hands. maybe you can get a better grip."

He got out, I got in. It definitely felt like a false backing. Whoever manufactured it knew what he was doing. There was just the tiniest space in the top right corner that felt as if a finger might get purchase. But not my finger. "Dale you're better at this, maybe your screw driver would help." More musical chairs.

She went to work, her shoulder lurched, and she peered into the compartment. "Oh my! Heavenly pellets! Carson, get over here." We crowded by the car and shoved Carson closest to the door. Dale withdrew her hands holding a large, strangely shaped, beautifully golden nugget. It was lumpy, flat, long and curved, as if somewhere deeply within an ancient formation, moving rock had stretched it like a piece of taffy. She placed it in Carson's hands and sank back into the dirty seat. We were speechless.

Finally Dale spoke, "You know, Carson, I can't help but wonder, you come out here, want to clean the place up, you call a dealer to haul away junk, it ends up in a crushing machine. Or you end up selling the place. You'd have to put in a just-in-case clause, charge another fifty thou because they might find nuggets you missed. Wouldn't your grandfather have thought about that? That these amazing things might accidentally be thrown away, or found by some person he didn't care about."

We raised our eyes to Carson. Something about the gold he held made us want to touch it, run our hands over it, feel its weight. He handed it to me. It felt as old as the world.

Carson ran his fingers through his red hair. "Yes, I've wondered about that sometimes. He wasn't much for possessions. He collected, and was given specimens all over the world. Donated them everywhere. I'm sure he thought about it, but I think he might not have cared. He might have even thought it was fun. He certainly wouldn't have cared about gold being crushed and ending up back in the earth, or even someone finding a surprise of a lifetime." He rose from his hay bale seat and brushed off his pants. "And I don't care either. Let's go get a beer."

He retrieved the scrunched water bottle and note from the front seat, shut the car door and patted the hood. "Good boy." Max handed him the nugget.

Ginny ran off again and came back riding her mother's cart. "Here, Mom, you need to use this."

Dale and I followed Max and Carson. I said, "It's difficult to remember that they're both recently out of the hospital."

Dale agreed. "Carson feels pretty good, but he still looks pale to me." She hooked her elbow with mine. "I was so glad to hear you got married."

"I wished you were there."

"Charlotte called and invited me and Carson, but I thought it would just be nice with the original four of you. And Carson was still in the hospital."

"It's good to see the two of you having fun together."

She smiled but didn't say anything more, and I didn't want to push her.

We sat at the table with the gleaming nugget for a centerpiece. Max ignored it, picking up the smaller quartz specimen with its impressive vein of gold. He inspected it from all angles, with and without the jewelers loupe. Then put it back on the table. His face was a study in thought. I'd seen that look before.

Dale brought out a platter of sandwiches, and Ginny took orders from the cooler. Max absently chose a sandwich and took a bite. The bite brought him back to us. "Mm, Reuben! This is wonderful! Thank you."

"You're welcome." Dale said. "At least it brought you out of your stupor."

"That was no stupor, that was high class thinking."

"I'm interested. Tune us in." I could see her gold antennas rising.

"I'm captured by that specimen as a clue. It indicates a lode. This land," he swept his arm over the ground around us, "is not conducive for gold, but if you add the words, 'look to the heights,' which we think is another clue, the idea of gold becomes more interesting. The only heights around here are on that butte."

We all looked at the graceful, tall, landmark that had marked its spot in the world for thousands of years.

Carson said, "It's been an integral part of this property forever. I'm sure Granddad explored every inch of it. If there's a secret to it, I'd like to know what it is."

"The important part of a butte is its top," Max said. "The hard rock that doesn't erode, or at least, doesn't erode as quickly as what is beneath it does. That's what creates a butte. There are all kinds of hard rock, but because this was a gold hunt, what came to mind was silica, which could be quartz, agate, jasper." He pointed at the quartz on the table. "There are such things as ancient fossilized hot springs that can consist of a lot of silica. It's unusual, but not impossible that a fossilized hot spring could be the capping of a butte and possible traces of gold could be found."

"There wouldn't have to be gold," Carson said, delighted. "That sounds exactly like one of Gramps's learning moments."

Max threw his arms up in the air. "Hey, hey, everyone. What about all that! Was I erudite, or was I not? Did you hear those words roll off my tongue like…like…"

I heaved a sigh of relief. The others, puzzled, started to laugh. I picked up his thoughts, "Like bits of gold slithering from under black sand."

"Right." Max laughed and pushed back his chair.

"Sorry for the commotion, but I've been concerned that my mind and memory might have turned into rubble from all the drug shots I received. That little bit of retrieved knowledge has been a crowning moment for me. But now, I'm dying to get a close look at that butte."

"Me, too," Carson said. "Anyone want to join us?"

CHAPTER 49

G inny was excited "I want to go to the butte, Mom. Can I, can I?"

"Don't be a pest, Ginny."

"We like pests." Carson put his hand on Ginny's shoulder. "We won't let her climb anything."

Max looked around, quietly checking the lay of the land. "I think we should all go, or none of us go. For safety. Remember the sheriffs said to be cautious."

"Well, snort, I've got a cell phone," Dale said. "Thea and I have already seen the butte. There's not much there."

"I don't have a phone," I said.

"I've got one." Laurel patted her pockets. "It's in the house, in my tote bag, and I'd like to get my leg up for a while."

Still worried, Max said, "Anyone you call will take time to get here, even the guys working at Stella's."

"Oh, you guys go on." Dale started cleaning off the table. "If I need a weapon I've got a tire iron in the back of my truck."

Carson laughed. "And my rifle is in the closet under the stairs."

"Good." Laurel chuckled. I might not know anything about gold, but I've been shooting cans off a fence since I was a kid."

I gave Max a kiss. "Hey, take the Rav instead of walking. If anything happens, we'll call you first. You'll get here quicker than anyone else."

"Okay, I give up. Ginny can go with us."

"I want to ride the cart there, Mom, is that okay?"

"You need to ride in the car with Max and Carson. If you want to take the cart with you, that's fine."

"Okay," Carson said," I'll put the scooter in the car, Squirt. You grab some water for us."

Max gave me a kiss, and they were off. At least they wouldn't wear themselves out before they got there.

The three of us cleared the perishable food from the table and took it in the house. On our way to the kitchen, Dale opened the closet door. "Ha! he's right, there's the rifle." Laurel and I peeked in and saw it propped in a back corner. "All that fuss over Jake the snake," Dale muttered. "He's probably hundreds of miles away by now."

"Doesn't hurt to be cautious," I said. "What I'd really like is to find another clue or treasure before they get back. Our clue is the house key, but I'm not crazy about poking around in Carson's house."

We took our ice tea into the living room, and got Laurel settled on the couch with her leg up on a pillow.

"A secret panel hunt would be fun," Dale said, "but like you, not without Carson. What else have we got?"

"I'm the amateur here," Laurel rearranged the pillow behind her back, "but I keep wondering why that squished water bottle was in the glove compartment. Could that be a clue?"

"Great idea. Maybe another 'duh' one like Ginny's. Water."

"The pond!"

"The pond's certainly weird enough," Dale said." Carson said it's the first thing he wants to take care of. It's just a hole in the ground. He thinks it should have a proper base, or lining, and a circulating water pump."

I agreed. "That would get rid of the scum."

Dale got up. "Let's take a look.

Laurel was content to stay on the couch a bit, but urged us to go investigate.

Dale and I went outside. The gold centerpiece shone in the sun, looking quite lavish on the white plastic table. We admired it again along with the other treasures. Dale shook the box with the gold pellets before we went to the pond.

We sat on one of the logs. Insects hazed the air above the scum but weren't bothersome to us.

I said, "Are you thinking that the gold pellets could mean there's some good panning here?"

"I don't know what I think. I've enjoyed today, the business of trying to puzzle things out. You and I have done a bit of digging in the creek bed. There's nothing obvious there, at least on the surface. Maybe if you dug down deep enough...

"I just don't know enough yet, Thea. Max has an advantage as a geologist. He can simply look around and know what kind of formations we're in, and what can be expected of them. I've decided it would be fun to take some geology classes. And I suspect this hunt of Carson's is going to be more than a one day affair. He might find himself with a much longer project."

Some instinct frizzled my attention, making me look up. A man stood by the end of the Quonset, watching us. I jumped to my feet.

"Hollywood," I said under my breath. "What's he doing here?"

"Distract him. I'll stash the gold." We both waved. He returned the gesture.

I went to meet him, Dale walked casually to the table.

He wore a two piece white athletic suit and amazing white Nike's, most likely in the thousand dollar range. I had to admit he had movie-star looks.

"Hello, Quentin," I said, trying for a pleasant expression. "What brings you here? I thought you left for California yesterday."

I maneuvered myself so I could see Dale, and he couldn't.

"This has been an incredible experience for me, and I wanted to say a final goodbye to the men still working at Stella's."

"Did you walk from there?" I saw Dale drop the quartz specimen into the box, close it, and secure it in a pocket.

"No, I've got my truck; I'm surprised you didn't hear it." We took a few steps and could see his large white pickup parked by the cottonwoods. He must have coasted in. Weird. Dale gave me a quick ok signal. I didn't see what she'd done with the big nugget; she must have had a large enough pocket for it.

He walked slightly in front of me back toward the pond. I followed, and Dale joined us.

He gave her a dazzling smile. "Haven't we met somewhere before?"

"I don't think so. But I was at the meeting yesterday with the sheriffs. You might have seen me there."

"I didn't think anyone would be here today, or I wouldn't have bothered you." He took in the table, the chairs. "It looks like you've been having a party."

"Of sorts," I said. It was an awkward conversation.

"There must be others here as well."

"Yes, they're off on a walk, but will be back soon. You may join us if you like." I was interested to see what his response would be.

"No, no, I have to be on my way, but thank you. Actually, I came to get my belongings." He gave a little laugh. "I hid some of my papers here the other day. Didn't want any of those thugs at Stella's stealing them. Nothing was safe there. I'll just get them and be gone."

He headed toward the pond at the same time I heard another approaching vehicle. Good, I thought, Max and Carson. Instantly, I knew the direction was wrong.

The sound became louder, closer, more furious. We walked away from the pond. I glanced back. Hollywood listened, too, then ran to the log seat at the end of the pond, got on his knees and furiously pushed the heavy log.

A dusty blue pickup barreled through the open front gate straight toward us at high speed. At sight of us, the brakes squealed in a wide turn, pointing the nose back toward the gate. The truck stopped and, engine still running, the door swung open and the driver jumped out.

Jake the snake Novak, murderer, the wanted man.

"Jake, you ass," Dale said. "What are you doing here?" She pulled her cell phone from a pocket and curled her fingers around it, hiding it.

He went for her, yelling, "The same thing you're doing. Shoulda known the two of you'd still be pokin' your noses around, lookin' to steal whatever you could find."

"Steal what, you dumbbell?" She turned her back, stabbing at the phone

I blocked his path.

He stiff-armed me, knocking me down. "Run, Dale!"

He reached out, snatched her ponytail, jerked her head back. She screamed.

He got right in her face. "Gold, gold, gold. What in hell did you think? And don't call me dumbbell." He threw her to the ground, grabbed her phone and threw it as far as possible.

I quickly turned to Hollywood, motioning with my arm to come help us, then dropped beside Dale.

She groaned, but with an oath, rolled to her knees and got to her feet. I jumped up, furious, and shoved past Jake, yelling. "Get out of here. Get in your damn truck and go. There's nothing here for you,"

"Oh, yeah, there's plenty here for me. Like you, you stupid bitch. I shoulda killed you when I had a chance. I shoulda dragged you out by the hair."

Max's house! The two guys. "So that was you! Scared to show your face. The two of you ran off like a couple of chickens."

His face twisted in fury. His arm shot out for a grasp. I jumped back. But he caught site of Hollywood, still trying to move the heavy log.

"Hey, you bastard! That's mine." He ran after him. "I saw you smash that old bitch in the head. That's my money."

What! Hollywood killed...? I stood, stunned.

"Not on your life, you stupid ass!" Hollywood snatched a bag from under the log, turned to run as Jake reached him. Jake grabbed Hollywood's sleeve, pulling him off balance. The fight was on.

I was on one side of the pond, Dale on the other. Hollywood managed a solid hit. Jake retaliated with a kick to the knee. I bounced, uncertain what to do. Out of the corner of my eye, I saw something whiz past behind them. The scooter? Jake landed a solid punch, which sent the money bag flying. It landed a few feet from me. I grabbed it. The two men ran for me, Dale close behind. I threw the bag in the pond. Hollywood jumped in after it. A strong push from behind sent me flying face first into the scum. As I hit the water, a thunderous roar blasted my ears, echoing twice in the water. All I could think of was scum and icky water. My left hand touched bottom and sank to the wrist when I tried to push for the surface. Yuk. The other hit something hard that tilted into my fingers. I clutched it, twisted around, shoving, kicking for the surface. I gasped for air, spat, and opened my eyes, blurred with scum and dirty water. Something white and green was halfway out of the pond lying on…I shook my head, blinked. Hollywood! Dale! He had his hands on her throat. Without thinking, I threw the disk I held like a Frisbee. It hit his shoulder blade and skipped off. His hands fell from her throat. She gasped and rolled away.

A couple of strokes to the side, then I grabbed the pond's edge. But Jake lay there on the path, moaning, clutching his knee.

I swished around for the other side, and saw Carson a few feet from the pond, rifle in hand, pointed at Hollywood. Laurel half ran, half hobbled to his side.

I reached for the edge of the pool, then hands grabbed at my shoulders and pulled me to the bank. "Max! How did you get here?"

"Later." He shook his head. "I don't know if I can pull you out, it's very slick. Help's coming."

"Something exploded." I said.

"Laurel shot a SOS with Carson's rifle."

"Laurel?" Too much, too fast.

"Yes, the men working at Stella's are almost here."

"They're here," I said, as three cars drove up behind Carson.

Two deputies ran behind Max. He rolled away.

"We'll get her, sir." One took hold of my forearms.

"The side is mud and very slick. Can you get purchase with either foot?"

"I think so." I dug a toe in. It slipped away. Tried again and gave a shove. The other man grasped my waist while Max held him taunt so he wouldn't slide in. The deputies swung me out and over. My feet touched solid ground. "Yay."

Ginny ran up with a blanket. "You look terrible. You have green stuff in your hair."

"Thanks, honey. I'm just glad to be out of there. Give me a hug."

"No, no." She giggled and backed off.

With a laugh, Max wrapped the blanket around me. "Don't worry; we'll get her fixed up." Laurel and Dale stood by the table. We joined them. The blanket helped soak up the wetness.

"Are you all right?" I asked Dale.

"Yes, thanks to you." She tucked the blanket more tightly around my shoulders. "Green scum becomes you."

I squeezed her hand. "What happened to Jake?" Two men and a woman were huddled over him.

"I'm not sure. Broken kneecap, maybe. I hit him as hard as I could with that nugget in my hand. Hurt my wrist, too."

Four deputies had taken over Carson's watch of Hollywood, one with a weapon while the other three hauled him out of the water. He still held the soggy bank bag. One of the men tugged it from him. Carson stepped to the pond, picked up something from the ground, and brought it over. He used his shirt tail to wipe off mud.

"Is that what I threw at Hollywood?"

"Is that what you did?"

"Yes. Is it a disk? I found it on the bottom of the pond. It felt like a small Frisbee, that's the way I threw it. It hit him on the shoulder blade, I think, and then bounced off. I couldn't see very well."

Carson held it up. I caught my breath. So did Max. He took his arm from around my shoulder. The disk was larger than a saucer, but not much. Where the mud was removed, we could see the glimmer of gold. "I can't believe it," he muttered.

"Let's go clean it up," Dale said. Another car came through the gate, drove up and parked behind the other vehicles. The county sheriff.

Carson handed the muddy plate to Dale. "You take it. I'll need to talk to the sheriff."

We followed Dale. "I'll want to talk to him, too," Max said, "but I'll see you to the house first."

"You don't need to do that." He stopped, wrapped his arms around me, and kissed me, filth and all.

"Yes, I do."

"Stop worrying about me. How did the sheriff know to come here?"

"I was half way up the butte and had good sight of the road; I saw that truck before he got here. Knew it was trouble by the way it was flying. When I saw it was going to turn in, I called 911. Got a decent signal from there. They got here so fast it must have gone from Rock Springs to Garnet Pass."

Laurel caught up with us at the front door. She held it open for me. "Come on, I'll help you wash that stuff out of your hair."

"Wonderful! I can hardly wait."

"Take care of her," Max said. "She needs watching."

CHAPTER 50

W e sat in the living room, except for Ginny who was sprawled sound asleep on Carson's bed, dreaming dreams of becoming the next J.K. Rowling.

Max and I snuggled discreetly on the couch. I had on a pair of Carson's sweat pants with the legs rolled up, a matching sleeveless sweat shirt, and his socks from the hospital. My hair, as always, was doing its own thing, but happy to be clean and slime free.

Carson sat in his grandfather's leather recliner, Laurel was in a wing chair with her foot propped on a pillow placed on the cooler, Dale in the other wing chair. The round coffee table was in the middle of the floor with our gold finds of the day beautifully displayed on top. The old house had lost its musty, forlorn feeling of abandonment and seemed to fold us into its contentment.

"I'm still confused." I said. "Too many things happened so quickly. Did I really see someone whizzing by on the scooter?"

Carson held up his hand. "That was me, the ride of a lifetime. When Max yelled from the butte that trouble was coming, all I could think of was my rifle in the closet. Max still had to climb down from the butte. I got the scooter. Ginny helped me and I took off. I figured that with the rifle I could manage a surprise or hold someone at bay. I worried that you gals were alone and might need help. Foolish, me. When I ran in the back door—scared the hell out of Laurel—she already had the gun out and loaded."

"You did scare me, but only for a second," Laurel said. "I heard the truck roar past, and was on my way to see what was happening when I heard a scream. That must have been you, Dale." She nodded. "I got my phone and hoped a 911 would reach the men working at Stella's, but I got nothing, so I went for the rifle. Fortunately, the ammo was right there with it. I figured the men working at Stella's would hear a SOS shot. Carson was exhausted when he came through the back door. He saw what I was doing, and motioned me out the door. I shot the three shots in the air. Once he caught his breath, I gave him the rifle. He could move faster than my hobbling."

"I didn't even know there was an outdoorsman SOS," Carson said. "I would have just blown some bullets in the air for attention. But who needed help? Thea and Dale had put Jake and Hollywood out of action. All I had to do was stand there and point the rifle."

There was a knock on the door. Carson called, "Come on in." Sheriff Jud stood in the doorway. "We're done out there. Just wanted to make sure everyone was all right."

"Come in and sit down." Carson pulled up another chair. "Can we ask some questions?"

"Sure, but I can't stay long."

"Me first," I said, with a thank you. "How did you get here so quickly?"

"Good luck and quick action. Max's 911 call got sent immediately to the men working at Stella Parker's place.

Some of them had already thought Quentin Cook's appearance there strange and decided to follow him. They were on their way when they heard the SOS shot. Others of us were out on the road checking a report that some guy had seen Novak's truck. So it turned out well."

Dale wanted to know what was in the bag they were fighting for.

"Money. A lot of it. The money Stella got for her part of the trafficking. We're not sure who stole it first, but will soon find out. Quentin Cook, or Hollywood, as you call him, wasn't a complete surprise for us. At any rate, we have both men arrested, charged for murder."

"If it will help," I said, " I heard Jake shout out that he'd seen Hollywood smash-in the old lady's head."

"Yes, he told us that, too, and we tend to believe him. We think that was Quentin's plan from the beginning. Maybe not to kill her, but to take the money."

"And Novak?" Max asked.

"Yes, that man has more than an anger problem. Virgil Parker has nailed him for Deefy's death, and probably Townsend, as well. We have a lot more investigating to do before finalizing anything, but I'm sure we're on the right track. I've got to get going now. If you have any more questions, feel free to ask me or Deputy Krause."

He stepped over to the coffee table, squatted to get a close look at the gold.

"You can touch, or pick them up, if you want," Carson said. "Or ask questions, Max is our brain man."

He stood, and shook his head. "I wish I had time. My nephew's going to be so jealous when I tell him about this. I know he'd like to meet both of you." He ran a finger across the nugget and the gold plate. "May I give him your names?"

"Of course," Max and Carson said as one.

They stood to see him out the door, Max saying, "And thanks for the rescue." Which we all echoed.

Ginny came out of the bedroom rubbing her eyes and sat on Laurel's lap. Laurel held her tight. "I want to thank you all for including Ginny and me in this amazing day. Believe it or not, this has been a healing day for us, and we welcome the new friendships and finding a new relative."

Carson grinned. "Just what you need, another cousin."

Laurel rose to her feet. "I've also found a new charity. I feel a responsibility for those poor girls. I'm going to get something started for Consuela Brown's home for girls. I'll call it my golden moment. But now it's time for me to take this child home."

Ginny ran around and gave everyone hugs. "Thea, can I still help you write your gold story?"

"Of course. I'll need help. There's a lot we can do together."

"After we get back from our honeymoon." Max gave her a high five.

It was one of those longish farewells when no one is quite ready to say goodbye. But finally the hugs, thank yous, and plans for future meetings were finished. We waved them off, and filed back in the house.

Dale sat again in the wing chair. "Laurel called her idea for a charity her golden moment. I had one today as well. I already told Thea about it. I'm going to take geology classes. I want to have at least some of the knowledge you have, Max. I'm as interested in the process of finding it, as I am in the gold itself."

Max raised a thumb. "You'll probably end up knowing more about it than I do. My specialty is petroleum. It's just another form of prospecting, but I've always been interested in the rock and mineral side of it, as well."

"And Thea," Dale went on. "I keep thinking of the

doodlebug. It made me sick to hear those guys tore it even more apart. I'd like to reconstruct it, or as much as possible. Carson, your grandfather, or maybe even your great-grandfather, honored that old machine. Would you let me do that?"

"Of course, I might even help, but what's all this fuss about a doodlebug?"

Dale and I groaned in unison. I held my hand out to her. We were too far to touch. "That was the beginning of all this…this adventure, if that's what you want to call it."

"Oh, snort, The Search for Max Holman is a better title. It's a long story, Carson. I'll tell you all about it later."

"I heard some of it last night." Max gave me a hug. "It has a happy ending."

"Yeah." Carson took the gold plate from Dale and studied it. "I have the actual gold we found, but a moment of regret, rather than a golden one. As a relative, Laurel felt responsible for those girls. I'm even a closer relative. Stella was my grandmother. My father's mother. I'd planned to meet her, maybe make a connection; repair some of the old wounds. I might have made a difference if I'd sought her out ten years or so ago. The chance is gone now. I feel guilty that I've waited so long."

Dale leaned toward him, holding out her hand. "Don't feel that way, Carson. It might not have worked, anyway. She had responsibility, too. Everyone battles with remorse for things not done or said."

"And don't forget that Alton Olmstead was your grand-father," I put in. "That's a good seed in your pack."

"You'll still need Granddad's papers, won't you, Thea?"

"Definitely, I have a new plan, too. I'm still going to tell the story of the old gold mining towns, and how one man built his career through them, but I'm not going to focus on the ladies of the night any more. Soiled doves of the Old West have been romanticized for a long time. Getting a first-hand look at prostitution and how girls, or women, can be treated like chattel has given me a different perspective. I'm not putting them down, so many had desperate lives, and few options. Some even did a lot of good. I'm simply going to change my focus. I'm going to look for the women who helped destitute young girls, the Consuela Browns of the day, to find other ways to make a living. I know those women are out there, I just have to find them: the cooks, the laundresses', the school teachers, even women miners. I'm going to give them my attention now."

Max smiled. "I like that."

"As do I," Dale said. "It will be different, and I bet your readers will like it."

"Thanks, but my real golden moment will always be the shining bits of gold swimming out from under darkness that you showed me. It's become an analogy for me that I'll never forget. We should have shown that to everyone, Dale."

"Next time," she said, "next time!"

Carson held up the small gold plate. "One can tell this little beauty is very old. The gold we found today was raw. This piece was manufactured by someone, shows what people have been doing with gold for thousands of years. It could have been a shipwreck piece, and that might have been why Gramps hid it in the water. But I'm going to trace its history, try to find out who that someone was. I'll find a place to put it, here in this room, so we can see it whenever we get together again, which I hope will be soon. I've decided that living in Wyoming will always be an adventure. That's my golden moment."

"Perfect!" Max said. We all agreed.

Max stood and pulled me up beside him. "And now,

Mrs. Holman, we should be off for the second day of our honeymoon. My only wish is that it might be calmer."

"Where are you going?" they asked together.

Max looked at me for the answer.

"Just a suggestion, husband, but I've been doing a lot of research recently, enough to show me that gold has always been magic in the West. Let's look for some of it." I felt like doing a Ginny run around. "South Pass City, Atlantic City, and Miner's Delight, all have rebuilt historic sites, mine tours, as well as creeks, and piles of mine tailings we could paw through. If I'm going to write about those towns I really need to investigate them."

"Gold fever!" Max laughed. "I should have known. I wonder if it's catching."

"You'll soon find out!" I grabbed his hand. "Come on, Dale, no next time. Let's show them now. We can do it in the kitchen. Carson, go grab a gold pan."

Dale patted her cargo pants. "I've got the black sand. Let's use the gold pellets we found today."

"Oh, Max," I said. "You've got to see it. You'll love it!"

The End

ACKNOWLEDGMENTS

This is a book of fiction. Parts of it are real, parts of it are imaginary. Even so, touches of reality are always needed. For those, I have so many friends, family and experts to thank for their information. I hope I don't forget any of them.

My first readers are writer friends. We've spent many years together, they're my toughest critics and greatest encouragers: Chris Goff, Yvonne Montgomery, Chris Jorgensen, and Susan Smith.

Special thanks go to Dan Hausel, Geologist; Cheryl Lete; Kim Anderson; Pat Devries; Suzy and Karen; and Hallie and Jeremy Grable. And once again, forever thanks to my husband, and children. Without their love and support I'd be nowhere.

ABOUT THE AUTHOR

Raised in a Chicago suburb, author Carol Caverly married into a Wyoming pioneer ranch family. Yes, it was a bit of a culture shock, but she quickly grew to love the stark dry landscape and, most of all, the people. Now Carol enjoys writing mysteries set in the modern New Wild West she loves.

www.carolcaverly.com